Island Thyme Café

Island Thyme Café

ANDREA HURST

It's never too late - never too late to start over, never too late to be happy.

~Jane Fonda

Cover design: Lidia Vilamajo
Developmental Editor: Cate Perry
Copy Editor: Martha Schoemaker & Cameron Chandler
Marketing & Publicity: www.2MarketBooks.com
Foreign Rights: taryn.fagerness@gmail.com

ISBN- 1540446123
ISBN- 9781540446121

This book is a work of fiction. Names, characters, places and events are a product of the author's imagination and are used fictitiously.

Dedicated to Billee Escott, my inspiration for the character, Betty, in this series, and in many other areas of my life.

Table of Contents

Chapter One

A warm breeze skipped across Grandpa John's face, causing his eyes to flutter open. He'd dozed off again. These lazy June days often led to a nap. He stretched his arms in the air and took a deep breath before settling back into the wooden chair. For a flash of a moment he thought he heard Maggie's voice in the garden. He glanced up, almost expecting her to be there, picking lilies and bright orange poppies and smiling back at him. But she'd crossed over about three years ago now. Lately, as he moved deeper into his eighties, the line between the here-and-now and the beyond seemed to blur just a bit more.

John gazed over to Maggie's old farmhouse where Lily and Ian now ran the thriving Madrona Island Bed and Breakfast. Love had skipped two generations with those two...his grandson and Maggie's granddaughter. The dogwood trees were in bloom and tall red hollyhocks towered over the garden fence. They'd been neighbors and fast friends for many years, through Maggie's marriage and the loss of John's wife. It didn't seem that long ago that Maggie had been widowed, and soon after put out her shingle for the B&B. He remembered the young, golden-haired Lily, running like a pony in the yard, rocking on the porch swing, and picking wild strawberries.

Despite his wife's decline and lingering illness, Maggie had done her best to keep their spirits lifted. She'd bake batches of cookies and bring them over, sit and have coffee, and talk the afternoons away. Ah, Maggie. They'd been through so much together and it had brought them closer than he'd ever thought possible.

Gretel came bounding over with a stick in her mouth, tail wagging and an expectant look hoping for a game of fetch.

He petted the top of her black head. "Thatta girl, my good girl."

Gretel dropped the stick into his hands and backed away a few feet in anticipation.

"There you go," he said, sending the stick flying through the air. He watched her run and noticed that her gait was slowing down as she approached ten years of age. Getting on for a lab. His heart clenched at the thought of losing her. At his age, he'd seen friends, family, and even a wife go. His neighbor, Betty, was not doing too well, and he worried about her. At least he'd been able to watch his grandson, Ian, build a strong family after his wife died and left five-year-old Jason for Ian to raise alone. And then miraculously, Ian found happiness with Lily.

John sighed, "Maggie you would have been so pleased to see those two together." He wished she were here now to get to know Kyla better and meet her husband, Luke. And then there was Jude. Even at the end, sick in bed, Maggie had worried over Jude's future. After Jude's daughter, Lindsey, had left her to live with her father, Maggie had fussed over Jude for weeks. That was her style, truly loving her neighbors and her friends.

He missed Maggie, but he was needed here.

Gretel, his faithful friend, dropped the stick at his feet again. He was one lucky man to have the time to idle away at his farm overlooking Puget Sound, to have his family and those dear to him so close, and to have known such love late in life with one Maggie Parkins.

Chapter Two

From the ferry deck, Jude admired the summer sun as it began its slow descent behind the Olympic Mountain range. She leaned over the railing and watched the foaming wake leave a trail behind the state ferry as it began its journey from Victoria, Canada, back to their home on Madrona Island. She leaned her head against Ryan's shoulder, and he slipped his arm around her waist and held her close.

"The colors are unbelievable," Jude said, pointing to the shades of pink and lavender reflecting from the sky onto the water.

"The striking golds remind me of Ian's paintings," he said. "Or a scene from a fantasy novel."

Jude agreed. Just like the magical few days they'd spent in Victoria staying at the Empress Hotel. It was grand and extravagant. Their first romantic get-away together had been perfect. She glanced over and admired Ryan's profile. A strand of sandy blond hair toppled across his brow. His hair was pulled back into a short ponytail that spilled across his collar and set off his cheekbones and rugged face.

Ryan's dark eyes met hers and her breath caught. This was real, she reminded herself.

He pointed to the sky where a blue heron glided just above them. "Look at that magnificent wing span."

Jude watched the prehistoric looking bird glide above them. "I sure didn't miss the 4th of July rush weekend," she said. "I'm glad we were kicked out of Island Thyme Café by the movie people, or we might never have left the restaurant all summer."

"And now we'll get to see what the café will look like with a new white exterior. Who knows," he said, "perhaps it will attract more customers."

The movie team had made a deal to transform the town into a quaint New England village for their set. In return, the merchants would have the choice of what color they wanted their exterior repainted after the shooting. Maybe Jude would leave it a crisp white and paint the shutters Kelly green to offset the flowerbeds. Kyla was having Tea & Comfort painted pale lavender with white trim.

Golden hues warmed the sunset and spilled light across the waters of the Sound as they crossed the border back into the U.S. How nice it had been not to have to wake and open for business for a few days. After all the work with Kyla and Luke's wedding, and the preparations for the movie to start shooting on Madrona Island, this was a much- needed break. They'd stayed awake both evenings, listening to soft music and sharing confidences. Walls slowly crumbled between them. Jude told him a little about her marriage and her estrangement from her daughter, Lindsey, who would be arriving soon for the summer. Ryan had listened intently and held her when tears threatened. He'd suggested Lindsey be his sous chef in the kitchen. It would keep her busy.

Jude smiled. "The hotel was like being in an English castle. I have to tell Kyla about the afternoon High Tea at the Empress. She'd love the china and the hotel's signature afternoon tea blend, and that elegant lobby with overstuffed furniture."

"It was a great escape," Ryan said. "Those just-out-of-the-oven raisin scones with that strawberry jam and Empress cream were worth the trip alone." He turned her toward him and lifted her chin for a kiss.

As she had all weekend, Jude melted into his arms. Space and time did not exist when she was with him. It had been so long since she'd let herself fall like this. Trepidation danced at the edge of her joy. Could she really trust a man again? In a few months she would be forty. For years now, she'd kept a smile on her face and been a friend to all who walked through the door of Island Thyme Café. She'd watched her two best friends, Lily and Kyla, find the men of their dreams and marry all in the last year. Jude couldn't be happier for them, but would it ever be her turn again?

Ryan kissed the top of head. "We're almost there."

The outline of Madrona Island emerged in the distance. They would be home soon. Back to real life. To Lindsey staying for the summer, and to the devastatingly beautiful actress, Peyton Chandler. Jude had probed a little on this trip. She'd seen Ryan's face when the actress's name was mentioned at the Farmer's Market last month, and it wouldn't take a tealeaf reading with Kyla to know there was trouble there. His voice had been level and his words crisp. "We dated briefly a while ago," was all he would say.

Best to let it go, Jude thought. She didn't want to hold on too tight or hope too much. Love needed loose reins. Love...she had no doubt that was where she was falling.

The lavender hues were turning to a deep purple and midnight blue as the ferry docked at the Madrona Pier for walk-off traffic only. In the summer, this newly added extra stop would bring even more tourists. They would find the island quite full for the next three weeks or more as the movie crew took over the town of Grandview. Ryan's sigh caused Jude to look at him. She could almost see him retreating back into his shell.

"I wish we could turn around and go back," he said.

Jude put her hand in his as the ferry slowed and dock workers moved into place. "On with the show," she said, trying to sound cheery.

Ryan only nodded.

Chapter Three

Early morning sunlight stretched across the back deck enticing Jude to read her morning emails outside. A foamy cappuccino in one hand, she lifted her iPad off the counter and called to Ryan who was in the kitchen prepping for lunch. "I'll be outside if you need me."

Ryan strolled toward her and stared longingly toward the café's windows. "Wish I could join you, but you know how it goes; the soup needs stirring, the thyme butter needs thawing. A chef's work is never done."

He attempted a smile, but his eyes were dark. Jude wondered again what was going on, but she still hadn't said a word about what was stirring in him under the surface. Ever since they stepped off the ferry from Victoria, Ryan had been somewhat distant. But she was determined not going to pry. He would tell her when he was ready.

She gave him her best "everything is great" smile and walked outside. The benches glistened with dew. Jude wiped it away with her hand before sitting. The clear, still water below resembled silk, and one lone, anchored sailboat swayed in the breeze. The jagged-peaked mountains in the distance looked like they were painted against a perfect sky background. She placed her coffee on the table, put her iPad in its stand, and opened her email. Usually this only took about five minutes, but with the movie Murder Most Magic scheduled to shoot in town for next three weeks, her inbox was overflowing. She'd read in the newspaper that shooting on Madrona Island had been a last-minute decision after another location fell through. It would be disruptive, but fantastic exposure for the merchants.

One email contained the list of local townsfolk who had made it through the auditions and would be paid as extras in the film. Jude was sure there'd been plenty of takers. Grandpa John's name was right on top. He would be a regular on set everyday. It would be nice to see him around more. She recognized a few other names scattered over the shooting days, including Ian and Lily's son, Jason, and Shirley with her new husband, Don. It would be fun to have them all together here in town.

Island Thyme Café had been contracted to provide lunches to the cast and some of the crew most days. Jude had to hire extra help, but it would be very profitable and help pay off the remodel on the back deck. And with Lindsey prepping for Ryan, everything should hum along smoothly. At least she hoped it would. The newly-painted town looked even more picturesque now.

Her fingers froze on the keyboard when she saw an email from her daughter, Lindsey. The subject line was marked important. It had only been a couple of weeks since she'd heard from Lindsey with a cryptic note saying her dad, Mitchell, was cruising in his yacht with new wife number three for the summer. Mitchell didn't want Lindsey alone in the Seattle mansion, so she needed to stay with Jude until her dad returned. Lindsey was finally reaching out to Jude, not totally by choice, but because she had no alternative. Jude didn't care the reason. She would have her daughter back with her on the island, and with the close proximity, maybe some reconciliation could occur.

Holding her breath, she opened the email and read it quickly. Lindsey would be arriving sooner than expected. Her boyfriend had recently dumped her, so all the plans to delay Lindsey's homecoming as long as possible had been ruined. Jude closed her mail and laid her iPad on the wooden table beside her.

White-hot regret shot through her. If things had been different in her marriage, perhaps she'd still be sitting in a luxurious home on Lake Washington with a loving husband at her side and a daughter who wanted to come home. But they had not. The indelible imprint of that night almost twenty years before would never leave her memory.

Jude remembered pacing the floor of their Seattle home trying not to look at the clock again. "Where the heck are you, Mitchell," she'd yelled at the front door.

Nine-month-old Lindsey let out a piercing cry from her crib down the hall.

"Oh no," Jude said, "You just went to sleep." She hurried down the hall toward the baby's room, fatigue dripping off her like perspiration.

"It's okay, little one. Shhh," she whispered, holding the baby close to her chest. She'd tried everything, but nothing seemed to help with Lindsey's colic. The doctor had told Jude to try and stay calm, that the baby might be raising her stress level. With no sleep and an undependable husband, staying calm seemed impossible. By day, Mitchell left for work and expected to come home to a quiet and clean home, with dinner on the table. But with a colicky baby that never slept, day or night, and could barely keep food down, it was all Jude could do to just get through the day and pray Mitchell would relieve her when he got home from work.

The clock glared at her...almost four a.m., and her husband was still not home. Cradling Lindsey in her arms, she walked back out to the living room and collapsed on the couch. The baby flailed and the incessant crying began again. Jude's last shred of self-control snapped causing her to burst into tears. With no relief in sight, it was all too much.

It was hardly the perfect scenario for a happy home. Lately, when Mitchell walked in and heard little Lindsey's cry, he'd blame Jude for being unable to keep her own baby content. It didn't matter what Jude said or did, or how she tried to make Mitchell understand. He'd just shake his head, turn around, and walk out the front door.

And tonight, she wondered, would he even come home at all? They'd barely been married two years and already he'd lost total interest in her and his own child.

Lindsey finally quieted and nestled into her arms. "It's just us girls," Jude whispered.

There weren't many options for her if the marriage fell apart. She'd be a single mom. All she had in the way of work experience was cooking and waitressing during summer breaks from school. There had been plenty of boys back then, and even before reaching drinking age, Mitchell had come along. He was one of the rich boys who lived in the big houses by the lake. He'd never paid attention to her in school, but that summer after graduation when everything seemed so perfect, they'd fallen in love. The whirlwind romance had ended with a quick wedding in Las Vegas followed by days of drinking and celebrating in the glitzy town.

She kissed the top of Lindsey's sweet head. "That's it, little one," she whispered. A car passed by and Jude watched the headlights move past her window. The clock ticked even later.

Her mind wandered back to when she'd found out she was pregnant with Lindsey and had been so excited to tell Mitchell. She remembered him sweeping her off her feet and taking her to bed.

The euphoria of having a baby together had lasted just long enough for reality to set in. They needed more money to pay for a child, and their "anything goes" lifestyle was about to end. Mitchell's parents were happy to finally have their only son working for them at their company, under their rules. The long workdays turned into long nights out at the bars or strip clubs before he would come home. "I have to blow off steam from the day, somehow," he would say.

And just how was she supposed to blow off steam? Jude rose cautiously off the couch and carried the now sleeping Lindsey back into their king-sized bed in the master bedroom. Hardly daring to move, she lay back on propped pillows and held Lindsey gingerly against her chest. Heavy-eyed, she felt herself finally drift toward sleep.

Headlights flashed through her bedroom windows as the familiar sound of Mitchell's car screeched across the driveway. Jude held her breath hoping Lindsey wouldn't awaken. She propped the baby between two pillows in the middle of the bed and walked out to the living room. Mitchell opened the door and startled when he saw Jude standing there.

"What the..." he said.

She glared at him. "Waiting for you."

His face was swollen and covered on one side with small cuts and bruises. He touched his eye and winced. "I was at the emergency room. Damn car accident."

Mitchell pushed past her and walked over to the bar to pour a shot of whiskey.

Jude doubted he needed any more; he reeked of alcohol already. "Why didn't you call me?" She moved in closer to assess the damage. "Are you all right? What happened?"

He downed the shot and waved her away. "I just want to go to bed."

"Lindsey's in our bed. You'll wake her."

Mitchell rolled his eyes. "What a surprise." He slammed down his glass on the bar. "I'll sleep in the guestroom."

"No concussion?" she'd called after him.

He answered by slamming the bedroom door in her face. Soon after, he walked out of her life entirely. Without the police paperwork she'd discovered in Mitchell's desk, Jude would not have had much of a life to turn to back then, and would certainly not be sitting on the deck of her own café and home on Madrona Island now.

She reminded herself that the police report and photos were discreetly stored in her safe deposit box on Madrona Island, and the deed to her building had been in Jude's name for years. She'd kept her promise to Mitchell and never said a word to their daughter about the incident.

She shook away the memories, calmed herself, and answered Lindsey's email, assuring her she'd be at the shuttle in town to pick her up. She snapped the lid closed on her iPad and grabbed her empty cappuccino. The once calm, peaceful morning had faded into a grating headache. She blocked her eyes from the stark sunlight and darted back inside. Jude was greeted by the smell of brewing coffee mingling with herby garlic bread baking in the oven.

Ryan was writing down the lunch specials while the two new waitresses they'd hired to keep pace with the summer rush set the tables. Jude watched them place the sprigs of flowering thyme in small glass vases next to the scalloped dishes of thyme and sea salt butter.

"You okay?" Ryan asked. "You're looking very pretty this morning."

He was standing in front of her now and she hadn't even noticed. "Change of plans," she said. "Lindsey will be here in two days."

His eyes crinkled with concern. "Should I smile or run?" he asked.

Jude leaned her head on his chest. "I'm not sure. Lindsey's boyfriend just broke up with her, so her mood was not too pleasant."

Ryan hugged her. "Don't worry. I'll have her so busy in the kitchen she won't have time to think about that guy or get in any trouble."

The café door sprung open and Audrey, the librarian, with the local writer's group in tow, piled noisily in after their morning writing session at the library. Wine corks would be popping all through lunch. Jude hurried over to greet them with her best smile, or at least the best she could manage today.

Chapter Four

Ryan pulled the car into the parking lot by the local library. The streets were so crowded he could barely find a place to put the car. He opened the door for Jude and admired her long, tan legs that were usually hidden under pants all winter. Hot days and shorts made summer even better. He escorted Jude down the hill, waving at neighbors and friends as they went. It looked like the whole town had come out for this meeting the movie people had called. They walked through the double doors of the Grandview Community Center and could barely make their way, much less hear each other over the noisy crowd. They spotted Lily, her baby in her arms, and maneuvered over to join her in the back of the room.

"I'd better go get us some seats," Ryan said. "You two, I mean three, ladies wait here." He did not want to leave out baby Gwyn in her pink sundress.

As he started to maneuver his way through the crowd, Lily called something back to him, but he couldn't hear what she said over the noise. He smiled and made his way toward the seating area, happy to spot Lily's husband, Ian, standing tall and waving him over to a row of empty seats.

Ryan shook Ian's hand. "Thanks for the save. Should I go tell the ladies?

Ian shook his head. "Lily knows where we are. They'll meet us here when Kyla and Luke arrive."

Ryan took a seat a few down the row, leaving room at the end for the others.

"How's it going at the café?" Ian asked.

"Super busy. How about you? How's fatherhood?

Ian yawned. "Sleepy, but happy."

Ryan could only imagine. Would he ever be lucky enough to be a father, he wondered.

People hustled across the stage at the end of the room setting up microphones and shuffling papers. Probably the movie crew, Ryan mused. He scanned the room, noticing many familiar faces including Dan, the sheriff, and Audrey, the librarian, in the front. But no one visible from his past. Yet. The cast would be behind the scenes. It certainly wouldn't be Peyton's style to make an appearance at an event like this.

Lily returned with Kyla and Luke, with Jude following right behind. Ryan and Ian stepped out of the row to let the ladies in first.

"What a crowd," Jude said, fanning herself. "I think the whole island is here."

A familiar face hurried over toward them. "Hello," Shirley said. "Nice to see you all."

Decked in a turquoise pantsuit and her usual long strand of pearls, Shirley waved over her husband Don. He shook hands with the men and nodded at the ladies.

"My word, this makes me feel like I'm back in the big city," Don said.

Ian stood to offer Shirley his seat, but she waved him to sit down. "Grandpa John saved us seats in front with my sister, Betty, so we can hear all the details. We'll see you after this thing is over."

"See you later," Jude called after them as they hurried toward the front.

A man who obviously, from the look on his face, took his job very seriously, finally took the stage and flicked on the microphone. He tapped his fingers across it testing for sound. "Attention everyone. We're about to begin. Please take your seats.

Jude rolled her eyes at Ryan. "I hope this doesn't take all night."

"Nothing moves fast in this business," Ryan said. "We'd better get used to it for a few weeks."

The man introduced himself as the production coordinator and went on to discuss safety concerns with the power equipment and lights and privacy issues regarding the cast. "Expect delays, but otherwise business as usual," he said. Then he introduced the location manager who would be handling basic logistics.

"I wonder how these several weeks of shooting will affect business at Tea & Comfort?" Kyla said. "Will people think we're closed?"

Lily smiled. "They told me the set would only be closed during filming. I think we are all going to be very busy. I have several of the cast staying at the Inn."

"And we are catering lunch for them," Jude said, "Marco at the bookstore came up with the brilliant idea of putting a coffee cart outside before any shops open in the morning."

As the producer droned on, Ryan's mind wandered. It had been several years since he had last seen Peyton Chandler, and she was an even bigger star now. The media had labeled her a temptress. Maybe to others, but he'd do anything to avoid this unpleasant reunion. He thought of Jude's heart-shaped face and sweet smile. The way her deep brown hair curled about her shoulders. He would never abandon Jude during such a busy time, despite his discomfort with having to see Peyton again.

A young woman no more than thirty took the mic. "The stores will remain closed during the shooting of the film, and open all other hours. A guard will handle traffic safety and parking as needed." The assistant director who would be supervising the extras was next. The AD announced which extras, including Grandpa John, would be used almost every day and where they were to report and at what time.

"I hope he can handle those long hours," Jude whispered to Ryan.

Ryan winked. "Between takes, we'll keep John well fed and rested at the café."

The talking droned on in the crowded, stuffy room. Ryan shifted around in his seat. The once familiar talk of filming movies grated on his nerves and reminded him too much of the old days with Peyton. He leaned over to Luke. "Let's get out of here. Get some air."

A big grin spread across Luke's face. "Sounds good to me."

Ryan whispered to Jude that he'd be right outside, then lowered his head and scooted down the row. Luke followed briskly behind him and out the back door.

"Phew, we did it," Ryan said. He turned toward the water and ran into Marco outside talking to Becca, the new manager for Tea & Comfort. Her bright red hair was unmistakable, and their flushed faces and smiles left no doubt about the chemistry between them. "I see you escaped the crowds too," Ryan said.

"We got the gist of it," Marco replied. "Lots of people, lots of hours, and lots of delays."

"That's about it," Luke said. "We're making our escape. See you guys later."

They walked down the sidewalk toward the entrance to the pier, past the shady bench nestled under the towering cedar tree. Sunlight spilled like a blaze of fire on the blue waters of the cove. Between the large volume of summer tourists and the movie people, Ryan wondered how much longer Grandview would stay a peaceful small town.

"Pretty fancy yacht they brought for the shoot," Ian said. He leaned over the railing and took a closer look. "I wouldn't mind a ride on that myself."

After all this movie stuff is over, and the old Captain's Schooner finishes repairs, we should all go out for a sunset cruise."

"Great idea." Luke said. "Speaking of the film's wrap-up, how does next week look for coming by my place? We can finalize the menu for the cast and crew closing night dinner in the vineyard for August."

"That'll work," Ryan said. "Did they turn in the final number of people attending?"

"We capped it at fifty. They moaned and groaned a bit, but that's all the space and the kitchen can handle. Work for you?"

"Yep," Ryan said. "In my spare time, I've started putting recipes together for a cookbook and was thinking of doing a section on vineyard dinners with wine pairings."

"Count me in on that," Luke said.

As Luke talked about possible decorating ideas, Ryan gazed across the water and recalled his last confrontation with Peyton. He had no idea how much time had passed when Luke nudged him with his elbow and said, "Where'd you go, Ryan?

The din of laughter and conversation coming from the community center signaled the end of the meeting and broke the quiet moment.

"We better go find the ladies," Ryan said.

Jude and Lily were right out front. Ryan waved Jude over.

Even wearing simple jeans and a T-shirt and her dark auburn hair pulled back in a ponytail, when he looked at Jude it took his breath away. "You two playing hooky?" Jude asked. "I don't blame you a bit."

"Tell us the truth," Ryan said, "Did we miss anything?"

"Not much," Lily said. She handed Ian the baby. "I think she wants her daddy."

Jude leaned against him with a sigh. "Let's go home. That was exhausting."

"Yoo-hoo," Shirley called as she approached them with Don who was trying to keep up her with her. Betty, in her classic jeans and plaid work shirt, and Grandpa John were in tow behind her.

"So what did you all think about that meeting?" Shirley asked.

"You two had the right idea skipping out," Betty said. "Darn long meeting with just a lot of hot air."

Shirley fussed with her pearls. "This is going to put Grandview on the map. Did you see that article in Celebrity magazine about Peyton?"

Everyone turned to hear what Shirley had to say except Ryan, who froze in place.

"No, I didn't see it," Jude said.

"Well...," Shirley drew out the moment in her usual dramatic fashion. "Seems right after Peyton's fortieth birthday, her husband, that big actor Todd Chase, left her high and dry for some hot young actress."

"It happens," Lily said.

Ian squeezed her close. "Not around here it doesn't."

Ryan, finding it hard to breathe, broke away from the group. "If you'll excuse me, it's getting late and I have a long day ahead tomorrow."

"I'll go with you," Jude said.

The streets were clearing out, so it took only a couple minutes to reach the steps leading upstairs to their apartments above the café. Jude invited him to spend the night in her room.

Ryan looked down at her warm, brown eyes and wanted to say yes, but the pounding at his temples was building.

He forced a smile. "Not tonight," he said. "I'll see you tomorrow."

Ryan paced the floor of his bedroom trying to calm his racing mind. He should have mentioned something about knowing Peyton to Jude sooner, before the cast arrived. He hated rummaging through his past, but he couldn't bring himself to do it when things were going so well between them. He was sure Jude would understand, but now, finding out this way it would seem he was trying to hide something. And he was. It would all probably come out now as part of some twisted plan Peyton had conceived. The local paper said Peyton chose Grandview after seeing the setting in Celebrity magazine when they did the special on Luke and Kyla's love story last February. Had she known he was here as well? He did not look forward to the three weeks of hell ahead, but he could only blame himself for not telling Jude sooner.

Chapter Five

"They're on their way," Jude called toward the kitchen. Waitresses scattered as Chef Ryan put the final touches on the buffet against the back wall. The shooting of the film, *Murder Most Magic*, had been going on in different locales around town, and in a few days they would be ready to shoot a scene at Island Thyme Cafe.

Through the window, Jude could see the cast and crew making their way over to her café for lunch. The front door sprung open and the hungry crowd piled into the dining room. Filtering the cast from the crew was easy to determine because of the makeup and costumes. The actors were more demanding in their needs for gluten free and paleo-friendly food options. The crew was happy with about anything.

With the movie's schedule so tight, lunch moved fast. A whirlwind of people and activity took over the café, and they all left in a mass exit within one hour. After clearing away the buffet, the dining room was almost empty. Jude took a seat at the bar and sipped a little chilled Chardonnay.

"Hard day already?" Ryan said as he dried his hands on a towel at his waist.

His alluring smile took Jude's breath away.

"You could say that," she said. "How many more weeks did they say they'd be here?"

Ryan's hands moved to her shoulders, massaging away the tension. "It'll fly by like magic."

As he kissed her cheek, the front door flew open and in walked the dazzling leading lady, Peyton Chandler, in a linen dress that showed off her curves. How could anyone look that perfect, Jude wondered. Her hands instinctively pushed her dark hair out of her eyes. What a mess she must look.

Peyton slid off her Channel sunglasses. "I hope I'm not too late for lunch." A coy smile did not disguise the way her eyes darted from Ryan to Jude in his arms.

Ryan let go of Jude and backed against the bar.

"Is that you, Ryan?" Peyton asked, obviously feigning surprise. She brushed back a strand of her raven black hair that flowed long over her shoulders and down her bare back.

He nodded.

"Well, I'll be." Peyton rushed over and threw her arms around him. "I'd heard you were somewhere in the Seattle area, but what a surprise to find you cooking out here on this little island."

Jude turned to Ryan. His eyes were a black contrast against his pale face as he stood rigidly, enveloped in Peyton's arms. Finally she stepped back and poised on the barstool beside him.

"You must tell me everything while we're together these next few weeks," she all but cooed to Ryan before turning to Jude, displaying a little shark smile that made Jude want to punch her.

The finely polished actress reminded Jude of a pouncing panther. One she needed to detour right now. Jude reached out to shake Peyton's hand. "I'm Jude, the owner of Island Thyme Café."

Peyton's icy blue eyes stared briefly at Jude's extended hand and then turned back to Ryan. "You must make me that divine chocolate mousse like you used to. The one you used to whip up for midnight snacks."

Peyton was actually blinking her long, black eyelashes at Ryan, who looked like he was going to be sick. Jude felt a bit sick herself. It was obvious these two had done more than date briefly. They knew each other, probably in every sense of the word. Why hadn't Ryan told her they'd had a serious relationship? Was that why he had been acting so anxious lately? Her heart dropped into her stomach. Just how much had he been hiding from her?

Ryan stepped away from Peyton. "It is good to see you again," he said coolly. "Now if you will excuse me, I have work to do in the kitchen."

Peyton placed a hand on his arm, "Of course, darling," she said. "I'll see you real soon."

Jude gagged on the long, drawn out "darling" as she watched Ryan hurry to the kitchen.

Peyton nodded at her. "What did you say your name was again?" she asked.

"Jude."

"Please make sure Ryan and the rest of your staff follow my dietary restrictions exactly. You should have received my list of acceptable foods and preparations from my assistant."

"We have," Jude said. Perhaps it would get conveniently lost, or better yet, Jude could accidently edit it a bit. She smiled to herself imagining all the butter she would add to Peyton's fat free dishes.

Peyton stood and scrutinized the café. "I just realized I'm not hungry after all." She turned without another word and let the door slam behind her as she left.

Heat raced through Jude's limbs and burrowed into her racing heart. Ryan had some explaining to do. She threw open the kitchen doors and walked over to Ryan who was slumped over the stove stirring his special clam chowder in a large pot. His face was drawn and she hesitated before speaking.

He turned off the flame and finally turned to look at her, but she recognized that faraway look he sometimes had, especially when they'd first met.

"Just how well did you know Peyton?" Jude asked.

"It was a long time ago," he said. "Trust me, it's over."

With that he walked over to the industrial refrigerator and began mechanically putting away food from lunch.

Jude stood and watched him go through the mechanical motions. Trust him? She had let her guard down and begun to trust again. And here she was, precariously balancing between a man she really didn't know and a beautiful woman who was obviously still in the picture.

Ryan threw off his chef's coat and hung it behind the door. It had been a few days since Peyton had made her entrance at the café and he was hoping it would be her last. Yet the actress had haunted his thoughts ever since. The pain on Jude's face when Peyton finally left the café had killed him, and he hated himself just a little bit more for putting her go through that.

The lunch rush wouldn't start for a few hours and he needed a break. Badly.

"Sierra, can you take over the prep from here?"

"Sure, Chef," the new kitchen helper answered.

He walked out the back door and headed toward the cove to clear his head in the fresh, early morning air. Wires were strewn everywhere as the crew busily set up lights and put props into place for the day's shoot. Ryan waved at Marco as he passed the long line in front of his coffee cart on the sidewalk outside Books, Nooks, and Coffee. The stand was mobbed. Great idea that young man had.

Rays of sunshine spread across his face and shoulders as he briskly walked down the wooden planks to the end of the pier. A blue heron perched on one of the pilings, still as a painting, while gulls screamed across the sky dropping mussels on the pier to crack open for lunch. Ryan leaned on the railing overlooking the water and exhaled the pent up tension he had been holding for days.

He'd once thought, in an alcohol-and-drug-induced daze, that he loved Peyton. Even now, the warmth of her body near him had stirred memories. But Ryan was no longer the up-and-coming-chef hungry for fame and fortune. Nor was he dazzled by the charms of Peyton Chandler, a creature of physical perfection so breathtaking no man was immune. Like the sirens of old whose enchanting songs led sailors astray toward their deaths, she had almost been the death of him. And now, when he was finally happy, his past was creeping up on him, like the tide below, to wash him out to sea.

He'd heard that she was separated from Todd Chase, so what was she scheming for now? When they'd lived together in San Francisco a few years back, Ryan couldn't believe the lying and games Peyton played with him and others. It never phased her conscience, no matter the pain her actions caused. They'd be shopping in some high-end store and she would steal stuff under his nose and then gloat gleefully when she showed him what she got away with.

What did she want now and how did he play into her spider's web? His stomach turned and beads of sweat broke out across his brow. He did not want to stick around for the next few weeks to find out. He'd run far to find the kind of people and life he wanted, a place he fit, and he'd finally found it on Madrona Island. He couldn't just take off now and leave Jude with this mess. He was done running and done with that crazy life, just like Kyla had been when she'd run from New York and the modeling scene. She might have some advice for him.

Ryan gazed out at the jagged peaks of Mount Baker towering against the backdrop of the azure sky and counted his blessings. He was grateful that he'd found this place. A lone kayaker paddled rhythmically across the still water.

"Pretty darn nice day," Betty said as her little dog Zinger dragged her toward Ryan.

Ryan reached down and scratched behind the dog's ears. "Good boy," he said.

Betty shook her head vigorously, her silver white hair catching in the wind. "Don't tell him that. He'll want a treat."

"Bring him by the café later. I'll give him some scraps or a good bone."

Betty stood beside him and muffled a cough. "You look deep in thought, young man."

"What do you do when your past catches up to you?" he said meeting Betty's eyes.

She cocked her head. "Depends what kind of man you are."

What kind of man was he? The kind that thrived on blinding flashbulbs and reporters swarming? The kind that was blinded by the instant fame as the boy-toy-chef of a famous actress? The fast-track life of drinking and drugging, of Peyton's lying and cheating, all led him down the road to that last night. She'd gone too far and he had walked out with total disgust for himself and her, shutting the door on that life forever.

One eyebrow arched, Betty looked at him waiting for an answer.

"I know the man I want to be," Ryan said.

"Then be it!" Betty said, patting him on the back. She gave the dog's leash at tug. "Come on Zinger, let's hit the road."

Ryan watched her scurry along the pier trying to keep pace with the curly-haired red dog. In her late seventies and she could still run circles around most people. That woman was a marvel. What you saw was what you got. He wished he could be that transparent.

Maybe he could put his past behind him and finally be happy.

Peyton always found a way to get what she wanted. But not this time.

Chapter Six

Jude wiped down the counter of the old oak bar that had seen many a year. She turned around and emptied glasses left by customers into the sink, and then placed them in the dishwasher bin. The volume of tourists coming in for lunch, on top of the movie crew, was keeping them busy beyond their comfort zone. It was almost 4:00 p.m. and she and Ryan had to leave to meet the shuttle for her daughter Lindsey in a few hours. She was half ready to lock the doors and put a sign out saying they were closed for dinner when the front door burst open. Jude looked over with dread.

"It's me again, I'm afraid," Grandpa John said.

Jude smiled. "C'mon in. You're always welcome." He was looking pretty exhausted and probably needed a good meal after being an extra all day on the film. And she always loved his company.

Betty, dressed in work clothes, scooted in behind him. "Got room for one more?"

Jude waved them over to the bar, but not before putting the closed sign in the window. If anyone complained, she would remind them they operated on island time here.

"Why don't you two sit at the bar, and I will wait on you personally."

Betty climbed up on a stool and sighed. "This extra work takes a lot out of me. All that sitting around and waiting for them to finally film the scene about drove me crazy today."

Grandpa John winked at Jude. "I kind of like being paid for doing nothing. Lots of 'hurry up and wait'." He opened the menu Jude had put before him. "I hope you don't mind me dropping in for an early dinner. I hate to bother Lily, with the baby and all. Plus the Inn is full and those cast members seem to always need something."

"You're right about that," Betty said. "Shirley encourages them to come by our house and ask questions anytime."

"Questions?" Jude asked.

"You know, about where to eat, drink, fish, that kind of thing. Mostly it's the crew. The cast doesn't bother with us locals much. And that Peyton, it's like 'the Queen Herself' arriving when she appears on set."

Jude placed an iced tea with a sprig of lemon and thyme in front of both of them. "On the house," she said. "I heard they are using the 100 foot yacht for filming out off the pier tomorrow."

Grandpa John sipped his tea. "Murder and mayhem," he said flashing a smile. "From what I overheard, the leading man, a magician, and his wife sail into the small seaport when the magician becomes mysteriously ill. Joe tells me the local ambulance has been repainted for the scene where they rush the guy to the hospital."

"Peyton, of course, is cast as a murderess, I presume?" Jude said.

"Oh yeah," Betty said. "And after someone tips off the magician, he escapes by night in a sailboat and the chase begins."

Ryan came out from the kitchen, wearing his black chef coat. Jude noticed his face looked drawn and he did not make eye contact with her.

"I thought I heard voices out here." Ryan walked over and shook Grandpa John's hand. "How's it going?"

"Just fine with me, but Betty's all tuckered out."

Jude looked closely at Betty. The dark circles under her eyes and the pale translucence of her skin looked like more than just fatigue.

"I'm fine. I could run circles around any of you," Betty said.

A dry cough followed Betty's words and it lingered just a bit too long for Jude's liking. She doubted Betty had set foot in a doctor's office for a long time.

Grandpa John laid his menu down on the counter and looked over at Ryan. "Any chef's specials tonight?"

"For you two," Ryan said, "The skies the limit. How about a plate of my freshly made lemon thyme chicken over linguini?"

Betty tossed her menu down. "Sold."

Grandpa John nodded his affirmation.

Ryan turned and headed back to the kitchen. Later, in the car, perhaps. Maybe he would open up to her about what was on his mind when they were alone.

"Glass of wine? A beer with dinner?" Jude asked.

"Not tonight," Grandpa John said. "I'm not sure I could stay awake to drive us both home. I bet you're ready to call it a day yourself."

Jude took a seat beside them and kicked off her shoes. "The movie people can be hard to please at times."

Grandpa John sipped his water. "I see Peyton popping in and out of here a lot. She must like the food."

"It's not the food she's interested in," Jude said. "It's Ryan."

Grandpa John placed his hand over Jude's. "Try not to let it bother you too much. It's obvious Ryan is only interested in you, and they'll all be gone in a few weeks."

Jude hoped he was right, but the knot in her gut said otherwise.

Ryan was glad he had offered to drive Jude to get Lindsey at the airport shuttle. Jude twisted her hands in her lap and stared out the window. He'd never seen her this nervous.

"How long has it been since Lindsey's been to the island?" he asked.

Jude turned her head toward him. "If you mean for longer than a day, it's been a long time."

He listened quietly as she told him how heartbreaking it had been when her fifteen-year-old daughter had decided to go live with her rich father and his new young wife. Ryan could only imagine how devastated Jude had been. He could understand a teenager being bored on this small island, but he could not understand the betrayal and callousness Lindsey showed when she left her mother behind.

"I'm sorry you had to go through this," he said.

Her brave smile was one of the things he liked about Jude. She worked to overcome her obstacles and find happiness wherever she was.

They pulled the car into the parking lot just as the shuttle arrived. Jude fidgeted in her seat.

He'd not brought the topic of Peyton into the conversation, because it would just add more stress in to an already tense situation.

Ryan walked around the car and opened the door for her. He forced a smile. "Surely the two of us can handle one little teenager."

Jude took his hand and stepped out on the gravel pavement. "Don't count on it," she said.

People exited the shuttle slowly, but there was no teenage girl in sight. Ryan looked straight ahead, willing her to appear. Taking her own sweet time, a young woman in cut-off denim shorts, a flimsy t-shirt hanging off one shoulder, and wearing strappy sandals slowly made her way down the stairs. She carried a pink backpack with the word MOM in black letters printed on it. Maybe there was hope after all. As she sauntered closer, Ryan realized the backpack displayed the brand, MCM. Lindsey made no eye contact as she stood by the back of the shuttle texting on her phone. Her entrance did not bode well with him, nor could he imagine with Jude.

Lindsey pushed her long blonde hair out of her eyes and finally looked up. Ryan could see the resemblance to her mother. She nodded toward them as if she was ready for them to retrieve her luggage. Jude walked toward her and Ryan followed slowly behind to let them have a little a moment alone.

Jude reached over to hug Lindsey and she leaned her head to the side to let her. "How was your trip?" Jude asked.

Lindsey pulled her long hair off her neck. "Hot and long."

The driver placed Lindsey's suitcase down next to them and Ryan scooted in to retrieve it.

"Who's this?" Lindsey asked.

"This is Ryan," Jude said. "He's the chef at the café and a friend."

He put out his hand, "Nice to meet you."

Lindsey eyed him suspiciously and then managed a weak handshake. She looked over at her mom. "You look different," she said.

"I do?"

Lindsey shrugged.

"How about we take off?" Ryan said. He walked over and put the suitcase in the trunk. He waited for everyone to get in and buckle up before driving back toward Jude's water view apartment above the café. He had the small single apartment next to hers that faced the street, so it was an easy drive home.

"Anyone hungry?" he asked.

"Sort of," Lindsey said. "What's good here?"

Jude flashed a hopeful look at Ryan.

Ryan laughed. "The best food on the island is at Island Thyme Café, if I do say so myself."

"You would say that," Lindsey said.

"I'll let you be the judge. I hear you like fine dining and cook a bit yourself."

Lindsey glared at him in the rearview mirror then pulled out her phone and started typing away. She was not going to make things any easier in their lives, but he was not going to let her get away with making things worse.

"You'll be working in the kitchen with Ryan this summer," Jude said.

"Dad gave me his credit card," Lindsey mumbled, eyes engrossed in her phone. "I don't need the money."

"I wasn't planning on paying you," Jude said. "It will be good for you to get involved, learn about cooking and be a part of things here."

Lindsey bolted, suddenly paying full attention. "What? I have to spend the summer here, deal with being dumped by my boyfriend, and now I have to work too?"

"That's how it goes," Ryan said.

Quiet permeated the car as Ryan pulled into the driveway to park. Jude was nervously biting her bottom lip and Ryan wanted to kiss it and make it better. He didn't dare look in the rearview mirror.

"Fine," Lindsey finally said. She flung open her door and got out. With a huff, she walked up the stairs to Jude's apartment.

Ryan carried her oversized suitcases and put them in Lindsey's room before returning to the living room. He sat down on the couch next to Jude and rested his arm gently around her shoulders.

Lindsey was curled up in the overstuffed chair across from them. "Awfully friendly for an employee," she said. "You two dating or something?"

Jude smiled. "We are. For a little while now."

Lindsey shrugged. "No wonder you look different." Her phone chimed and Lindsey pulled it out and started texting again. They no longer existed to her.

Ryan winked at Jude and got to his feet. "Let me know if you need anything. I guess I'll be going now. Let you settle in. Nice to meet you, Lindsey. I'll see you in the kitchen at

6:00 a.m. for prep tomorrow. We have a film crew coming in at 8:00 sharp."

"You have to be kidding," Lindsey said, jumping out of her seat. "I just got here and need some sleep."

Ryan stood firm. "When it comes to work, I don't kid."

Lindsey looked to her mother.

"He's the boss when it comes to the kitchen," Jude said.

"Some welcome home," Lindsey said. "Any other surprises?"

"I'm sorry we didn't get much time to talk after you sent your email," Jude said. "Perhaps tomorrow we can do some catching up?"

"Fine, whatever." Lindsey turned and headed to her room.

Ryan kissed Jude on the cheek. "Get some sleep. I'll let myself out."

This was one night he was glad he was sleeping in his own place.

Chapter Seven

Jude woke to the sound of Lindsey slamming things around in the guest bathroom. She propped up in bed and took a deep breath. It meant everything to her to try to rebuild her relationship with Lindsey this summer, but since living with her father the girl's attitude had changed, and not for the better. She remembered the sweet, curly blonde-haired daughter she'd pushed on the swings in Grandview Park. The little girl who loved to bake cookies with her mommy and be read the nighttime fairy book at bedtime. They'd always been so close until Mitchell decided he wanted to be back in the picture. He'd so totally abandoned them when Lindsey was little that Jude had almost forgotten about him. But not Lindsey. She wanted to know her father. Jude couldn't blame her and had purposely said nothing negative about her dad, just that he was a very busy man. It was a perfect storm the year Lindsey had turned fifteen and Mitchell remarried. None the less, Jude was determined to find a way to bond with her daughter this summer.

Lindsey burst into her room. "Do you have any hair straightener? I can't find mine."

"I don't use one," Jude said. "We can get some at Island Drug later if you want."

Lindsey rolled her eyes and fled back to the bathroom.

Jude got out of bed and pulled on her robe. A long, hot shower might help, followed by a triple mocha. She heard Lindsey slam the front door and clomp down the steps to the café. 6:00 a.m. sharp. Jude was impressed.

It was going to be an extra stressful day all around. The set designer from the film had put everything in order for a shoot that would take place at the table by the window in the café. A menu had been given to Ryan, and Jude noticed it included chocolate mousse.

The warm water pounded on her back and neck as she hummed softly in the shower. She inhaled the calming scent of her favorite lavender soap from Tea & Comfort, and imagined the water rinsing off all her tension and sending it down the drain.

After towel drying, she returned to her room to dress. Her house was silent and, she had to admit, peaceful again. In her mind, she blessed Ryan for coming up with the idea of Lindsey working with him in the kitchen. The girl needed a routine and something to do to feel good about herself.

Dressed and ready, Jude headed downstairs. She avoided the kitchen and went directly to the espresso machine behind the bar. They wouldn't be open for almost an hour, but there was a lot of prep to do first. The crew members and cast would need beverages and morning snacks. The smell of fresh baked blackberry muffins drifted in from the kitchen and made her stomach growl. Jude turned on the large coffee makers, ground the fresh roasted local coffee beans, and started the brewing. For herself, she brewed two shots in the espresso maker, covered it with foamy steamed milk, and added a generous pump of chocolate. She took a seat at the bar with her iPad for a quick email check. There was a note from the assistant director requesting a few changes to the menu. She gulped her mocha, slipped off the stool, and headed into the kitchen.

It made Jude smile to see Lindsey wearing an apron over her shorts and T-shirt. Her sun-streaked hair was rolled in a bun and she was chopping vegetables furiously. The smell of garlic and thyme filled the air.

"Good morning," Ryan said.

"Maybe," Jude said. "A few requests for changes in todays menu. Now they want fresh squeezed orange juice for the scene and the muffins to be gluten free. Can you do that?"

Ryan nodded. "That's why we're hustling in here. I figured there would be last minute changes. We won't officially open for lunch until the scene is complete."

"I'll take care of the chilled wine and make sure each glass gas a strawberry in it," Jude said. She walked over to Lindsey and admired the platters of vegetables she had sliced. "Good morning," she said. "Did you get some breakfast?"

Lindsey cocked her head toward her mother. "Ryan threw together an omelet. It wasn't half bad." She turned and went back to her chopping.

"If it's okay with Ryan," Jude said, "Why don't you come out and watch them shoot the scene today in the dining room?"

Lindsey looked over to Ryan. "I'd really like to."

Ryan eyed the pile of cut vegetables. "I think I can spare you for an hour or so."

Jude could hardly believe her eyes. Ryan was taming the wild beast she called her daughter. Maybe... she stopped herself before she set herself up with more expectations.

"I'll let you know when they arrive," she said before rushing out.

Just as she got back into the lobby area, the crew was piling in with all of their equipment, and she knew she'd better get the coffee ground and ready. As people clamored in with lights and other equipment, she saw the set designer arranging plates and glasses, and trying different flower arrangements at the table. Meanwhile, the cameramen checked angles and figured out where to shoot. The extras were brought in and placed at their tables.

Jude rushed to get cups of coffee out on the bar and have pitchers of ice water ready. She knew that everyone was waiting now for Peyton to arrive. With that thought, the door opened, and in walked Peyton Chandler followed by her entourage. Wearing dark sunglasses, a skimpy red sundress, and carrying a pricey Gucci bag, she strutted in for all to see. Jude noticed Lindsey standing by the door to the kitchen, watching the entrance intently. Her eyes never left the actress. Jude waved Lindsey over for an introduction. Lindsey seemed quite interested in being a part of what was going on.

"Hi, everyone," Peyton said. "Are you waiting for me?"

Jude almost choked. Lindsey stood beside her, and it was obvious that she was very excited to meet Peyton.

"Well, hello," said Peyton. "And who is this pretty young girl?"

Jude stepped forward. "She's my daughter, Lindsey."

Peyton shook Lindsey's hand, showcasing her best smile. "Are you here for the summer?"

"Yes, I'm helping Chef Ryan out in the kitchen as his sous chef. It's so great to meet you."

"Well, thank you," Peyton said.

The director walked over and took Peyton's hand. "Good morning, darling. We're all set up and ready for you." He guided her over to the table so the shoot could begin. The young actor who was playing the local reporter looked familiar to Jude, maybe from TV. He took his place at the well-set table for the lunch scene and took a sip of water.

"Quiet everyone," the director said. The actors got into place, cameras were readied, and a hush fell before he said, "All right, action!"

A low buzz of conversation and the clattering sound of coffee cups hitting saucers began. Extras were mixed throughout the café in booths and tables. A waitress moved among them filling coffee cups, just like a regular day at the café. Jude watched as the two main actors began their conversation. Peyton crossed her hands in front of her on the table, and smiled innocently at the man across from her. She was obviously wrapping that local reporter around her diamond-clad finger as she weaved her story.

"I'm so worried," Peyton said. She leaned over toward the reporter, revealing ample cleavage. "My husband and I finally had some time alone. He's so busy with his career, I barely see him. And then," Peyton dabbed her moist eyes. "All of sudden he was so pale and passed out right in front of me. I told the captain to find a hospital immediately. And now, I just don't know if he will make it."

The reporter seemed sympathetic and quite mesmerized by the actress's charm. "I'm sure he'll be fine, Mrs. Blackwell. I'll see to it personally."

"Call me Lizbeth," she said coyly.

"Lizbeth, then," he said. "Is there anything I can do for you? Find you a place to stay, call a relative?"

Peyton looked at him with grateful eyes. "Thank you for your kindness. I'll just stay on the yacht for now. But you could..."

"What?" he said.

"Keep the story quiet, just for a little while?"

The reporter's face sank. "Of course, whatever you need."

"Thank you. You know what will happen if people start finding out the infamous Blackwell is here; we'll have no peace."

The reporter rose and handed her his card. "I totally understand. If I can be of any service, you know where to find me."

The way he looked like he wanted to devour her, Jude thought he was probably hopeful that Lizbeth would take his hand and bring him back to the yacht with her. But no luck. Lizbeth lowered her head and faked more tears.

"I will let you know," she said and watched him exit the scene.

It seemed like hours went by as they shot the scene three more times. Fresh food had to be brought in, hair and make up were checked with each take.

"Working on a film would be so cool," Lindsey said beside her.

"Right," Jude said. That was about the last thing she hoped Lindsey would do with her life.

In the middle of saying her lines, Peyton lifted her hand in the air to stop the shoot. She pushed back her dark, silky locks, and came abruptly out of character. "Cut, break," she demanded. "This doesn't seem real. I think the chef should come out in this scene and ask us if we want anything else."

Jude sighed. That was quite a chess move on Peyton's part. But she forced a smile and went into the kitchen. "Ryan, your presence is being requested by Peyton. She would like you to come out and ask how their meal is going on camera."

He rolled his eyes, dried his hands on a towel, and buttoned his chef coat. "I don't remember signing a waiver to be in the film and I damn well don't want to."

"Just come out then and humor her a minute. She's holding up the shoot."

Ryan marched over to the table as ordered.

"Wait," the director said. "Let us get the cameras rolling and then walk in and ask for their order."

A dark frown crossed Ryan's face. "No release."

The director nodded and motioned for Ryan to move to the table. "We'll take care of that later."

He mock bowed before Peyton. "And how was everything today, ma'am? Can I get you anything else?"

Peyton looked at him with fury in her eyes. No young, attractive woman liked being called ma'am. Jude guessed Ryan threw that in specifically for that reason. He had more spunk than she thought.

"I'd just love a chocolate soufflé," she drawled.

Ryan hesitated. "May I suggest a lighter dessert?" he said, glaring at Peyton. "I could bring out a dish of our homemade grapefruit and thyme sorbet with a couple of our special macaroons."

Peyton pouted. "If you don't have what I really want here, then I guess that will have to do."

It was obvious to Jude that they were locked in a power struggle and neither was going to back down.

"I guess it will," he said.

Ryan turned abruptly toward the kitchen, just as the director called a halt to the

scene.

Peyton stood blocking Ryan's exit, and faced the director. "Do we have it?" Peyton asked impatiently. "Is my alibi handled now?"

The director looked put out, but acquiesced. "Why don't we call it a wrap? The crew can break for lunch, and we'll meet back on the pier for the shoot on the yacht at 2:00 p.m. sharp."

The crew began to disperse, but Peyton was not finished with Ryan. She touched his shoulder, and whispered in his ear. Jude could not hear what she was saying and moved closer.

"You know how I love your, rich, creamy chocolate mousse," Peyton cooed.

Ryan shook free. "I'll put it on the dinner menu this week," he said.

"That would be so sweet of you."

"No problem," Ryan said, "now if you will excuse me ..."

Peyton tried to get another word in, but Ryan showed her his back as he hustled back to the kitchen. Hands on hips, she glared after him. Realizing she was being watched, Peyton turned to her audience. "It's nice to have an "in" with the chef," she said winking.

Jude wanted to strangle her long, perfect neck, but reminded herself she had work to do. The shoot was over. Peyton showed up, worked for a few hours, and now she'd be off till the afternoon. Jude could only imagine the seven figures the actress was paid. She noticed Peyton still staring toward the kitchen and knew exactly what was on her mind, but before Jude could react, Peyton glided right through the doors into Ryan's private domain.

Jude hesitated. It would be best not to follow her and let Ryan handle it. She went back to the bar and supervised cleanup as the crew returned their dirty coffee cups before leaving. Lunch today would probably be quite crowded, and she didn't have much time to turn things around before the hungry tourists and regulars started arriving. Luckily, Lindsey was back in the kitchen helping Ryan, and the waitresses had arrived early, so everyone was hustling to put the restaurant back in order.

Jude couldn't hear what was going on in the kitchen, but without a doubt, Ryan would be escorting Peyton out fairly quickly. And of course, she was right. But not completely. She was surprised to see Peyton exit with Ryan following her out the back door. They sat down at a table in the middle of the deck, in clear view of everyone in the café through the dining room windows. It was obvious the actress was setting the scene to be sure Jude and everyone else who was still in the restaurant would see just how cozily she was sitting with the chef.

Laughing, smiling, flirting, Peyton put on quite a show. When she reached over and put her hand on Ryan's leg, Jude's chest tightened. For one minute, she wondered if Ryan and Peyton were an item again. Was Ryan lying to her? It all looked so real, but then with an actress how could you ever tell what was real and what was fake? Was this just staged? Staged by a professional to cause more problems? She sighed.

Ryan, red-faced and frowning, finally walked back in. He waved to Jude and headed back into the kitchen. Peyton made her exit much like her entrance, pretentious and attention grabbing. Jude sighed. One down. How many to go?

Fortunately they had cancelled dinner service tonight because they'd had no idea how long the shoot would take and how late lunch would run. Jude wanted to ask Ryan what was going on. Why hadn't he told her he had a past with this woman before she arrived? All Jude knew was that she might want to rethink their relationship. At least question him a bit more. He'd assured her that his relationship with Peyton, or whatever it had been, was long over. But could she believe him after what she saw today?

Ryan strode back into the kitchen before saying something in public he would regret. He didn't want Jude exposed to the depth of his anger before he could calm down and explain everything to her. Ryan couldn't believe Peyton. "If you come right now, we can settle this," she had told him. He had no idea just what they were settling, but he'd taken the bait. And in turn she'd brought him out there, flirted with him, and purposely tried to make a public scene. When he'd asked her what she wanted to clear up, she grinned and said, "Us, honey."

What must Jude have thought? He diced the celery and the onions in prep for the lunch special. With each knife cut he imagined chopping Peyton out of his life, word by word. If he just ignored that woman, maybe she would go away, but of course he knew that would never be the case.

Lindsey walked over and admired his handiwork with the knife. "Could you believe how beautiful Peyton is? She's such a good actress. And you knew her."

Ryan just rolled his eyes.

"Do you think Mom would mind if I watched some of the shoot down at the pier after we finish here? They told me it was okay. It might run late."

"You better ask her," he said.

"I'll be right back."

Lindsey was out of the kitchen faster than he'd seen her move all day, and back almost as fast. From the smile on her face, Jude must have said yes. He hoped Jude wasn't too disappointed that Lindsey was heading out on her first afternoon in town.

"What time will I be done here today?" she asked.

"You've only been here a few hours," Ryan said.

"Mom said I could go to the shoot, and I don't want to miss too much.

Ryan wiped his hands on a towel. "About 3:00. In the meantime, could you get the avocados peeled? We're going to have people coming in for lunch any minute."

"All right, all right," Lindsey said. "Peyton told me I could come watch her shoot any time. It sure was fun watching. It must be amazing working on a movie set."

"Yeah, I'm sure it is," Ryan said. "Meanwhile, you're working in the kitchen."

"I know," Lindsey said with a sigh. "I'm on it."

She propped herself on the stool by the counter and began peeling avocados for sandwiches. The daily special was crisp, apple smoked bacon, local lettuce, tomato, and Coho salmon sandwiches.

"Two specials and a shrimp salad," a waitress yelled through the order window.

Ryan checked the temperature of the grill. It was sizzling hot, so he could start searing the salmon. He'd baked the savory garlic thyme bread last night and would cut it thick for each individual sandwich.

Lindsey assembled the sandwiches and dressed them with a pickle at the side and a scoop of homemade potato chips fresh from the fryer.

Ryan dropped another handful of sliced potatoes into the oil and watched them sizzle until golden brown. Sizzling was probably what Jude was doing. He was going to have to tell her more than he wanted to even remember much less share that part of his life. After the morning antics, he had to prove to her that he was not interested in Peyton.

An idea came into his mind. There was no dinner service tonight, and Lindsey was going to be out for a while. What if he made a wonderful early picnic supper for just the two of them? He sighed, for the first time letting out the breath he'd been holding all morning. He would open that exquisite bottle of Chardonnay that a friend had sent from the Napa Valley. It was already in the wine chiller. He would serve it in crystal glasses.

As he worked, he created the meal in his mind. Salmon salad sandwiches. What would be better? He would put aside some of the salmon into a bowl and add fresh squeezed lemon, cut up fresh picked tarragon, very thinly cut red onion and celery, and blend it with mayonnaise and whipped cream cheese. He'd add a hard boiled egg, a dash of salt and pepper, and *voila*, salmon salad.

A waitress hook Ryan out of his daydream by calling in another order. "Two soup and sandwich specials, one lemon thyme chicken pasta."

Lindsey moved into action with the chicken dish alongside the new prep chef he was training. Ryan continued making sandwiches. The orders continued to pour in. Ryan would have to wait for a down moment to catch Jude's attention and mention the picnic. It seemed that everyone in town had decided to eat there today. He hoped Jude was handling everything well in the front. Just as he thought of her, she appeared in the doorway. Her classic smile was there, but her eyes were tinged with sadness.

"Sorry for the rush guys, it's finally slowing down," Jude said. "You're doing a great job back here."

Ryan wiped his hands on a towel and nodded to Lindsey to take his station. "And how are you holding up out there?" he asked.

Jude shrugged. Her face was noticeably pale.

"You look like you could use a break," Ryan said. "How about we go outside for a few?"

They walked out of the back door and along the wooden walkway behind her building that overlooked the sea green water. The sky was clear again today, giving Ryan a perfect view of the crew setting up at the end of the pier near the large yacht. He was glad they wouldn't be coming back to the restaurant again. Jude looked exhausted. He offered what he did best, a comfort meal.

"I have a surprise for you."

"You do?"

"So remember there's no dinner service tonight."

"Of course, I remember," she said.

"I have a special picnic planned, just you and me, an early supper alone and a perfectly chilled bottle of your favorite Chardonnay."

A smile softened her face. "That sounds pretty good," she said. "I think we could use some time to just be together. Lindsey is already bailing on me her first evening home."

"She's a kid," Ryan said. "Maybe she'll meet some of the young people in town, make some friends."

"Maybe," Jude said.

He knew he should say more about the scene with Peyton, but this was not the time or place. Later when they were alone and rested would be better timing. He didn't want to add to Jude's already full plate. He appreciated that she was waiting for him to bring it up. When the time was right, he told himself.

Ryan drew her into his arms and kissed the top of the head. "Don't let all this movie business get in the way. It's just that. The movie business. It has nothing to do with real life."

Jude nodded. "It's more than I bargained for. The glamour faded pretty quickly."

"It's all smoke and mirrors," Ryan said. "We'll have our island back soon enough."

Jude searched his face and he wondered what questions lingered in her mind. She yawned and released it with a sigh. "What time were you thinking of having our picnic?"

"How about this?" Ryan said, "After lunch, maybe we both could get a nap?"

"A nap," she said, perking up. "Sounds heavenly."

"Afterwards, I'll pack my handy picnic basket and we'll decide on a location."

She threw her arms around him. "Thank you, Ryan."

"You don't need to thank me. Thank you for agreeing to come."

His lips moved to hers, the kiss deepening as they pulled each other close. Jude was the most precious thing in his life now. There was no way he was going to lose her.

"Jude, where are you?" A waitress called out toward them. "There's someone in the front who needs you."

"I'll be right there," she yelled back.

"I'd better get back too," Ryan said. "Lindsey is holding down the fort alone with the new prep chef."

Once back in the café, Ryan hurried into the kitchen, which had gotten chaotic without him there to supervise. The new prep chef, Sierra, was peeling potatoes as fast as she could while trying to pull salmon off the grill at just the right moment. Lindsey plated and put food at the window for the waitresses. They made a good team. Jude had commented that the two extra summer waiters were doing great as well. In between orders, Ryan prepped everything for the salmon salad. He would make the sandwiches at the last minute before meeting up with Jude.

What else could he make? He wanted the meal to be special. Of course, he'd forgotten dessert. But what should it be? He looked over at the fresh strawberries that were just delivered today. They were as sweet as any dessert could be. If he packed fresh whipped cream, they could just dip the strawberries in it. He could sprinkle a little cinnamon in the whipped cream as well, or chocolate. Oh yes, chocolate whipped cream. A little container, fresh strawberries, and that would be it. He imagined placing the luscious, chocolate covered strawberry in Jude's mouth and kissing the whipped cream off her lips.

They finished the last order and began clean up. Ryan demanded a neat workspace in his kitchen, so it wouldn't take too long for the three of them to have the kitchen immaculate and ready for tomorrow.

While the others finished cleaning the pots and pans, Ryan dug out the rustic picnic basket that was used for special to-go orders from the cafe. There were blue and white-checkered linens that went inside it. He added the crystal wine glasses, wrapped well in napkins. Some forks, some plates, and it was set. He put everything aside until right before they left. Then he would make the sandwiches, wrap them tight, and they'd head off.

Lindsey watched him over his shoulder. "Going on a picnic?" she asked.

"Actually, while you're out, I'm going to treat your mother to an early picnic supper."

"Trying to be romantic?" She asked.

"Trying," he said.

"Good, then I won't worry about being home late," she said. "Anyway, I was going to check out that coffee shop down the street too. It's the newest looking place in town."

"Marco just remodeled the shop before re-opening it. He knows his coffee."

"Cool," Lindsey said.

Ryan pointed to the stacked dishes that still needed to be loaded. Lindsey glanced at the clock and paused. It was already after three.

"All right, go," Ryan said. Lindsey had put in a hard day of work, and he was pleased she would be joining him in the kitchen this summer.

Ryan pulled off his chef coat, threw it in the laundry basket, and headed upstairs. He was serious about taking a nap. He needed one, and so did Jude.

When he got upstairs, he saw that Jude's front door was open to let in the cool breeze. He walked in to join her. She was sitting on the couch in a pale blue sundress that showed off her legs, a chilled drink in her hand. The apartment ran warm because of all the picture windows that were exposed most of day to the sun.

"Want some iced tea?" she said.

"No thanks. By the way, Lindsey just raced out of here. She was curious to check out Marco's place."

Jude grinned. "He certainly will catch her interest, but I'd say he's taken by Becca."

Ryan sat beside her on the couch and put his arm around her shoulder. Jude's body felt warm and soft sitting so close to his. She smelled like fresh air and spring flowers. Jude was a beautiful woman, inside and out. He could hardly believe his luck finally meeting someone like her.

Jude laid her head on his shoulder. Her fingers drifted across the front of his T-shirt. "I'm so glad we have some time alone," she said.

Ryan stroked her cheek and let his fingertips trace her full mouth. He lifted her chin and brushed his lips to hers. "Jude, my Jude," he said.

She encircled him in her arms, the kiss becoming urgent. It was more than passion, almost a question seeking reassurance. And for a moment, it was only the two of them, fiercely in love against anything that could threaten them. Ryan stood and took Jude by the hand. He wanted her, wanted her more than anything in the world. He walked her down the hall to Jude's bedroom and closed the door behind them. They fell onto the bed wrapped in each other's arms. Ryan knew they may not fall asleep right away, but they would get their nap eventually.

Jude awoke to the sound of her cell phone chiming by the bed. Lindsey had sent her a text. Lindsey, thank goodness she hadn't come home and found them here.

"Watching the movie shoot with Marco and Becca. Will grab food. Back later."

Jude hated the idea of Lindsey being anywhere near Peyton, but Jude was glad something on the island was catching her interest and that she was meeting some of the local young people.

Jude looked at the time: it was after five. "Don't be too late," she texted back.

"Thought you and Ryan were going out for a picnic?"

Right, Jude thought. She hoped Lindsey didn't feel left out. Then she remembered her anxious plea to be allowed to go watch the afternoon shooting of the film.

"Ryan, wake up," Jude said.

He shook himself awake. "What?"

"Did Lindsey know about our picnic before or after she asked to watch the filming?"

"I only came up with the picnic idea after she said you told her it was all right to go."

Of course, Jude thought. Her daughter couldn't get out of the house fast enough. "Lindsey met with Marco and Becca and they're out watching the movie shoot. It's going to run late."

"That's good. Isn't it?"

Ryan rose in bed. His hair fell across his face and down his bare shoulder. "Maybe giving her some space is a good idea. Let her have some fun?"

Jude texted back. "Stay close in town and be back by nine."

"Thanks. Later," Lindsey replied.

Ryan pulled her down next to him. "That was quite a nap," he said.

Jude nestled close. Her first night home and Lindsey was staying out as late as possible. Jude tried not to take it as a rejection. Her stomach growled loudly, demanding food. "I guess I'm hungry."

Ryan winked at her. "For food or...?" He laughed, "I know. Let me get some pants on and I'll run down and get those sandwiches made, pack the basket."

"I'm too hungry to wait to drive anywhere," she said. She pointed out her front windows. "Best seat in town is outside on my back deck. And that way we won't be gone too long either."

Ryan paused "Right, I'll get it all ready and we can sit there in style. I'll be right back."

Ryan hurried down the stairs back to the café kitchen. After slicing the fresh bread, he toasted it brown and crispy, then scooped on a hearty helping of the deep pink salmon salad. The sandwiches were dressed with butter lettuce, thin-sliced beefsteak tomato, a pinch of salt and pepper and then cut in half and arranged on a plate. He added a side of the homemade chips, cool now, but still crispy and delicious. He let the glistening strawberries and chocolate whipped cream stay chilled until later. He was about to leave when he remembered the wine. Basket full, Ryan took the stairs back two at a time.

Out on the porch, Jude had put some silverware and a bouquet of dahlias on the table. Ryan added the checkered tablecloth underneath for ambiance and laid out the luscious spread. He opened the Chardonnay and poured it into the long-stemmed glasses. Its golden glow caught the sunlight. The turquoise sky reflected off the surface of the water, mingling with shades of silver.

"A toast," Jude said when he joined her at the table.

Ryan held up his glass. "To good food and ..."

"And what?" Jude stopped. Ryan looked at her.

"And to us," he said. The smile on Jude's face was worth everything. They sipped the wine and then dug into their stacked-high sandwiches.

"Oh my gosh," Jude said, "This is heaven on bread. This is the best salmon sandwich I have ever tasted. We have to put this on the menu."

"Of course. It could be one of the specials. We'll have to add thyme. I put tarragon in this time. Our salmon salad thyme special. It'll be expensive," Ryan said. "But it'll be good. They'll come from miles around for this one."

They munched on their juicy sandwiches and crunchy potato chips. The setting was the perfect complement for the meal. In the distance, the Cascade Mountains still had a tiny bit of snow on their caps. Seagulls screamed overhead, dive bombing the beach below.

"Look at that," Ryan said, pointing to the wet sand below. A huge bald eagle, its white head stark and regal, stood at the tide's edge looking out over the water.

"You don't often see them on the ground," Jude said.

Ryan winked at her. "Maybe it's lazy, or it just likes mussels."

Her face finally broke into a smile. It had been a hard few days for her, and he was determined to help her unwind.

"Are you finished?" he asked.

Jude shook her head. "Stuffed and happy."

"Just the way I wanted you." Ryan stood and took the plates away. "But I have one more treat for you."

Jude held her stomach. "I'm so full."

"You'll like this."

He returned to the kitchen for the dessert that he'd placed on a glass platter in her refrigerator.

"Voilá," he said, placing the platter of strawberries and a small tub of fresh chocolate whipped cream mixed with a pinch of cinnamon and lavender on the table. He dipped one of the strawberries in the luscious cream and held it to Jude's luscious mouth. She took a bite, the red of the strawberry oozing over her lips.

"And I thought I'd already gone to heaven," Jude said. "What is in this?"

Ryan laughed and pulled a chair beside her. "Oh, just a little magic."

She took a strawberry, dunked it in the dark cream, and held it out to him. He took the whole thing in his mouth and tried to take part of her finger. She laughed and pulled away. Next thing he knew, Jude scooped some whipped cream onto her finger and held it to his mouth. He sucked the whipped cream off, licking her finger ever so softly. Looking into her eyes, he thought maybe they'd be going back to bed soon, even if it wasn't dark yet. And then he remembered Lindsey. Anything else would have to wait for another day.

Chapter Eight

Jude propped up in bed and held the cell phone to her ear. With Lindsey there, she didn't want it on speaker during her call with Lily.

"I'm sorry to hear that," Jude said. "I'm glad Betty finally went to the doctor. I had a bad feeling about that cough of hers."

Jude listened as Lily explained about the extensive cancer treatments the doctors were recommending. "I'll come by later today. And count me in for helping in any way I can."

The filming had been going on for over a week now, and Jude was glad she finally had an afternoon off. She glanced at the clock and couldn't believe she'd slept so late. She remembered waiting up last night for Lindsey to come home, and then nothing until Lily's call now. It was almost 11:00. This was not like her at all.

She took a quick shower and fixed her hair. After throwing on some linen drawstring pants and a cool cotton shirt, she headed out to the living room. Lindsey was curled up in a chair by the window reading her Kindle with her feet on the coffee table.

"Hi, Mom, did you have a good sleep?"

Lindsey had her hair pulled up, and with no make-up on Jude could see the hint of her little girl she used to take to the swings in the park. "I did," Jude said. "How are you doing? Good book?"

"It's pretty good. You know, it's another one of those, two teenagers; they fall in love then one gets sick and is dying. I'm getting a little tired of this storyline."

"I can see why," Jude said. She'd just heard upsetting news herself about her friend, Betty, and that was real enough.

Jude went into the kitchen scouting for food, but nothing looked good. "Have you eaten anything, Lindsey?"

Her daughter's nose was back in her book. "Had toast," was all she said.

Toast sounded doable. Jude made a cup of tea while she waited for the toast to pop. Her usual morning coffee didn't sound appealing. She took her brunch with her and joined Lindsey in a chair by the window. "I'm headed over toward Madrona Island Bed and Breakfast to visit a friend. Do you want to come with me?"

"Oh, I don't know," Lindsey said.

"Going to go see Betty who isn't feeling too well. She's been one of the extras in the film. You've met her in the café, but not her new dog Zinger."

Lindsey perked up a little. "What kind of dog?"

"A curly red poodle rescue. Very cute. They have a lovely cottage right on the Sound next to the B&B."

Jude waited for Lindsey to lay the Kindle down. "Come on. Let's get out of here. We'll get some ice cream while we're out."

"I'm not five years old, Mom."

"I know. I know," Jude said, "But everyone likes ice cream."

"All right." Lindsey put the Kindle on the table, unwrapped her legs, and slid her feet into her flip-flops. "Give me a sec to brush my hair."

Jude waited while Lindsey fixed herself up. She tried not to hum and show how happy she was her daughter was coming along. This was the first time they'd really had any time alone, and now they would have a whole, bright, sunny afternoon together.

"Okay, let's go." Lindsey had put on some very short shorts, sandals with higher heels, and some lip gloss. She was a beautiful girl, even if she did look a lot like her dad. Mitchell had always been a handsome man. That had been part of the problem when Jude was young.

They hopped into the car and headed out of the town center. Jude took her time, keeping to the 25-mile speed limit in the town limits before getting on the main thoroughfare. "Would you like to see the bluff where we spotted the whales last year?"

"Sure," Lindsey said.

Jude took the exit toward the state park. The road wove along windblown trees and open farmland before opening to the gate of the forested park overlooking Puget Sound. "I'll park by the lighthouse," she said. "It has the best view."

"This way," Jude said after exiting the car. Lindsey followed her up a short bluff where they could see the glistening water and rocky beach below. "Lily, and Kyla who owns Tea & Comfort and I saw them right out here."

They scanned the water looking for a telltale dorsal fin or air spouts.

"What's that island way out there," Lindsey said, pointing north.

"It's actually Canada. Vancouver Island. Perhaps we could take a ferry there one day and go shopping."

"Can we go inside the lighthouse?" Lindsey asked.

"Sure thing. You can even take the steps to the top and look out."

"Let's go."

They wandered through the museum area on the bottom floor and then climbed the narrow steps to the top. "This was a military base during World War I," Jude said. "Lots of history here."

Once out front again, Jude took them on the upper trail into the woods. Sunrays pierced the pine needle laden forest floor, highlighting the tiny pink wildflowers that lined the path. They continued past the campsite area and down to the old army bunkers. Even though the conversation was minimal, Jude couldn't be happier.

Lindsey perched on a spot overlooking the bluff. "It's a great park, Mom. Hey, do you think I could borrow the car sometime and come over here?"

"Sure," Jude said, "You've got your license and insurance, right?"

"Of course I do."

"I figured you did. So, how's your summer going so far?" Jude asked.

"It's okay. Ryan is a pretty good guy, you know. I like working in the kitchen. He's letting me experiment on new recipes with him and take the food shots for the book proposal."

"You always had a good eye for photography," Jude said. "And Chef Ryan's a very talented man."

"Yeah, he is. I just wish there were some more people my age around."

Jude thought for a second. "You know Marco and Becca now, and they're not much older than you."

"I went in to Tea & Comfort. It's pretty in there and all, but kind of smelly. All that lavender. Kyla wasn't there, but I did buy some hand cream Becca said would help with my new dishwater hands."

"Most people like lavender. It has medicinal properties, too."

Lindsey raised an eyebrow. "Now Marco, he is one hot guy. I might just spend a lot more time over there."

Jude let that one go by. They were doing so well. She would choose her battles wisely, and this one was low priority.

Lindsey leaned against one of the towering cedar trees. "I can see why you like it here. But I think I'd be bored out of my mind if I had to live here all year."

"Well, it's not for everyone." Jude stood beside her daughter. "It sure is nice to have you here for the summer."

Lindsey shrugged. "I know it's been kind of hard for you with me living with Dad and all."

"I just want you happy," Jude said. "You're the best thing that ever happened to me."

Lindsey's eyes softened. "Thanks, Mom."

"You have a lot more opportunities living with your dad. I can't say I haven't missed you, but I want you to do what makes you happy."

"Dad's pretty active, he keeps things busy. I'm away at school now, studying and trying to figure out what I want to do with my life."

"Got any ideas?" Jude asked.

"Well, my major is business, mostly because Dad made the choice for me." Lindsey walked across the emerald grass and stood at the edge looking over the rocky bluff. "After being here this summer, I'm thinking about doing something more creative. Maybe something with writing and photography and or maybe food."

"That would be an exciting career," Jude said. "You could write while you travel and take pictures. And eat!"

"I thought about that. Maybe I'll start taking some journalism or creative writing classes when I get back. I have a year to go, but I think Dad will be pissed if I don't graduate with a business major."

"Your life isn't about making your dad happy. It's about making you happy."

Lindsey smiled. "Yeah, but dad's paying the bills."

"That doesn't make him in charge of what you choose to do for a career," Jude said.

"I know that."

"I'm really happy that he's paying for your education. But just remember, it's still your life."

"I guess so."

"You guess so?" Jude said.

"Let's walk some more," Lindsey said.

Jude followed her down the dirt trail. "So you might remember where we're going today? It's a beautiful old turn of the century bed and breakfast,. Lily inherited it from her grandma, Maggie. You met Lily last week."

"She seemed nice. I do remember Maggie too. She used to bring those scones and cookies to the shop, right?"

"Oh, that's right, of course. You loved her cookies too."

"She was a really nice lady. You guys were pretty close, right?"

Jude sighed. "We were. Maggie passed away a few years ago, leaving a hole in all of our hearts. Lily is her grand-daughter. She came here after a pretty bad divorce in Los Angeles."

"Oh, divorce. It seems like everybody's getting one."

"Not everyone," Jude said. "I think Lily and Ian are headed into a lifelong happy marriage."

Lindsey just nodded. "We should probably get going now. What's wrong with your friend?"

"Betty has cancer," Jude said. The word caught in her throat. She couldn't even imagine Betty sick. Betty, who had just climbed on a roof last week. Betty, who was help-ing to build the animal shelter and always one step ahead of everyone. Betty, who just had her first chemo treatment.

"That's too bad."

"It's somewhat advanced," Jude said. "But her treatment is going well so far."

As Jude opened the car door, hot stuffy air poured out from it. "We probably should have brought something for her."

Lindsey fastened her seatbelt and rolled down her win-dow. "Knowing your friends, she's probably got everything she needs and more."

Jude turned down the lane toward Betty's home. "I don't know. Lily's probably cooking for her. Her sister, Shirley is a pretty good cook, too, so I doubt Betty needs any food. She has her sweet dog, Zinger, too. He'll cheer her up."

"Sounds good, Mom."

The day was going well. It seemed Lindsey was starting to mature and understand that her mom was just a person, too. When they pulled into the B & B, there were a few other cars there. Jude's heart dropped when she saw the doctor, shoulders slumped, walking out of Betty's front door toward the driveway.

"How's Betty doing?" Jude asked the doctor.

"That woman is amazing," he said. "I think she'll outlive us all."

"Oh, I hope so."

"Don't stay too long," the doctor said. "You don't want to tire her out. Not like anything tires that one out. She'll probably be mowing her lawn next week." He shook his head and got in his car.

Jude and Lindsey walked to the door and knocked. Shirley greeted them, dressed as always in full makeup and sporting a coiffed hairdo. "Hi, good to see you, Jude. And Lindsey, yes?"

"Yes."

"I'm Shirley, Betty's sister. Come on in, join the crowd."

Betty was sitting on the floral couch with her feet up on an ottoman, a hand-knit shawl draped over her shoulders. Zinger was at her feet. She waved them over. "You guys, too? What's the whole town come to visit me? I'm fine, I'm fine."

"Betty, you remember Lindsey."

"Of course, I've been seeing her around your café. Nothing wrong with my mind. I remember when she was a little girl." Betty patted the couch beside her. "Come on, sit down."

Lindsey sat at the end by Zinger and petted the dog's head.

Lily, Ian, and Luke were sitting off to the right and Jude introduced them to Lindsey. The concerned look on Lily's face made Jude nervous. She took a seat in the pink wing-back chair next to them.

"So, did you see the doctor on your way out?" Betty asked.

"We did," Jude said. "He said you're amazing!" She did look pretty good considering. A bit weak, but steady.

"Of course I'm doing great. Don't think anything is gonna keep me down. You girls, stop worrying. I'll beat this thing, you'll see. Besides, I've got a whole lot of projects. If I don't get them done, who will? Certainly not Shirley, sitting there in her nice outfit. She won't even lift a hammer. And that dog shelter's counting on me."

At the word dog, Zinger sprung into the air and landed on the floor. He turned in circles with an expectant look aimed at Betty. "Hey, Zinger. You need a walk?" Betty started to rise. "You're not going anywhere," Shirley said.

"I'll take him," Lindsey said. "I'm happy to take him for a walk."

"Okay," Betty said. "He'll go with you if you rattle the leash."

"Come on, Zinger," Lindsey said, shaking the leash.

Jude watched as Lindsey leashed the dog, petting and talking to him sweetly. They looked cute together.

"Just take him right down the path there," Betty said. "He likes walking along the sand. It's a nice beach, but don't get too close to the water here."

Jude moved over to the window. "Looks like the tide's pretty far out. You should be fine."

"I know what a tide is," Lindsey said. "I'll keep a watch. We'll be back soon." She headed out the door with the dog traipsing behind her.

"Come, sit next to me," Betty said to Jude. "Tell me how everything's going with you?"

Luke took Jude's place at the window, and she gave him a grateful smile. The tides could change in a flash.

"The restaurant's packed with movie people for a few more weeks. I did they are staying on the island longer than planned. Lindsey's working in the kitchen to help Ryan out," Jude said.

"Everything looks good out here," Ian assured them from where he stood by the window. "Ryan mentioned Lindsey's a talent in the kitchen and is going to assist with the wrap-up dinner at the winery, too."

"A relief for me," Jude said. "So, where's Kyla?"

"Kyla had to go into the shop today. Becca had some plans with Marco, so Kyla went in to relieve her for the day."

"Becca's that new girl, right?" Betty asked. "How's she doing running the shop?"

"Pretty good," Luke said, "And it's nice to have my wife home more, even if she is in the lavender fields half the time"

"So have you and Ryan worked out all the details for the closing dinner?" Jude asked.

"We sure have," she said. "Cast and crew only."

"It should be quite an affair," Lily said. "Let me know if you need help."

Shirley came out of the kitchen carrying a plate of heavenly smelling chocolate chip cookies.

"Cookies anyone?" she asked, passing them around.

"None for me," Betty said.

Shirley frowned. "But they're your favorite."

"All right, leave one."

Shirley made sure everyone had their share and then sat down on the rocker next to her husband, Don.

Jude let Betty know she was there for anything she needed, any time. The grateful smile she received warmed her heart. She couldn't imagine life without Betty. She was an intrinsic part of the town and very close to Jude's heart.

Betty yawned. "How am I supposed to get any rest with you guys watching over me? I'm telling you, I'm going to be fine." She waved for them to go.

"Okay, okay," Lily said, "I get the hint. Come on, Ian. Let's give this lady a little rest." Lily and Ian headed for the door. "Just let us know if you need anything. We'll stop by later either way."

"You don't need to stop by later," Betty said. "But thanks."

Jude waved goodbye. She was happy to see Lily and Ian were so close by, but she hated seeing Betty like this. She could tell Betty had lost weight and her once sun-worn face was now pale.

Jude started to stand, but Betty stopped her. "You wait here with me until your daughter comes back."

"So, Betty," Jude said with a smile, "It must be about killing you to have to rest."

"You know it girl. I'm not convinced that rest is the best thing. Tomorrow I'm getting into the garden a little."

"You sure you're up to it?" Shirley said.

"What, I'm going to sit around like you all day?"

"I can take care of it," Shirley said.

Betty laughed. "And get your manicured hands dirty!"

Shirley threw her hands in the air. "All right, well, if you'd don't need me then, my husband and I have some errands to do. We'll be back with dinner later."

"Fine, fine. I could use some peace and quiet," Betty said.

Jude reached over and took Betty's hand. "I know you're going to beat this. I've never seen anyone more vibrant and alive than you."

"Thanks," Betty said. "I do too, but it's nice to know someone's on my side."

The two friends enjoyed a few minutes of local gossip before they were interrupted by the sound of steps on the front porch.

"We're back," Lindsey said, popping in the door with Zinger. She released the dog's leash and Zinger bounded up, jumping onto the couch and right over Jude into Betty's lap.

"It's time for Zinger and me to take a nap," Betty said. "You two head off. I know you have work to do."

Jude reached over and hugged Betty. "Please let us know if we can do anything."

"And if you need a dog walker," Lindsey said, "I'd be happy to help."

"I may take you up on that," Betty said.

Jude and Lindsey walked to the car. "It's a beautiful place, isn't it?" Jude said.

"Yeah, I wouldn't mind living on a farm like this some-day, right on the water, maybe married and with my own dog and—"

"Oh really?" Jude said. "You see yourself married and settled?"

"Not right away, Mom. Don't get excited."

"Oh, don't worry. I don't want to see you marrying too soon. And by the way, Marco and Becca. They're kind of in a relationship."

"Of course. The only young people in town and they're both into each other."

"Doesn't mean you can't be friends with them," Jude said.

"Yeah, maybe I'll head down there when we get back. We chilled the other night together. They did seem kind of into each other."

Jude turned the corner on Main Street and pulled into the drive. "Why don't you go off now, have some fun?" Jude said.

"Thanks, Mom. I'll see you later."

Chapter Nine

$\mathcal{J}$ ude watched the assistant director holding court at an almost predawn breakfast meeting that took over the large table in the dining area of the cafe. Joining him were several of the key crew members and Kate, the publicist for the film. Jude had been instructed by the AD that this meeting was important and was not to be disturbed except for the delivery of food. Whatever they wanted was fine with her. She asked a waitress to come in early to wait on the table and be as inconspicuous as possible.

Things had been going pretty well the last week, but she was counting the days until these ever-demanding movie people were long gone. Between trying to feed them and handle the summer rush of tourists, she was exhausted and summer wasn't half over yet. At least things were going fairly smoothly with Lindsey.

Jude ground coffee and stocked the cream and sugar containers for the morning coffee service. The chocolate syrup dispenser was full. She was considering how long to wait between her first cup before she could have a mocha break on the deck, when the meeting started to disperse.

The crew members herded out the front door for another big day of shooting. Jude was just about to lock the door until opening time when the AD and Kate walked over to the bar, took two seats, and ordered cappuccinos. The meeting was obviously not over yet.

Jude started their drinks and caught bits and pieces of the conversation between grinding and steaming the coffee. Mostly gossip, Jude decided, and let her thoughts drift elsewhere. She placed the foamy drinks before them and they barely acknowledged her presence. Not local folk, for sure.

"Morning," Ryan said as he walked out of the kitchen. "Early start today. How'd it go out here?"

"Sure is," Jude said. "Great breakfast, thanks." She rolled her eyes toward the two at the bar. Ryan winked at her, a mischievous smile widening across his face. They were both ready for normal business hours to resume again soon. Summer rush had taken on a whole new meaning with the Hollywood cast and crew in town.

"Here's the menu for the specials today," Ryan said. "Fresh baked honey bread, crab quiche, and blackberry cobbler starting at 10:00. Full menu at 11:00."

Jude noticed the AD staring at Ryan. Protectively, she stepped in front of Ryan to block their view. "Do you know them?" she asked.

Ryan glanced over to the bar and shook his head. "I've seen them around town. Who's the well-dressed woman?"

"Kate is the publicist for the film."

Ryan frowned and took Jude's hand. "I try to avoid the press," he said. "I think I'll go back to my domain and handle lunch."

Jude couldn't help but watch and admire him. His dark shirt was cinched at the waist by a black apron tie, and his sun-lit hair, tied back in a ponytail, playfully spilling over his collar. She wanted to follow him into the kitchen and take him in her arms.

"I'd heard they scored Chef Ryan Folger as the chef at this place, hard to believe he's dropped so far from his days in San Francisco."

The words from the AD drifted over to Jude and she froze in place by the kitchen door with her back to the bar. What did they mean by "so low?" She wanted to turn around and pound them.

"Maybe he's hiding out here," Kate said. "You know, after all the scandal around that chef's death."

"Yeah, maybe," he said. "Peyton couldn't dump him fast enough after that."

Kate sipped her cappuccino and lowered her nasally voice. "Well she does seem to have her claws out in his direction again."

Jude turned slowly until her gaze settled on the two seated at the bar.

The AD was smirking. "We all know Peyton's unquenchable appetite."

Jude had heard enough and wanted them out of her café. She returned behind the counter ready to say something, but as soon as they saw her, they changed the subject abruptly.

"Are you finished?" Jude asked, staring at their empty coffee cups.

The AD seemed to look right through her. "No we're not," he said. "I believe we have reserved the place until 10:00."

At least Kate had the decency to look down at her cup rather than engage in the rude eye contact this man was now making.

Jude removed their cups and slammed them down in the sink. Her jaw clenched as she fought to hold back a threatening storm of tears.

She motioned for their new waitress, Carol, who was bussing tables, to join her. "Can you handle the counter too for a few minutes?"

Carol nodded. "Sure thing, we're still not open for a few hours, so take your time."

Jude walked slowly through the dining room, trying to hide her frustration. She opened the sliding door that led to the deck and stepped outside into the chilled morning air. Their words had cut through her gut. If a heart could drop, hers plummeted into a dark, familiar pit. Despair, her once constant companion, returned to its residence in her mind. The mood swing was so fast and insidious that Jude had no time to put up barriers.

Betrayal stung like no other wound for her. She'd told Ryan all her deepest secrets, and in return he'd supposedly told her his own. But obviously not all of them. The other day at their picnic he'd told her it was long over with Peyton, and he only had eyes for Jude. But what else was he not telling her? Years ago, she'd trusted Mitchell, only to be dealt a devastating blow. "Never again," she'd promised herself, "Never trust a man fully." But she had.

Jude looked over the wooden railing to the water below. The searing tears were winning over her resolve not to cry. She turned and raced up the stairs to her apartment to beat the outburst of tears that followed. She locked the front door behind her and leaned against it for support.

"Why am I so stupid?" she yelled at the ceiling as she dropped into a chair. Images of her crumbling marriage filled her mind. She'd been left alone with a young child, and so afraid. The tears built as her body trembled. "Even my own daughter abandoned me for a father who never loved her." And now, she had no choice. She had to let Ryan go. She would be alone again. But safe, ever so safe. She buried her head in the throw pillow and let the tears come. Even as she cried, she knew she was indulging self-pity. But sometimes a good cleaning out was needed before a new direction could be forged.

She felt rung out. "Pull yourself together," she told herself. "Deal with the problem, like you always have. Face on."

Jude dried her eyes and fixed her hair before going back down to the kitchen. Was it only an hour ago that she had wanted to race into his arms? Ryan was alone when she got there with no Lindsey in sight.

"Where's Lindsey?" she asked Ryan.

"She went out for a walk," he said. "She's been doing quite a bit of that lately. I figured that was good for her, get up, have a long morning walk, maybe get some exercise or meet some friends."

Jude put her hands on her hips. "What about her working?"

"She wakes early, helps me, then takes off."

"And you didn't think to tell me this?" Jude asked.

Ryan looked confused. "It seemed fine."

His innocent smile reminded her of a little boy. But then the image of him on the deck with Peyton flashed across

Jude's mind. She glared at him. "It would to you." "Is something wrong? Do you need me to ..."

"Never mind," Jude said. She headed out the back door, leaving Ryan in mid-sentence.

What was Lindsey up to? Jude had assumed her daughter's mornings were being spent in the kitchen. It was time to investigate; her talk with Ryan could wait. She took a few steps uptown, unsure of where she was headed, before spotting cameras at the end of Front Street. The scene was set with a thriving farmer's market, and all the townsfolk, families, and kids were milling around. No wonder the sidewalks were so empty. Everyone was down there.

Jude saw Grandpa John sitting on the bench in front of Tea & Comfort. He must have been in half the movie. It would be fun to all watch it together when it was released. She walked over to where the guards were stationed at the edge of the set and watched for a little while. She really hadn't seen much of the shooting outside the café.

The farmer's market looked unbelievably real. It was obvious to Jude that all of the local farmers with their produce were stationed at the carts and make-shift stalls built for the film. It looked like a typical, lazy summer day in a small coastal town, unexpectedly still and quiet until the directed yelled, "Take one. Action."

All at once the scene came alive. Everyone started chatting and sampling the goods as they walked through the street market. A young couple on bikes rode down the Main Street hill followed by their two kids and a shaggy dog.

Jude wasn't sure what was going to actually happen in this scene until she saw the lead actor, Michael Medford, come walking down the sidewalk with Peyton. He didn't look well. His face was dead pale. Peyton supported his weight as he stumbled along toward the pier where their sailboat was docked.

As the camera zoomed in, Peyton spoke, and Jude could see the sound boom moving in silently just above them to catch the dialogue. This must be the scene where she dragged him out of the hospital to take him back onto the yacht to finish the deadly deed. Jude watched as they shot the same scene three times. The director finally yelled, "Cut! That's a wrap."

At just that moment, Jude caught sight of Lindsey sitting with some crew members in front of one of the make-believe storefronts. As Jude walked over closer, she realized Lindsey was sitting right next to Peyton. They were chatting away with another man who Jude did not recognize. Who was he? Jude thought back to the original town meeting. She believed he was the person that organized everything. What was his title? And just what was her daughter doing here in the thick of it all?

She could feel her skin burn. Just how many mornings had this been going on? She saw Peyton and Lindsey laughing and the man writing something down. It looked as if her daughter was about to sign something. That was all she needed to see. Jude stamped through the set, across the fake farmer's market, and over to where they were sitting.

"Good morning," she said, looking straight at Lindsey.

Lindsey looked shocked. "Good morning, Mom."

"And just what's going on here?" Jude said. "Ryan said you were out for a walk."

"Oh no," Peyton said, her sharp, shockingly white teeth peeking under her smirk. Obviously, she had caught the drift right away. "Lindsey's been helping us every morning. Didn't you know?"

If Jude could strangle that woman, she would. "No, actually, I didn't know," Jude said, looking at Lindsey.

Peyton looked adoringly toward Lindsey, and then turned to Jude to gloat. "Your daughter is wonderful. She's so supportive to me. Our producer raves about how fantastic she is with the catering. She even took some publicity shots for us with her camera."

"What do you mean, the catering?" Jude said, hating the look of triumph on Peyton's face.

The other actors around them started to disperse, probably wanting to avoid the conflict. But the assistant with the contract remained.

"Lindsey helps us out with the food choices on the set. She's been invaluable," Peyton said, watching Jude's every move. "We were just discussing how she might be able to come with us when the action shifts to San Juan Island."

Rage moved through Jude like a torpedo searching for a target. She had to squelch the impulse to grab Lindsey by the hair and drag her away. Instead, she looked over at the man holding the contract. "I don't know who you are, nor do I care. But you need to be aware that my daughter is under twenty-one, and I am her legal guardian. So before she signs anything, or agrees to anything, I think it would be best—"

"Mom, stop," Lindsey said. "I don't have to be twenty-one to work in the USA, even here on this little island. You only have to be eighteen."

"Is that right? We'll see about that. Don't forget that Ryan is counting on you in the kitchen," Jude said. Peyton's glare brought her to a dead stop. The last thing Jude wanted was for Peyton to see just how uncomfortable she was. Sweat pooled at her back and her heart picked up speed. She could tell the woman was enjoying every moment of this little exchange.

"Don't worry, Lindsey," Peyton said, "I'll talk to Ryan. I'm sure he will be reasonable. In fact, he told me the other day how well you were doing. I'm sure he can spare you."

Jude's face flushed hot. The other day? Peyton and Ryan had been talking in the last few days? Did Ryan know what was happening all along? Had he lied to her?

"Lindsey, did Ryan know that you've been coming over here and helping?"

Lindsey looked Jude straight in the eye defying her mother to doubt her. "Yes, of course he did."

Jude was pretty sure her daughter was lying, but for that moment she didn't know who was lying anymore. She just wanted out of there. "All right. It's time to get back. Ryan needs you to help prep for lunch."

Lindsey turned to Peyton. "I'll see you tomorrow."

Over my dead body, Jude thought.

They walked back to the café in silence. Lindsey scuffed her feet along the sidewalk and huffed. "You embarrassed me, Mom."

Jude could only sigh. She didn't know what to say. In fact, if she was honest, she just wanted to take Lindsey and shake some sense into her. "I didn't mean to embarrass you, Lindsey, but it's time you realized that I'm your mother and your guardian for the summer. Anything you do here, you need to run by me. And you've made a commitment to Ryan, to work with him in the kitchen for the duration of the summer. So that is where you belong each day."

"Fine. But as I remember you kind of forced me to work in your kitchen. And I could make money working on the film."

Jude stopped and looked at her daughter. "I thought you liked the work. Do you want to quit? Is that it?"

Lindsey shook her head. "No, I mean yes, I do like it, and no, I don't want to quit. I just like working for them too. Peyton is helping me learn the business."

I bet she is, Jude thought. But her motives were plain to Jude. Peyton had no interest in Lindsey except as a way to get to Ryan.

"For now, I want you to stay away from the set."

Lindsey walked begrudgingly behind Jude to the cafe and let the back door slam behind her when she entered.

Ryan glanced over when they entered, but Jude ignored his questioning expression. She didn't want to even look at him, much less talk now. But how could she not? She took a deep breath to compose herself, hoping she would come off saner than she felt.

She met Ryan's eyes. "Did you really think she was taking a walk?"

Ryan looked confused. "Of course."

Lindsey scooted in next to him, eyes wide. "Remember Ryan, I told you that I was helping Peyton out with a few things."

Ryan froze, looking between the two women. "No, I don't really remember you saying anything about that."

Lindsey, hands on her hips, looked like a little girl having a tantrum. "Peyton said she told you."

"Not true, I haven't spoken to her," Ryan said, firmly stepping away from Lindsey.

The room spun as emotions overwhelmed Jude. There was enough staff working today that she could walk out and take a day off, and that's just what she planned to do. She needed to get out of this kitchen, get away from everyone, be by herself, and pray for some clarity.

"I need to leave for a while." Jude said.

"Everything all right?" Ryan asked.

Jude looked right at him and said, "I don't know, you tell me." He looked surprised, but only for a second, then he frowned. Jude wondered what that look was. Guilt? Worry? Sadness? She didn't care right now.

Her daughter was sitting and writing notes at the counter. More work for Peyton?

"Lindsey, aren't you supposed to be helping Ryan out?"

"I am," she said, "He asked me if I would write down some recipes for the cookbook, and that's what I'm doing." Lindsey's expression was fierce. "Is that okay with you?"

Jude turned to Ryan, "Are you working on a cookbook?"

Ryan nodded. "Jude, I didn't want to tell you until I was sure that it was definitely going to happen. I wanted to surprise you."

"Well today has certainly been full of surprises," she said.

Ryan continued. "I've been thinking about putting together a book proposal. One of my old chef friends told me that his agent's looking for some new work. He suggested I come up with an outline and said he'd pass it along to him."

"I see," Jude said. "Don't you think you might have mentioned this to me sooner?"

Ryan took a step closer, but Jude backed away.

"I was going to sit down and talk to you about the idea as soon as we had a minute and I had something more concrete to show you. Lindsey is keeping track of everything. I was thinking of featuring some recipes from Island Thyme Café. That would promote the restaurant too. What do you think?"

"I can't really think about it right now," Jude said. "I'm sure it's a great idea. I'm glad you're helping out, Lindsey."

"I've taken some photos too. I'm really good with that Nikon Dad got me last summer."

Of course her dad would have bought her some expensive camera. "I'm glad that you're finding something to do here at the cafe. I just wish someone had told me."

Her daughter looked up, her eyes afire. "At least this is interesting for me. Maybe if my stupid boyfriend hadn't dumped me, I wouldn't be stuck here so long with nothing to do. At least if you let me go with the caterers to the next location..."

Jude stood firm. "No, you're staying here for the summer."

Lindsey crossed her arms across her chest. "You have no say over me."

Jude noticed Ryan's worried expression. He looked over at her for a cue to step in, but this was her problem. She had known Lindsey was used to city life and might be bored on the island with less to do, but after their hike the other day she thought they were making progress. When Jude had seen her working with Ryan in the kitchen with her hair up and apron on, it had given her some hope.

"I'm not trying to control you, Lindsey. I was hoping this summer we could enjoy some good times together again."

"Well, maybe you should have thought of that before you made Dad leave," Lindsey said.

Jude was stunned. Where had that come from? She walked over to her daughter. "You know," she said, "Your dad left all on his own."

"He says you made him leave."

Jude just stared. She was not ready for another battle, but backing down under attack would not send a good message either.

"Stop right there, Lindsey. I've always wanted what was best for you, even when you wanted to go live with your dad."

"I was going whether you wanted me to or not. You weren't being fair to dad either. Taking me here to this island and not letting him see me."

Jude's heart sank. Lindsey looked like a pouting child. "You don't know the whole story," Jude said.

"And whose fault it that?" Lindsey said.

Ryan started to speak but Jude cut him off. "Let's talk about this later in private, Lindsey."

"You never have time to talk about it."

Lindsey was right there. Her daughter was older now and hurting. "Think what you like," Jude said. "At this point there's probably nothing I could say to change your mind."

Jude walked toward the door, stopped and looked back. "So I assume you can both handle lunch without me, because I am heading out."

Chapter Ten

Jude raced out of the kitchen, wondering if she'd ever return. The fatigue that clung to her lately would not let up. She hopped in her car and cleared the driveway, not caring where she went as long as it was away from the café. Away from Ryan and the oppressive movie people. If she saw one more person with a camera or a light or dressed in a costume in heavy makeup, she was going to scream. The turnoff heading toward the ferry caught her eye and she made a sharp left at the stop sign. Summer sunlight filtered through the towering pines and little yellow and pink wildflowers grew in the shade. The beauty calmed her as she drove. Thankfully, there were no tailgating tourists hurrying her to drive faster, so her mind began to slow.

Lindsey's words echoed in Jude's head. Waves of nausea almost had her pulling the car over. Could she trust Ryan? Her mind screamed no, but her heart still held hope. His reassuring words dissolved before her whenever Peyton walked into the café. Peyton's attraction to him was impossible to miss. Clearly she was a woman used to getting what she wanted. He said there had only been chemistry between them, not real love. But with all her beauty and charms, he no longer found her attractive. Peyton's spell spread like a spider web dazzling her prey in its deadly snare. Every man in town swooned when he saw her.

Sunshine Lane was coming up at the next turn. As if by instinct, Jude had driven to Lily's house. She'd go there, have a cup of tea, and be with her dear friend. Jude followed the dirt road leading to Madrona Island B&B and parked her car on the gravel drive. There was not another car in sight, not even Lily's. The place was deserted. Everyone was probably in town filming. Jude left the car and went to the front door to knock, just in case. No friendly face greeted her, not even a furry one. She collapsed onto the front porch swing, frustrated, and let the tears come.

Would she ever find love? She was almost forty years old and had given up hope before Ryan came along. Why did he have to come here to this island? Life for her had become a comfortable routine with work and friends. That had been enough. Almost. Family, she wanted most of all, and she had already almost lost Lindsey once. She'd been so hopeful this summer would bring them close again. Love, she hardly dared to long for that. But Ryan was everything she'd ever wanted in a man. Everything but completely available and totally honest, she reminded herself. She sniffled and wiped away tears with the back of her hand.

"This might help," a deep voice said.

Jude turned abruptly to see Grandpa John walking up the steps holding a handkerchief in his hand. She collected herself and gave him a smile.

"Don't go trying to put on a happy face for me," Grandpa John said. "I know all about sadness." He pulled a rocker over beside her. "Mind if I join you?"

Jude wiped the last of her tears away. "If you don't mind joining my pity party, please do."

Grandpa John smiled. "I've always liked a good party." He sat down in the wicker rocker beside her.

Even at her worst, this man could always make Jude smile.

"So, what's going on?" he asked, tipping his hat.

"I have a daughter who hates me, and a boyfriend who hasn't been honest with me and who might be in love with someone else. Other than that it's been a perfect day."

Grandpa John rocked back and forth, staring out at the Sound. She could tell the wheels were rolling in his head.

"You know, Jude, I remember after my wife died, I never thought I'd find love again. I moped around, just let hope slip away, but Maggie was not not about to let that happen."

"Maggie was truly special," Jude said. "I remember staying here at her bed and breakfast after Lindsey left the island as a teenager. It felt as if she saved my life. I never thought I'd be happy again."

"And you were," he said. "Happy again."

She looked into John's kind eyes. "I wish Maggie was still here with us. She'd be so proud of Lily too."

Grandpa John nodded. "It's hard to lose someone you love, but it's also hard sometimes to let your heart stay open to another love. Don't let that Peyton Chandler spoil what you and Ryan have, honey."

"If I only knew for sure he loved me and I could trust him."

He patted her hand. "Nothing is for certain. There are no guarantees when it comes to love. But you have a choice to make. Is love worth the risk? Worth the fight?" He paused, "Look, if an old man like me could have a second chance at love, certainly a beautiful, kind-hearted young woman like you can!"

A cool breeze circled the porch and wind chimes swayed making sweet melodic notes. Jude folded the handkerchief in her lap. "I never thought of love as a choice before. Fear seems to overshadow everything when it comes to my heart."

"You're a fighter, Jude. Look at all you've accomplished. I remember when you first showed up here on the island, a young single mother all alone trying to start a business."

He put his hand reassuringly into hers. "And now look at you, the owner of one of the most successful businesses on Madrona Island and one of the most loved people in town to boot."

Jude looked out over the glistening water. She'd let herself slip away from her positive view of life. From being grateful for all she had and all she could share with others. She'd fought hard to make the café a success. When she knew what she wanted, she did whatever it took to make it happen. Did she want Ryan? She had to be honest with herself and push her fears and her past aside. Did she want him? With all her heart, yes!

"You're right," Jude said. "Thank you for reminding me I don't have to passively step aside for anyone. Not even Peyton Chandler."

"That's my girl," Grandpa John said, patting Jude's hand. "I was just on my way to check on Betty," he said.

"How is she doing?" Jude asked.

"Darn good," he said. "She's got to stay busy, so she's knitting doggie vests and coats for the dogs at the shelter."

Jude smiled. "Glad to hear that."

The sound of tires kicking up the stones in the drive had both of their heads turning.

"Well, here comes one of the posse," Grandpa John said as Lily pulled in.

Lily waved as she stepped out of her car and hurried to the porch. She took one look at both of them and said. "What's going on?"

Jude stood. "Here I am, crying on your porch swing and waiting for you to get home."

Lily threw her arms around Jude, squeezing her tight. Then she turned to Grandpa John. "Looks like you had some company."

"Oh yeah, really good company," Jude said. "And not a minute too soon."

Lily sat down on the porch swing beside her. The two were as comfortable with each other as sisters. "Do you want to talk?" The chair creaked as Grandpa John rocked back and forth. "Should I leave you two ladies alone? Go relieve Mary with little Gwyn?"

Jude let out a long sigh. "You've heard my sad tale so if you want to go..."

He shook his head. "Think I'll stay awhile with you girls."

"Is everything okay?" Lily asked.

Her sweet friend beside her put Jude at ease. "I overheard some talk in the café today about Ryan's past. It sounded dark. And then I found out Lindsey, who was supposed to be working in the kitchen with Ryan, had been sneaking out and joining Peyton at the morning film shoots. She said Ryan knew all about her escapades, but he denies it. I don't know what or who to believe any more."

"Maybe it's time for us to call Kyla and meet for coffee and catch up," Lily said.

"Absolutely. Sounds wonderful." Jude looked at her watch. She stood and motioned for Grandpa John to stay comfortably in his rocker. "I really do have to get back. I've skipped out on everyone during lunch, and I'd better not skip out on dinner service too."

Lily walked Jude to her car. "Why don't I give Kyla a call and see if we can meet early tomorrow morning at Marco's coffee shop? We can get in a cozy table by the window, get away from our own businesses, and talk."

"That sounds great." Jude hugged Lily one more time.

"Don't worry." Lily smiled. "I know just what to do. During my divorce when we needed some evidence on Brad, Google was our best friend. Marco's Café will be perfect. We'll do a little investigating of our own."

Jude knew she should have looked into Ryan's past when he first came to work for her. She'd checked his references and they were glowing. She'd done an in-person interview and had been satisfied. Now, the idea of secretly investigating his past made her a bit nervous. But what was that saying about all is fair? Besides, he'd obviously kept things from her.

She took the main road back to the café and tried to focus on what she needed to do today. She was a lucky woman to have friends she loved, to get to live in this wonderful town, and to own Island Thyme Café. The rest, she hoped, would fall into place.

The next morning, Jude rose extra early so she could sneak out of the house and head down to Marco's coffee shop. Last night she'd gone to bed exhausted after a grueling dinner service. She'd avoided any discussion with Ryan until after today's research. The town was still sleepy with most of the shops closed and only the local black cat stretching out in the sun on the sidewalk. Delivery drivers parked their trucks along the side of the road to deliver food and supplies for the day's shoot.

Jude didn't want to run into anyone and have to make small talk, so she dashed head-down to Nooks, Books, & Coffee where she knew Lily and Kyla would be waiting for her. They'd all decided the earlier the better with their busy schedules, and Marco was the first one open in town. Not to mention, Jude had to admit he made the best coffee on the island.

Jude walked into the newly remodeled shop and was instantly greeted by Gatsby, Marco's new golden, long-haired dachshund. She bent to scratch him behind the ears and he thanked her with a slippery kiss on her cheek. "He is the cutest dog ever," Jude said.

"He is a cutie," Marco said from behind the counter where he stood grinding fresh, locally roasted coffee beans. "You're up early today."

Marco was a striking young man, who looked a bit like a rock star with coarse black hair that hung just to edge of his of his faded gray t-shirt. Jude was surprised Becca wasn't over here before work too. She'd certainly seen her popping in frequently and sitting close to Marco at every opportunity. It was obvious they were attracted to each other, and they made a cute couple. Ah, young love, she thought.

"I'm meeting my friends here. What brew would you suggest?"

Marco pointed to the bag of Island Bay coffee.

"I just got these beans in. Organic. Fresh from the local roaster. It tastes like nips of chocolate mixed with a smooth dark blend. How about I make you a wet cappuccino?"

Jude smiled. "It's nice to have someone else make the coffees for a change. That's what I'll have." While she waited for her drink, she glanced around for a good table. She put her purse on the one by the open window overlooking the cove. The cool breeze washed over her. Seagulls screamed overhead, and the ebb tide was just working its way in and inching up the pier. She turned when the front door opened and Kyla entered. Her red hair was pulled back into a low ponytail, making her look like a kid.

"I would say good morning, but it's too early. I need a mocha, fast," Kyla said. She winked at Jude. "Sorry, Jude. I'm not cheating on you with Marco's mocha. I love yours, too."

Jude and Kyla hugged. It'd been a few days since they'd seen each other and Jude was happy to have her friends nearby, especially right now.

"How's everything out at the ranch?" Jude asked.

"All wonderful. The grapes are coming in, the 'tasting room' is full every day, and we have bookings for weddings in the vineyard starting to trickle in, too."

"And how's married life?" Jude asked.

"Couldn't be better," Kyla said with a sly smile. She turned and looked around. "Lily isn't here yet?"

Jude pointed to the door. "There she is." It was impossible to tell that Lily had recently had a baby. She was right back to her trim self.

"Sorry to be late," Lily said as she hurried in. "We had to make sure all the breakfasts got out to the guests. Luckily for me, Mary came in early to relieve me at the B&B so I could meet you both here. What are you two having?"

"A cappuccino and a mocha," Marco said over the sound of the coffee grinder.

Lily hesitated. "I want your fresh pour-over regular coffee. I love watching you pour the water in and see it drip through to fill the cup."

Marco pointed to the wall.

"These are the different roasts with the different flavor points. Let me know which one appeals to you."

Lily studied the board. "I'll have the light roast. And I'm paying for all of them."

"All right, ladies," he said. "Go grab your table and I'll be bring your drinks right over."

The three women sat down at the table Jude had picked. Jude stared out at the minus tide. The beach was smooth as fine silk. Some early foragers, probably locals, were out digging for clams. Perhaps Ryan was with them, seeing what he could harvest fresh for lunch.

"That young man has sure done a great job decorating this place," Kyla said. "The books look new and fresh, and I like the way he has the covers turned out. With the cozy tables, free Internet, and the heavenly aroma of fresh coffee, no wonder this place is always crowded."

Lily took out her laptop and put it on the table. The Internet password was on her receipt. "So, ladies," she said. "We are here on a mission to find out all about Ryan Folger."

While they waited for her computer to boot up, Marco arrived with a tray of steaming drinks.

"Here you go, ladies. If you don't mind, I'm going to go outside and start setting up the stand for the movie folks. If you need me, just yell."

"Go ahead," Lily said. "We'll be fine."

Jude held her breath, not quite sure she was ready for this. "All right," she said. "Google away."

Kyla watched as Lily opened the browser. "You know, I remember Googling my real name when I was on the run to make sure no one knew where I was. It was a good way to see what people were still saying about me."

Lily typed in Ryan's name. "It's amazing what you can find out about yourself just by Googling your name. I tried it once. The most exciting thing was my name next to a recipe for our special brownies on Pinterest."

"Maybe I should Google mine," Jude said, "but I'm not sure that there'd be much of interest to find."

The others laughed, "Oh, sure there would," Kyla said.

Lily hit enter. "All right, let's see what Chef Ryan Folger has in his past."

Jude put her head next to theirs and watched as about a hundred Google search links popped up. She took a sip of her coffee for fortification.

"Look, and there are images, too. Let's hit those," Lily said.

There were quite a few pictures of Ryan in his black chef coat. Some were from his younger days, where his hair drifted past his shoulders. Jude glanced at the headlines under them.

"Hottest new chef. Yeah, he was hot," Kyla said. "Should we click on some of these and see where they take us?"

Jude bit her lip in anticipation.

Lily clicked on a picture of a crowded room of beautiful people.

"Oh," Kyla said. "I remember this."

"What is it?" Jude and Lily leaned over.

Kyla pointed to a picture. "I remember this scene in front of that famous private club down in San Francisco. It was a few years back. There was this giant scandal about the chef at a grand opening of some fancy restaurant, and how he stepped outside and died right on the sidewalk. They believed it was a drug overdose. He was seizing..."

"Oh, my God," Jude said. "What does that have to do with Ryan?"

Kyla read the article aloud. "Famous chef Andrew Wakefield dies on opening night of the trendiest new restaurant in San Francisco. Many celebrity chefs were at the party, including Chef Ryan Folger and his fiancée, Peyton Chandler."

They all looked at each other.

"Peyton Chandler and Ryan were engaged?" Jude said. "I don't think I want to know more."

The room spun. For a moment Jude thought she was going to be sick.

"It was a few years back," Kyla said.

"But still, he could have warned me before she stepped foot on the island."

Lily clicked to the next page. "It's time that you know exactly who he is and what is going on."

The article went on to say it was the grand opening of Chef Wakefield's upscale new restaurant, but all was not bright. There were rumors his cooking show was going to be canceled by the network due to his drug problem. The coroner's report said he'd had a severe case of pneumonia and a lethal combination of drugs and alcohol in his system."

"How sad," Jude said. "It makes me wonder if Ryan was involved with the drugs, too."

"Oh," Lily said. "I didn't think of that. That could be why he's always seemed withdrawn."

"I knew there was a secret there. I knew it from the minute I saw him he was on the run," Kyla said. "Takes one to know, I guess. But I'm sure he's not on drugs now. I would've felt it. I would know."

Jude agreed, "I don't think so either, but I'm certainly going to be asking him.

Lily clicked on other links, but there was nothing about Ryan and Peyton marrying. In fact, all the articles and pictures of them at red carpet events ended suddenly close to four years ago. There was nothing on Ryan for a while after that until he was mentioned in Seattle, cooking at Land and Sea, and how lucky they were to have a chef of his caliber in their kitchen.

"Ryan was named the most up and coming chef from Gourmet Cuisine & Spirits that year too, but not much else of interest," Lily said. "Several high Yelp ratings wherever he was working and that's about it."

The Ryan Folger who had been engaged to Peyton Chandler had just disappeared, basically changed his identity. But why, Jude wondered. Now he was here on Madrona Island. And so was Peyton.

Chapter Eleven

Grandpa John sat on his back porch in his favorite rocking chair, gazing out at the sunlit view before him. Summer was always his favorite season on the island. The last time he'd painted these old chairs, Maggie had been beside him, paintbrush in hand. He glanced over at the empty rocking chair and remembered Maggie sitting there, the two of them drinking fresh-squeezed lemonade in the afternoon and laughing. There was always so much laughter with Maggie. Today seem especially quiet without her. Ah, but there was Lily coming up the drive.

Lily parked her car beside the barn and walked toward him. As she got closer, he noticed her face looked drawn.

"What's up, girl?" He asked.

Maggie had always been so proud of her granddaughter. John wished she could see Lily now, a grown woman, just as beautiful inside as outside, married to his grandson Ian and the mother of sweet little baby Gwyn inside sleeping. Not all the time asleep, he laughed to himself. He was getting used to the crying. Thank goodness Mary came over sometimes and watched the baby. Mary was a wonderful helper, as she'd always been when she'd helped Maggie at the B&B.

Lily slumped in the empty rocker and looked down at her feet. "I'm worried about, Jude. You know what Google is, right?"

"I might be old, but you know that saying, I'm not stupid," John said with a grin. Yes, I know Google. You guys have really had something amazing to grow up with. We were lucky if we owned encyclopedias. My family could hardly afford them. We had to buy them used."

Lily laughed.

"At least they were sturdy and well-bound," Grandpa John said, trying to cheer her up. "What's going on with Jude?"

"Things with Lindsey went sour again, and on other fronts, rumors started flying about Chef Ryan's dark past. Jude adores him and got worried that Ryan wasn't telling her the whole truth. So this morning we took a closer look into the background of Ryan Folger and Peyton Chandler."

Grandpa John shook his head, "Miss Chandler. She's not happy unless she's creating total havoc. So how did you go about uncovering Ryan's past?"

"Jude, Kyla, and I went over to Marco's café early this morning. He has a pretty good setup down there and the best Internet in town. Of course we had some of his great coffee. And then we Googled him."

Grandpa John chuckled. "Didn't Jude ever check his references?"

"She did, she checked the restaurant references, but after that, you know, it is the island. She didn't exactly go searching for a detailed background check or anything."

"So what did you find?"

"Lots of gossip about him and Peyton. It seems they'd been in a hot and heavy relationship when they lived in San Francisco. They were even engaged to be married."

"Engaged? That nice young man engaged to her?"

"Well, it seemed maybe Ryan wasn't the nicest guy back then, at least from the pictures. He was an up-and-coming chef, very handsome and debonair. Probably moved in the same circles as Kyla when she was in New York. There were lots of pictures with celebrities, and he was nominated for several awards for best new chef. The spotlight was certainly on him and Peyton together."

"Hmm, I can see that," Grandpa John said. "So?"

"Something happened, but it's not really clear what broke them up. There was a big scandal around a restaurant opening with a famous chef who died of a drug overdose. Ryan was there and he was a close friend of the deceased chef. No charges were filed. But after that incident there's not much about Ryan anywhere. It's just like he went dark."

Grandpa John let out a long sigh. "And Peyton?"

"Peyton's star shined ever bright with lots of movies and appearances. The next big news was when she married Todd Chase, the actor she's still married to now. At least, I think she's still married. There are all kinds of recent pictures of him and some young starlet.

"So what are you trying to say?" Grandpa John said.

"I guess Peyton has been flirting with Ryan and having Lindsey work on the movie with her. She's stepping hard into Jude's territory, and not in a friendly way. There are too many of red flags around whether Ryan's telling Jude the whole story, and just what Peyton's intentions are."

Grandpa John was quiet for a moment. He thought about Peyton, about Ryan, and about how Jude had been through enough.

"I just can't imagine it. I really can't." He said.

"I hope you're right."

He winked at Lily. "I usually am."

"You are," she said, "You usually are."

She smiled at him and for a minute John thought it was Maggie's smile. The family resemblance was growing stronger.

"If you get a minute can you talk to Jude?"

"I will, don't worry," Grandpa John said. He patted Lily's shoulder. "I always look out for you girls."

She stood and kissed him on the forehead. "You're the best. I'm going to go and check on little Gwyn. Has she been a good girl today?"

"An angel, as always. She's sleeping right now, so be real quiet."

"Like a mouse," Lily said. "I'll just slip into her room and watch her sleep."

John watched Lily enter the house. He was happy her burden had been lifted a little by talking. But he was a little worried about Jude. Jude had been through so much, too, and now she wanted this love with Ryan more than anything. He remembered when she'd first come to the island, a single mom, starting a café. John had known more than he really should about Jude, because at one point Maggie had confided in him. "That woman needs our friendship," she'd told him. He'd frequented the café quite a bit, bringing in new customers and trying his best to be there for Jude. Pretty soon her beautiful smile and her wonderful heart had charmed half the island. Under her watchful eye, Island Thyme Café had become a real success.

But John knew Jude was hiding her broken heart under that sparkly smile. As little Lindsey grew up, her daughter had been her pride and joy. Jude loved that little girl, and the town doted on her.

He leaned back in his rocker. Clear as a bell, the memories came flooding back of that day. Lindsey was in her early teens then, a real beauty and headstrong as a horse. Restless and pouty, she'd been hard to reach for a while. John had come into the café for lunch and asked where Jude was. A waitress had pointed to the back room where he found Jude crying.

He'd sat down beside her and waited until she was ready to talk. The pain he'd seen in her eyes was almost worse than when she'd first arrived on Madrona Island. Jude poured out the story to him of how Lindsey's long lost father, who'd barely been around or managed child support all these years, had remarried a woman not much older than Lindsey. Mitchell was starting a new lease on life and started communicating with Lindsey again. Jude had no idea that was happening.

John remembered the conversation well.

"My daughter," Jude had said. "He wants her to live with him now. She's all I have, all I care about."

"Well, he can't have her," John said. "We're all here to help you."

Her eyes filled with gratitude. "Thank you, but it won't help. Lindsey's made up her mind. She's bored here, hates the island, and wants the excitement and travel that living with her dad can bring."

John nodded. "Those teenage years. If only we could reach them with our wisdom now, but they need to learn on their own."

"I know," Jude said. "I love her and want her happy. Whatever it takes. She's so happy now that her dad is finally paying attention to her. And his golden checkbook is being dangled before her, too."

"Mitchell knows the way to a teenager's heart, it seems," John said.

Jude sniffed and wiped her eyes. "Lindsey wants to move to Seattle next month and live with them. Permanently."

It was clear Jude was devastated, but there wasn't much she could do. Jude was wise enough to know she could fight Mitchell, but then Lindsey would end up hating her. John was sad to see Lindsey leave the island, but he could understand why a teenager might feel restless here, and how the flash and glitter of her father's money would sway her.

"I'm worried how she will change, what she'll become under his influence. And now, I'll be truly alone."

Grandpa John had hugged her tight. "You'll never be alone here on this island, Jude. We all love you too much."

Soon after, Jude closed the café for several days and came to stay at Maggie's bed and breakfast. Maggie cooked her food and piles of brownies. He'd see them walking the beach every day, and they'd joined him right here on this porch and cried together. They assured Jude that someday her daughter would come around, but after Lindsey left and Jude finally went back to work, they weren't so sure.

"Maggie. Oh, Maggie," he said to the clouds. "You knew how to make everyone feel better."

If only Maggie were here to speak with Lindsey now that she was back on the island and possibly causing even more trouble. She was a good girl at heart, just a little lost. Maybe he'd have a talk with Lindsey himself; after all, he'd known her since she was a baby. He guessed she wouldn't listen. The young rarely did.

Chapter Twelve

After a quick taste of the spicy mixture, Ryan added another pinch of salt to the marinade before placing the large shrimp into the bowl.

"Make that one-and-a-half teaspoons of salt," he said to Lindsey.

He watched her sitting on a stool at the kitchen island, her fingers flying across the keyboard as she entered the ingredients for his Lemon-Lime Spicy Shrimp recipe on her laptop. "Thank you for helping with these," he said. "At the rate I type, the book would never get finished."

Lindsey shrugged. "I have nothing else to do."

Ryan washed and dried his hands before taking a stool next to her at the butcher-block island. "A good attitude goes a long way to making things better," he said.

She spun around to face him, obviously ready to pounce. Ryan held up his hands. "Hold on, Lindsey, let's talk about this in a calm way."

He watched her shoulders droop and her face soften slightly. "You know and I know you lied to your mother about my knowing where you were off to the last several mornings."

"What I say to my mom is my own business."

"Not when it includes me," Ryan said.

"She never lets me do anything I want. I was hoping you'd support me. You're following your passion, even if it is on Madrona Island."

Ryan noted Lindsey's change of tactics. He hoped Peyton wasn't rubbing off on her. "I've worked a long time to figure out just what I want to do and find the right place to do it. You are talented girl, but you are a lucky one too, to have a mom who loves you so much."

"If she loved me, she'd let me do what I want and not keep me trapped on this island all summer."

He was not getting through to her, or more likely, she didn't want him to. "My understanding is you asked to come here for the summer."

Lindsey pushed her hair back from her face. "It's not like I wanted to or anything. I had no where else to go."

"Really," he said. "I find that hard to believe."

"All right, so I wanted to come home, see my mom, and just chill this summer. Working with you in the kitchen is great, and Peyton helped me get some work on the set."

Ryan paused. "When Peyton Chandler is helpful, it is almost always because she wants something from the person and is setting them up. I'm not saying you didn't deserve the work or do a good job. Just watch out."

Lindsey stared at him. "What would she want from me?"

How much should he tell her, he wondered. Undoubtedly Peyton had a plan, and she wouldn't hesitate to use Lindsey as collateral damage to get what she wanted.

"At this point, it might be better if you stop meeting her in the morning until and if your mother changes her mind about you going. Agreed?"

Lindsey's face fell into a pout. "Whatever."

"One more thing," Ryan said. "I want you to tell your mother the truth about me, that I did not know what you were doing."

"Why don't you tell her?"

"I already told her I thought you were taking morning walks, but it would make things clearer if it came from you. She needs to understand that I wasn't helping you hide a secret."

"Fine. Now let's get back to work. We have two more recipes to finish this morning."

Jude entered the kitchen and eyed the food lying out on the counters.

"We're finalizing some recipes for the cookbook," Ryan told her.

She shrugged. "It's a good idea. It'll help business."

Relief flooded Ryan. "When would be a good time for us to sit down and go over the cookbook idea so you can make your suggestions and approve what I have so far?"

"I don't know," Jude said. "Not today." She walked over to where Lindsey sat typing. "I see you're working here this morning."

Lindsey nodded and said nothing.

Jude flashed a look at Ryan. "I'll be making coffee," she said before turning her back to him and walking out.

She'd said everything he wanted to hear, but her voice had been flat and her eyes weary. Not today, she'd said, like a warning to stay away. Perhaps a day or two would be best, give Lindsey time to fess up to her mother and set things straight. But somehow his gut said something was sliding way off track, and not in a good direction.

Chapter Thirteen

Jude paced the floor of her living room. It had been a couple of days since the Google discoveries and she'd waited to calm down and think things through before confronting Ryan. They had arranged for him to come upstairs to her apartment when he finished today, and he would be here any minute. She knew it was time to talk to him. They'd barely spoken since the blow up over Lindsey. He'd tried a few times, and at one point he'd kidded her about him "being in the dog house," but she hadn't found it funny. She'd been walking around in a daze, worried, sad, and lonely for him all at once.

She checked the time and tried to calm her racing heart. This stress and worry was making her sick. Every day she felt less and less like eating, less like her normal self. All she wanted to do was curl up in her bed and sleep. One more week, she told herself, and the extra work caused by the film people will be finished. After that, all she had to get through was August, the biggest tourist month on the island. Jude yearned for a vacation. A real long one.

Ryan's footsteps were noticeable on the stairs, and she took a deep breath. He knocked at the door. Jude waited. He was getting more formal. Usually he knocked, then popped his head in. She opened the door and met his eyes. Something was shifting between them and it made her feel off balance.

"Come on in," she said.

Ryan walked in a few steps and stopped, as if he didn't know where to sit or stand.

"You wanted to see me?" he said.

His eyes were sunken like he hadn't slept in days either. Shoulders slumped, he looked beat up on the inside, and her heart went out to him. "Would you like a glass of wine?

"That would be nice," he said.

She walked into the kitchen and opened a bottle of the local Pinot from Luke's winery with the warm black cherry aroma, and poured two glasses. Luke and Kyla's winery now, she reminded herself.

She pointed to the couch. "Let's sit down."

Jude sat on a chair facing him, making sure she was not too close. She had something important to say and did not want to be swayed by his physical proximity. He barely sipped his wine, although when she thought about it, that was really all he ever really did. He obviously was not much of a drinker now.

"Have you ever had a problem with alcohol?" she forced herself to ask.

He looked blindsided. "What do you mean? I barely drink the stuff."

"I noticed that," Jude said, "but that's not how it always was, is it?"

He thumped the wine glass down on the table. "No it wasn't. What's this about, Jude? You certainly know I'm no alcoholic."

"Were you ever?" she asked.

"Is it your business?"

She flinched at his reply. That fact that he was holding out on her flamed the fires of her fear.

"I think it is," she said. "As your boss, it's my business to know if you are doing drugs or abusing alcohol."

"You're my boss. Is this an employee talk right now? I thought we'd moved a little beyond that, Jude. I know it's your café, but pulling rank and accusing me of doing drugs is a bit much. What's going on?"

"Well," she caught her breath, "I never officially checked your resume and recently some things have surfaced."

"What made you check it now?" he asked. "I've been here for over a year with a perfect record. I've always been there for you and helped build your business. Why now, Jude?"

"Obviously, there are things you haven't told me. I know you're a private person, and I respect that, but now things are more complicated. We work together and..."

"We're lovers," Ryan said. "If it's Peyton, I told you there's nothing there. Did Lindsey confess the truth to you about her accusation?"

"Reluctantly, she did. But it's not just about that." Jude sighed. "You and Peyton obviously have a past."

"I told you that was over."

"Ryan, please just let me talk."

"Okay."

"It's obvious the two of you were together and she'd like to be again."

Jude put her hand up to stop him from saying anything else. He sank back in the couch.

She continued. "So, I know you've told me it's over, and I see your face when Peyton walks in and it's not pleasant. But, I also see your manner when she touches you and how you respond. I get it. She's gorgeous. What man could resist her? But that's not the point. I don't know what to think about where that leaves us in our personal relationship, but at least our business relationship needs to be clean." She looked him right in the eyes. "I Googled you, Ryan."

"Why?" he asked.

His hurt expression cut right through her. "I Googled you to find out what you haven't told me and exactly who the man really is who's working with me everyday and I'm building a relationship with."

"Who do you think I am?"

"You know what I'm talking about," Jude said.

"What are you asking, Jude?"

"I...I...I don't know how to put this Ryan. I'm sure you're not, but it came to my attention that there is some history with you connected to drugs and..."

"Fine," Ryan said, "if you want, I'll do a drug test."

"Of course not. Just tell me the truth, all of it. You know I have to be careful."

His face was pale as he inhaled deeply to calm himself. Jude wanted to hug him, but first she had to get it all out.

"You never told me you were a celebrity chef. You never told me that you and Peyton were engaged, and you never told me why you just left and went off the grid. What are you really doing here Ryan?"

She watched him drum his fingers on the coffee table.

"What am I doing here? I'm trying to have a life, a clean life, a happy life with someone I really care about. I'm working in a kitchen where I feel challenged and appreciated. Not for what I look like, not for what money I can make for people, but because I make good food. Obviously, I want you to make a profit, Jude, but my life in San Francisco was a nightmare. Constantly struggling, trying to be the best, trying to compete, smiling in front of the camera. Do you have any idea what kind of hellish life I had with Peyton Chandler? The incessant paparazzi, adoring fans, and constant pressure. And the more successful I became, the more she accused me of competing with her. It was absolutely insane!

"She'd say to me, 'Ryan, you've got to try harder, get seen, build your career.' But the minute I did she felt threatened and would do anything to make me feel not good enough."

"Did you love her?" Jude asked.

"I don't know what I felt for her. It was several years ago, Jude. I was much younger. Yes, we were drinking, that was part of the scene. There were drugs everywhere. Did I try them? I did. Mostly I tried to stay away from them, but it was impossible when we traveled with that crowd."

"What about the chef who died?"

All the blood drained from Ryan's face. The vein in his forehead pounded. His eyes teared up.

"I'm sorry," she said. "I saw the article, and it said that you and Peyton and some of the other people were involved."

"Andrew was my friend," Ryan said. His voice was quivering. "We were close. We went to cooking school together. His charisma, talent, and drive brought him too much media coverage and too much success too fast. To deal with it all, he did more and more drugs."

Ryan's chest heaved. "That last night, Peyton drove me to Andrew's grand opening party for his dream restaurant. She was so wired on something and relentless that I use this event to make connections and be seen with her."

He looked at Jude. "I haven't told anyone about this, Jude. And I hoped I would never have to."

She wanted to hold him close and make the pain go away, but she knew it wouldn't work. "It's best to get it all out," she said. His pain was palpable, but burying the truth would not serve either of them.

Ryan nodded a few times. He closed and reopened his eyes and then began. "I saw Andrew in the bathroom earlier in the evening, slurring his words and stumbling. When I tried to convince him to let me take him to a hospital, he laughed it off and brushed me away. I told Peyton about my concern and she said to forget it, he was just high. And to mind my own business. A good friend's welfare is always my business. But that night, I did what I was told and let it go. My friend died right outside his restaurant, on opening night. I watched him seizing on the ground. I watched as people scrambled to flush drugs down the toilet and flee out of there and as far away from Andrew as possible."

"Peyton grabbed me by the arm yelling, 'Let's go, let's get out of here.' All anyone cared about was being caught. All I could see was my friend lying dead on the sidewalk, and that I might have been able to help him if I'd insisted."

Jude stood and moved over beside him. "That must have been horrible."

"It was. I hope you never have to face that with someone you love."

"I've had my own tragedies to go through, Ryan. I understand loss and self-recrimination." She waited for him to say more, but he was silent. "Is that when you left San Francisco?"

"I knew I still loved cooking and feeding people. That was all I had left. I could barely look at myself in the mirror. Any feelings I had for Peyton died on that sidewalk with Andrew. I couldn't get far enough away from Peyton Chandler. She couldn't care less about me, and she married Todd Chase within a month. I later found out I was about the only one who didn't know she'd been cheating on me the whole time with the actor."

"That must have stung," Jude said.

"Not a bit, actually. I was relieved she wouldn't be coming after me. Peyton does not like to be the one left behind. Now that I think about it, probably this whole act with her coming on to me right now is about Todd Chase. It's all over the media he's off with some young actress from his latest movie. No one rejects Peyton Chandler."

He could be right, Jude thought. It made sense, but could she trust her instincts right now? It was time for her overdue confession as well.

"Ryan, I don't know what to say. There's so much to think about. You have to understand that I haven't told you everything either. We were both feeling things out, I guess."

He squeezed her hand. "Might as well get it all out on the table."

Jude took a moment to collect her thoughts. She owed him the whole story.

"You know my husband cheated on me, but not how I found out. I opened the local newspaper the morning after he came home so late, and there it was. There'd been a car accident and another woman was sitting in the passenger seat. What was not reported was that Mitchell had been very drunk and ran a young boy on a bicycle off the road with his car. Thank God the boy only suffered a broken leg. Everything about the accident got swept under the rug. His family had the money to bury anything."

"I'm so sorry, Jude. It's good you got away from him."

"I almost didn't. I confronted Mitchell about the accident after I found the police report in his desk. I told him I wanted a divorce. He said to keep my mouth shut and my nose out of it, if I wanted to keep my daughter. We eventually negotiated that if I filed an uncontested divorce, and I kept my promise to him and his well-to-do family to never reveal the incident, than he would allow me full custody of Lindsey and a decent divorce settlement."

Jude waved her hand over the apartment. "How do you think I afforded this property and this cafe? His parents. That was part of our deal."

So here we are, Ryan. Each of us running, each of us paying for our past. Where does that leave us? You know about me. I know about you. And we're both a bit broken."

"We can build the trust again," Ryan said.

"I don't know," Jude said. "Trust is hard for me. I just need some time to take this all in."

She was so exhausted she couldn't even wrap her mind around their conversation. Her feelings were such a confusing mishmash that all she could think of was that she needed some space from him. "This might be a good time to take a break and let this all settle."

"A break?" Ryan said.

"Just from our personal relationship to figure out what's really there. We'll keep working and do what we need to keep things running. We'll just back it up a little bit. Slow it down."

"If that's what you want, Jude," Ryan said.

She looked at him. It was the last thing she wanted, but she couldn't risk being hurt anymore. "Yes Ryan, for now that is what I want."

He stood. "Whatever you say, boss."

"Ryan, don't go like that."

"Jude, you can't have it both ways. I'm going to go to my room and get some much-needed sleep. I'll see you in the café in the morning."

She leaned back on the couch and watched him leave. Her mind wandered in a hundred directions. She couldn't remember if she'd had dinner. The room spun around her, turning her stomach. She didn't want to lose Ryan. Lose this last chance for love. But the pain of past betrayals ran deep. Before she risked her heart, she needed more time. Jude sleep-walked to the bedroom and crawled into bed. The constant exhaustion was overtaking her. Tomorrow she needed to go see the doctor and find out what was wrong. Maybe she was anemic again. She turned off the light and sank into the darkness of her dreams.

Chapter Fourteen

Jude woke, ran to the bathroom, and threw up. How could she go downstairs and act like nothing had happened the night before? Ryan would be in the kitchen with Lindsey, and here she was being sick and not even wanting to go down to her own café. She took a shower and got dressed. I'll go over to Tea & Comfort before they open, she thought, to see if Kyla or Becca is there. Maybe one of them can give me some tea to calm down, something to help with these nerves and settle my stomach.

She slipped out the side door. Ugh. The movie people were already setting their equipment outside. She waved at Marco as he readied his coffee cart across the street. Luckily, she knew the back way. The sign on Kyla's shop said Closed, but she could see light through the window and someone stirring inside. She went around to the back door and knocked. "Kyla, are you in there?" she said. The door opened and Becca, looking perky despite the early hour, greeted her.

"Hi, Jude, we haven't opened yet. Can I help you with something?"

"I hope so. Do you mind if I come in? Is Kyla here?"

"No, she's not coming in until late today."

"Okay, well, maybe you could help."

Jude walked into the lavender-scented paradise and strolled over to the counter.

"Tell me, what's bothering you?" Becca asked. "You look a little pale."

"It's just been really stressful," Jude said, "with the movie people and the constant scheduling."

"Boy, do I know," Becca said. "I've got to be here early, do twice what I'm used to, and some of the people aren't so nice."

"I understand they're under a lot of pressure," Jude said.

"Oh, that Peyton Chandler. She pokes her head in, looks around once, smells some of the cream, and walks out saying she doesn't like lavender."

Jude laughed.

"What a piece of work," said Becca. "Well, what can I help you with?"

"I was wondering if you have some kind of relaxation tea, something I could drink to calm the nerves a little. I've lost my appetite, and this morning I even threw up from all the stress."

"Are you sure it's only from stress?"

"It doesn't feel like the flu—no fever or anything."

Becca was looking at her now very closely, "You know something, Jude? You look just like my sister when she was pregnant, and your symptoms sound identical."

"Pregnant?" Jude took a step back.

Becca stared at her. "Is it out of the question?"

Oh no, it was certainly not out of the question, Jude thought. That wonderful weekend in Victoria with Ryan, how many weeks ago had that been? But she was almost forty years old. Pregnant? A wave of nausea surged through her. She grabbed at her stomach and ran. "Excuse me," Jude said as she ran back towards the back bathroom and threw up again.

She rinsed out her mouth and looked in the mirror. There were dark circles under her eyes. The truth was staring back at her. "I'm pregnant," she said to her reflection. It certainly was possible, but oh my God. What would she do now? What would Ryan say? What would Lindsey say? A baby, now? Jude could barely face herself in the mirror. She walked back into the shop. Becca looked at her with such a sweet expression that she almost burst out crying.

"I think maybe I'm right," Becca said.

"You might be." Jude took a deep breath.

"How about this," Becca said, "before I give you any remedies, why don't you do a pregnancy test and then we can talk to Kyla."

"Oh poor Kyla. What will she say?" Jude thought about Lily who had just had her baby, and now if Jude was pregnant after Kyla had been trying so hard...Everything was such a mess.

Becca put her arm around Jude's shoulder. "She'll be happy for you. And so will everyone else. Now you go and get a pregnancy test, and let me know the results. We have lots of remedies for morning sickness."

"Right, right," Jude said. She was in total shock. "I guess I'll go to the drug store and do the test after the lunch crowd today."

"I'll be right here, waiting to hear," Becca said. "It would be kind of nice huh, little baby sister or brother for Lindsey?"

"I don't know how Lindsey would react," Jude said.

"Babies bring good luck," Becca said, "you know that. Look what it's done for Lily."

"Right," Jude said. But it hadn't been that way with Jude's first baby. All the bad luck she'd experienced with her husband, the accident, the divorce. Maybe this time it would be different. She was barely speaking to Ryan right now, so she wasn't going to tell him yet. Not until she knew for certain that there was something to tell. "Please Becca, promise me you won't tell anyone."

Becca winked. "Don't worry, my lips are sealed."

Jude walked out the back door. She was so disoriented she almost slid down the top step. In the back courtyard she leaned against the sturdy pine tree bordering the driveway. Could this be true? It would explain everything—her moods, her super-sensitivity, being sick in the morning, not wanting to eat. She didn't want to buy a pregnancy test here in town and get everyone talking. She'd have to drive up island and find one of those big box stores where no one would recognize her. She wasn't sure she was ready to face the results. She pulled her cell phone out and called Ryan, "I'm going to be late getting back this morning," she said.

He answered back, "Okay, I understand."

No you don't, she thought. "See you in about an hour."

She clicked off the call and dropped the phone into her purse. She pulled out her keys and walked unsteadily back home to get her car. The drive went by in a blur. In the drugstore, she casually slipped the pregnancy test in with some supplies for the café, casually, so no one would notice, not at this busy place. Tonight, after everything was over for the day, she would take the test.

Ryan wondered why Jude was going to be late today again. Worry pitted in his stomach. She'd seemed so pale and not herself lately. Yesterday had been tense enough after their talk the night before. They'd spend the day passing each other politely as they worked, but barely saying a word otherwise. Now he had no idea where she was going.

"Morning," Lindsey said. "The fog's starting to lift out there. I could barely see the pier on my coffee run to Marco's this morning."

"Gets that way sometimes," Ryan said. "By the way, your mom called and said she was going to be late getting in."

Lindsey shrugged. "I guess we're on our own this morning then."

She started cutting vegetables for a shrimp stir-fry marked on the board for today's menu. Her knife cuts were precise and even.

"You're becoming quite a pro in the kitchen," Ryan said.

She graced him with a smile and just for a moment he got a rare glimpse of vulnerability. It was nice to see one flash across her face and replace the perpetual pout. Ryan wished he could tell Lindsey just how hard Jude struggled to be a good mother, but Jude had sworn him to silence on anything she revealed during their conversations.

At least Lindsey was working at top level and staying put in the kitchen since their conversation the other day. "Are you here voluntarily?" he asked.

Lindsey laughed and held out her wrists. "Look, no handcuffs. And you're a great instructor." She wiped a wisp of hair from her brow. "Did you get the chapter on Pacific Northwest seafood written for the cookbook?"

"I've been working more on the marketing plan for the proposal. According to my James Beard award-winning cookbook friend, I need a platform, whatever that is. So, I had to dig up some old stuff, you know, put in some of the things I was known for, how long the book will be, and the number of people that come to the restaurant every year, plates served, etc. From that they figure how many books we can sell directly on the island. And the good news is, we only need two or three sample chapters."

"Great," she said. "Hey, I forgot, I have some more food shots for you." She wiped her hands and pulled her camera off the shelf. "Have a look."

She turned the screen towards him.

Ryan flipped through the pictures. "A plate of paella glistened under the lights complemented by the bright lemon wedges and fresh green herbs. Another perfectly featured a summer special dessert, blueberry peach tart with a vanilla glaze. "These are impressive," Ryan said. "That's some of the best food photography I've ever seen, and I've seen quite a bit."

Now, Lindsey was beaming, "So am I hired? Do I get photo credit for the whole book?"

"Whoa," Ryan said, "I'll try, but from what I hear, publishers tend to pick their own photographer. And you'll be back at school."

"I could take time off for this project," she said.

"Not sure how your mother would feel about that, but I'll see what I can do. With your skills, this could be a career direction for you Lindsey."

"I'd like it, I think. I could see being a food writer, taking pictures, working with chefs."

"And you're one fine cook, too."

She gave him a mischievous grin. "Maybe I'll even do my own cookbook some day."

He wasn't sure this was the same girl who'd been stomping about a few days ago. Whatever the reason, he was happy to see her enthusiasm.

The dining room door sprang open and Jude entered the kitchen. The exasperated look on her face kept Ryan from asking where she'd been.

"Everything okay back here?" Jude asked.

Lindsey nodded. "We're doing great, but you don't look so good."

Jude just stood there staring at her daughter. "That's not nice to say."

"I didn't mean it like that Mom, it's just, you look tired. Is everything okay?"

"Everything's fine," Jude said. "Just go on back to what you were doing." She looked over to Ryan. The pregnancy scare had unnerved Jude, and she couldn't shake the feeling that she'd been too hasty in suggesting a break. Maybe what they really needed was some time to heal together.

"Do you think I could have a minute with you?"

He looked at the shrimp waiting to be peeled and veined. It could wait.

"Of course," he said. "Lindsey, you're in charge."

Ryan was glad Sierra would be coming in soon to help with lunch. They needed all the help they could get. He hoped she remembered to keep her mini-collie outside this time.

Ryan trailed Jude into the dining room. The tide was turning again between them and he felt unsteady.

"Why don't we go upstairs," Jude said, "where we can talk quietly for a moment."

Now Ryan was nervous. Another talk felt ominous. "All right, whatever you want."

"Really?" Jude asked.

"Really." His eyes pleaded for her to believe him.

Ryan followed her upstairs to her apartment above the café. He took the chair opposite and let his gaze wander out the window. Her place really had a magnificent view. His place overlooked Main Street, but from here, now that the fog had cleared, he could see Mount Baker and the Cascade mountains towering against the crisp blue sky. It was a paradise here in the summer. He glanced at Jude, her head back against the couch, eyes closed.

"How are you doing?" he asked. His voice was warm and tender.

"Just feeling a little dizzy," she said. "I haven't had any breakfast."

"You want me to cook you something? I can whip something up in your kitchen. You shouldn't go without eating."

"I don't know. It's just, I'm nauseous, and don't feel much like eating."

Ryan stood. This was finally something he could fix. "Come on, I'll make you whatever you like. French toast?" He saw a little bit of a smile peek out. "With orange lavender syrup?"

"All right, maybe you can talk me into that," she said.

Jude still looked a bit reluctant, so before she could change her mind, Ryan gathered the ingredients in her kitchen. Jude wandered over and slid onto a stool at the breakfast bar to watch him whip some eggs, then soak a few slices of the local egg bread with the mixture. He dropped in a pinch of the lavender, a teaspoon of vanilla, a sprinkle of cinnamon, and a fresh squeeze of orange juice. Lily had shared the recipe from her B&B, and it could win anyone's heart. He grilled the bread in a pan of sweet, sizzling butter, and then placed a stack on a plate garnished with a fresh strawberry and sprig of mint.

"Go ahead, eat up," he said, "you'll feel better."

He watched her pick at the food. His chest tightened. What was worrying her now? He knew damn well it could still be Peyton. He would kill Peyton if she'd said or done anything else to upset Jude. Whatever it took, he was going to stop her from causing any more trouble. He didn't know what the actress was up to, but he was certainly going to find out.

Ryan washed the pan, and then sat down on a stool beside her at the eating bar. "Feeling any better?" he asked

Jude turned and gave him a weak smile. "A little, thanks."

"Did you want to talk?" he asked.

"Ryan," she hesitated. "When I said I needed a break from our relationship, I was at the breaking point inside of me. That is not what I really want."

"Truce for now?" Ryan asked.

Jude stared into his eyes. He wished he knew what she was really thinking. Neither of them had said the three simple words yet... I love you.

"Truce," she finally said.

He gave her a quick hug, careful to keep it friendly. "I understand."

"You better get back to the kitchen and help Lindsey before she burns the place down."

"All right," Ryan said. "You sure?"

"Yes, you go ahead, I'll be down in a minute."

Ryan hurried downstairs, walked over to his station, and slammed his hand on the top of the kitchen counter.

Lindsey turned. "What's wrong?"

"It's nothing," Ryan said." It's just—"

"What?"

"You don't need to get involved Lindsey." He paused. "I don't know if you've noticed, but Peyton and I knew each other before."

"Yeah, I've noticed. You two have a thing?"

"No, absolutely not," he said, "I knew her several years ago, that's all."

"Really?" Lindsey said. "That's not how it looks."

"I'm telling you the truth."

"It better be," Lindsey said. "I don't want you hurting my mom."

He was surprised and pleased to see Lindsey defending Jude. Maybe there was hope for those two after all. He also knew words alone were not going to fix this mess. Action was needed, but he was not sure what. "Let's get back to work," he said.

Ryan needed to be careful not to cut his finger off with the knife as he vigorously chopped the onions and minced the thyme. It was going to be a hot day. That afternoon he needed to squeeze lemons and mix in some strawberries and thyme for the special house drink, Strawberry Thyme Lemonade. Everything he had to do today raced through his mind. He didn't know where to begin. At least he and Jude had called a truce for now and he could breath again.

He looked over at his calendar and realized this was the afternoon he was supposed to meet with Luke out at the winery after lunch to discuss the cast and crew wrap-up dinner that was only a week away. More things to handle today. They needed to figure out the menu and wine pairings and go over last minute details. On top of his regular workload, he needed to create and execute a meal for fifty very picky people. The best part was that when this dinner was over, it meant Peyton would be walking out of his life very soon after and hopefully everything would return to normal.

"What a beautiful spot," Ryan said. The view from Luke's deck soothed his nerves. The property included rolling hills covered in trellises of grapes with clear dirt paths between the rows. Afternoon sun lit the old wooden tasting barn that was nestled in the tall trees. Ryan was glad to be out of the kitchen and spend some time outdoors for a change.

"I love living here," Luke replied. "I've never spent even one day regretting my decision to buy this winery. It's a beautiful place, made even more beautiful by sharing it with my new bride."

"Married life seems to be agreeing with you and Kyla."

Luke reached down and petted Bailey whose thumping tail shook the deck. "Is it that obvious?"

"You look content." Ryan had almost said barefoot and content.

"Are you saying I look like an old married man?" Luke said with a laugh.

Ryan waved his hand out at the vineyard and forest beyond. "I wouldn't mind settling in a place like this myself." Bailey rolled over and stretched toward Ryan.

Ryan scratched him behind the ears. "Great dog."

"You should get one," Luke said.

He thought about it. Ryan once thought a dog would be a good companion, but between living in an apartment and working long hours, it didn't make sense. Dogs needed time, and he didn't have much extra of that right now. "My lifestyle at the moment doesn't really cater to one."

"True. What about a cat? Kyla's two are easy to care for and very affectionate. We try to keep them inside because of the coyotes out here."

"Perhaps sometime in the future," Ryan said.

"Well, feel free to come over and play with our Bailey anytime."

"I might just take you up on that." Ryan said.

A cool breeze moved through the leaves of the big leaf maple tree near the koi pond. Ryan closed his eyes for a moment, letting the peace wash over him.

"So what do you think about this hoopla they're planning out here for dinner?" Luke asked.

"I'll be glad when this movie is done shooting," Ryan said. "Every day with Peyton Chandler is one day too many."

Luke looked at him. "What do you mean?"

Ryan paused, "In case you haven't heard, I had a past with her. We dated years ago. It was not a good time in my life and things happened I'd rather forget. That's celebrity life. A complete lack of reality."

"I'd heard something," Luke said.

Ryan rolled his eyes. "I bet."

"I know what you mean," Luke said. "My parents are New York society people and they were not too happy when I was dating Kyla in her super model days. There were newspaper articles, untrue scandals, and then all the junk they put out when Kyla was running from the paparazzi."

Ryan looked over at Luke, "So you do know how it is and how the press can make it look even worse. How did you handle it all?"

"Once I found Kyla again and made up my mind I loved and wanted her, I didn't let anyone stand in my way. Not even my family."

Peyton seemed an immovable force to Ryan, but he knew once her scheme got her what she wanted, she would drop him like he never existed. "I want Jude to know how I feel about her, to believe me."

"If you are sure you're ready to commit to her, my best suggestion is to just tell her the truth, and do it as soon as possible."

"I know," Ryan sighed, "I was thinking of telling her after the cast dinner when the movie people leave."

"That works. But don't wait too long."

Too long? How long was too long, Ryan wondered. And would she believe his feelings were real? And what if she rejected him? He couldn't let his mind go there or he'd never say a thing, and he knew where that would lead him.

Luke pulled out his notebook. "So what were you thinking for the menu?"

"Mid-summer produce is at its best now, so I've put together a list of some menu items that would pair nicely with your wines and possibly a dessert that would be complemented by a bottle of your red wine."

Luke reviewed the sample menu. "Looks good to me. Roasted mushrooms with browned garlic and thyme butter goes well with our harvest too. We can decorate the tables with flowers. If it's not windy, we could even put a few candles out placed in grapevine holders. I'll make sure everything looks high-end."

"I'm sure you will, Luke. It won't take much in this picturesque place."

Bailey took the red ball from the deck into his mouth and then dropped it in Luke's hand. Luke threw it way out into the field and the dog went chasing after it.

"You do have a nice life here," Ryan said.

Luke caught Ryan's eye. "Like I said, don't wait too long. I know how you feel about Jude, and love like that doesn't come along very often."

Chapter Fifteen

Jude locked the bathroom door behind her. She sure didn't want Lindsey walking in. She took the test out of the box and read the directions. It was pretty simple. After you tested your sample, if the color turned pink on the strip, you were pregnant. If not, it was negative.

Step-by-step, Jude took her time and followed directions to collect and test the specimen. Three minutes was all it took. She could hardly believe it. When she was pregnant with Lindsey, it had taken two days to get the results after a trip to the doctor. The test did say they weren't always accurate, and to retest in a few days if in doubt. But there was little doubt in her mind which way this was going.

Her cell phone stopwatch clicked off the seconds. One more minute. It was already starting to show color, and she could feel her stomach dropping, her breath catching. She sighed, trying to calm herself. "It's going to be okay," she whispered. "It's going to be okay."

Ding went the stopwatch, startling her. Eyes closed, she held the test in her hand, willing herself to finally look down. There it was, as positive as positive could be. She was pregnant, and it was definitely Ryan's baby. There had been no one else in a very long time.

Emotions spun through her, from elation to despair. She lowered the toilet seat, sat down, and took a deep breath. In her mind, she counted backwards to their romantic trip to Victoria in early July. What would the due date be? "If this is August," she murmured, "I'm probably around six weeks pregnant now." She counted the months in her head. A March birth. Well, at least she wouldn't have to go through a summer pregnant like she had with Lindsey.

"I'm pregnant," she said aloud. Her heart stirred. Jude never thought she'd hold another baby in her arms. She'd given up on ever having a second child, but she'd always wanted one.

She stood and let a smile slip across her face. "A new baby." She and Lily, and hopefully Kyla, too, could all be mothers together. First steps. First tooth. First night they slept through all the way. Oh, my gosh, how would she go through all that alone? She'd have her friends, but they wouldn't be there in the middle of the night. Would Ryan? Jude sure hoped so.

Ryan. She had no idea what he would think about this. He kept telling her how much he loved her. He kept trying to show her, but she still wasn't sure how much she trusted him. How much of her fear and paranoia were from her own past, and how much was legitimately based on events in the present? After Googling Ryan, she didn't feel quite as stable, but, then again, everyone had a past. As did she. What about her future? She really needed to talk to Kyla and get some deeper insight. That woman could see through everything. Jude was lucky to count her as a best friend.

She crumpled the box and put the test in the garbage. Just to be sure, she grabbed the basket and walked downstairs to get rid of it in the outside dumpster. There was a cool breeze coming up in the night air. Jude walked behind the building, tossed everything, and stood there looking at the sky. The twinkling of millions of stars reflected back to her. Overwhelming beauty at the vastness of it all soothed her. Jude put the trash basket down on the platform and walked over to the railing that protected the deck from the water below. The tide was in, almost to the top of the retaining wall. The water glistened in the moonlight. Everything was quiet except for the sound of her own breath.

Ryan was tucked away upstairs in his room, and she was alone down here. Should she tell him now? And Lindsey? Her eyes took to the sky again just as a shooting star shot across it to the north. It looked like it was going to land right in the water. "Make a wish," she told herself.

Jude closed her eyes and made the true wish of her heart.

She opened her eyes. Could she believe in her dreams? Could she trust that her wish would come true? Her hands tightened on the railing. It was too late to call any of her friends and morning seemed thousands of hours away.

"Don't think about the past." Jude could almost hear Maggie telling her as much, as she had the many times as they'd sipped coffee on the porch of Madrona Island Bed & Breakfast. Oh, if only Maggie were still alive. She'd been like a grandmother to them all.

Memories flooded Jude's mind of the time she'd spent with Maggie at the inn after Lindsey had left to go live with her father. Maggie had given her a book during that terrible time, a book about mothers and being positive. It was in her hope chest at the foot of her bed. She was sure of it. That's what she needed right now.

The reassurance of Maggie's words spurred her up the stairs and into her bedroom. She opened the heavy lid to the antique chest with its wood carvings and metal latch. Years ago, she had painted it white to match her bed frame, and it was a good contrast with the spread.

Inside, sitting on the very top, was Lindsey's baby book. She retrieved it and hugged it close to her chest before opening it to the first few pages. In front were pictures of Lindsey wrapped up like a little bundle of joy in her blanket, and others with Lindsey with a little pacifier in her mouth. Jude wondered, "Do mothers still use those?"

There was a picture of Lindsey's first birthday, a little piece of her blonde curly hair. Jude scanned through the pages. There'd been a lot of joy in being a mother, despite all the problems with Mitchell. And there would be again, she reassured herself.

Jude placed the pink baby book down on the bed and looked through the other contents. There were many keepsakes from her past, but there, buried almost at the bottom, was a little book about comfort for mothers. That was it: Comfort for the Heart of Every Mother.

"Thank you, Maggie," Jude whispered. How well she remembered seeking refuge at the bed and breakfast when she was a complete basket case after Lindsey had left the island as a teenager. Maggie had put her in the special bridal suite, of all things, and nurtured her with a calm, warm strength. They had morning coffee together, and delicious croissants, muffins, scones, and plates of chocolate brownies to Jude's content. Before Jude left to go home, Maggie had sparked her will to go on, and given her this book. Maggie had told her, "Just keep loving your daughter. She'll come back. They go through so much, but they always come back to the love in their heart, and you're such a good mother."

Those words rang in Jude's ears, *such a good mother.* She knew so much more now, and with Ryan's help, perhaps that's exactly what she would be.

Chapter Sixteen

Ryan was in the kitchen, going through the motions of cleaning everything after the last cast lunch they would be serving for the movie people. He was grateful that he didn't have dinner service tonight. Jude was still barely talking to him. She was friendly, but still a bit distant.

Even Lindsey noticed. "What did you guys break up?"

He didn't know what to say to her. "Not exactly."

Lindsey shrugged. "Whatever."

He felt trapped, trapped in secrets he was still keeping, trapped by that woman who would not leave him alone. She'd been texting him all morning and he hadn't even give her his cell phone number. There was no end to her sweet charm alternating with threats in each message. Just what did she want?

"Meet me for dinner or else."

Or else what? "What is that suppose to mean?" he texted back.

"I don't think you want it to show on your phone. You know what I mean," was her reply.

He did know what she meant. She, of all people, knew his shame and guilt for not insisting his buddy, Chef Andrew, go to the hospital that night at the restaurant, and how close he'd come to following in his friend's drug habit himself. Peyton would happily share his private life with anyone who would listen.

"Dinner?"

He texted back, "I'm not hungry."

"How about just a drink then?" She texted a wink after the message.

"A short one," he answered.

Her last message said, "Meet me at the Captain's Cove. 7:00. I'll be in the bar at the back of the restaurant."

Did he dare ignore her? Perhaps one conversation face-to-face would put an end to this.

The meeting place was a lovely, tavern-type bar right on the water overlooking Muscle Cove. Ryan remembered it from New Year's Day when they'd been here for their wonderful brunch. The chef had a large herb garden right on the property, which Ryan envied. He hated the thought of being seen with the actress, but it was a Monday night and it wouldn't be crowded. He could run up there, have a drink, and finally figure out what she was after. Forewarned is forearmed, and all that. Ryan took a shower and put on a button-down shirt. He wasn't dressing for her, but he sure didn't want to look like he'd just stepped out of the kitchen. It was a nice place, even if the company would be anything but.

He got in the car and drove it down the tree-lined road that bordered the cove. It was just starting to get dark—the sun didn't set this time of year until after 9:00 p.m. Shadows of the trees reflected across the water and the red bark of the Madrona trees had a fiery glow when they caught the muted evening sun. They'd be able to see the full sunset from the bar; at least he could enjoy that. He reminded himself that he needed to stay on guard at all times. Just what did Peyton have in mind? She was always scheming, and he had no doubt that this was part of a big one. Ryan wasn't leaving tonight until he found out exactly what she wanted from him and made sure she knew anything they might have once had was completely over.

The parking lot was nestled under some old growth pines. He found a spot and parked the car on a bed of the copper colored pine needles that covered the lot. The restored old sailboat the restaurant used for tours and private parties, was anchored at the end of the short pier for tours and private parties. He'd love to take Jude out on it for a sunset dinner cruise sometime. The golden sunlight spotlighted the hills just across the cove where Kelly green light filtered down across the grassy knolls.

Ryan wished he were here with Jude and not on this dreaded mission, but it was time to get this over with. He pushed through the red front doors and nodded to the receptionist.

"Just heading to the bar," he said. He walked through the half-empty formal dining room toward the tavern area. Even if it was high season, Mondays were not a big day in town as most of the tourists were gone.

As expected, there was Peyton Chandler in all her glory sitting at the largest table, of course, the one that had the unobstructed view of the water. As if staged by a set designer, an oversize bouquet of roses wrapped in gold tissue paper lay on the table next to a candle with a flickering flame, a bottle of champagne chilling, and two glasses filled with the sparkling wine.

"What the...?" he murmured under his breath.

She waved and blew him a kiss. His stomach clenched. His pace slowed as if he were moving toward her in slow motion.

"Ryan," she said sweetly, displaying her classic smile. "I'm so glad you could make it."

He pulled out a chair and sat across from her. "What's with the flowers?"

"Aren't they beautiful?" She lifted them and held them under his nose. "Have a smell."

He leaned over to smell the flowers, and the next thing he knew there were flashbulbs going off. Paparazzi reporters and photographers jumped out from behind the bar and snapped pictures of them. As if on cue, Peyton rose and moved over behind him. She threw her diamond-clad arms around him, pressed her body into his back, and kissed the side of his face and neck. Flashbulbs added to the surreal scene.

Ryan pushed her off and broke free of her grip. "What is all this?" he said. The flowers, the wine, Peyton dressed in a slinky red sundress cut down to her naval. It was falling into place.

"What is going on, Peyton?" he demanded as he pushed back his chair.

She smirked, her eyes piercing his like daggers. She stepped aside and clutched a champagne glass in her hand. "To us," she said, smiling at the cameras again.

Ryan's face burned as the cameras went off, catching the perfect romantic scene expertly designed by Peyton. Just the two of them, dressed up and in this cozy bar that they had all to themselves.

"Why, Peyton? Why?"

Her lips curled. "Why not?"

Ryan shook his head in disbelief. "What do you want from me?"

"Don't worry, honey," she said, "I just got what I wanted. Now we'll see how well it works."

It took all the restraint he could command to not take her long neck in his hands and squeeze it with every drop of strength he had. "Don't ever contact me again," he said between gritted teeth.

"With pleasure," she all but purred.

Ryan looked at the cameramen and shook his head, "It's not what it seems."

"Right, right," they said, snapping more shots.

The flashes blinded him and he covered his eyes. He turned to run out of there and half tripped over a chair. More flashbulbs. They'd probably say he was unsteady on his feet, and that he was off the wagon again

He didn't care, he just wanted to get out of there as fast as he could. When he got safely in his car, he gripped the steering wheel and tried to catch his breath.

I stepped right into it, was all he could think. What a stupid mistake. On the dirve home, he could see how perfectly she'd set him up. Would anyone believe him?

Ryan woke extra early the next morning to take a long walk and try to shake off his tension and anger out from the night

before. Now in the kitchen, he pounded the garlic with the knife harder than he needed to. Whatever Peyton had planned was bound to materialize into trouble soon. Last night he'd tried to write the whole scene off in his head, tell himself no one would pay attention. But that hadn't worked at all. Then he'd

paced his living room floor for half an hour trying to figure things out before knocking on Jude's door. He knew the best thing to do would be to tell her the truth about everything. But in the end, his feelings of shame had got the better of him. Maybe things wouldn't look so bleak in the morning. It would be better to talk to her in the light of day when he had a better perspective on things.

Ryan also didn't want to do anything else that might play into Peyton's scheme. What would he say to Jude? "I saw Peyton last night in order to clear the air between us, to end things once and for all. But she set me up with flowers and wine and candles. She even had the paparazzi there to take pictures. But you have to believe me, it wasn't what it seemed." It sounded like a lame excuse even to his ears. He had to warn Jude, but he wasn't sure if he could find the right words to make her understand. So far, when he'd tried to make things right between them, he'd only ended up making them worse. Everything between them was so fragile right now, and something like this could easily cause a break.

Ryan heard Lindsey tromping down the stairs. She was a good kid and had been a tremendous help with the cookbook, and her photography of the food was beautiful. It had actually been quite fun working together.

Lindsey peered into the kitchen. "Morning, Ryan. I think you might be in the doghouse."

He dropped the knife on the counter and whirled around. "What?

"Hey, don't blame me. I'm just the messenger," Lindsey said.

She hopped on a bar stool, flipped her hair out of her eyes, and waited for a response. Ryan weighed his options.

"What do you mean?" he asked.

Lindsey held up her iPhone. "Uh, do you ever go on Twitter?"

Breakfast flipped in his stomach. "Sometimes. Why?"

"Well," she said, pausing and obviously enjoying the moment, "you're trending there right now."

"Show me," Ryan said. He moved behind her to get a better view of the screen.

"All right, just give me a minute to pull it up on my phone."

Ryan leaned on the kitchen island, while Lindsey connected to her Twitter account. She held the screen to him. "There you go. See," she pointed. "Pictures of you and Peyton."

He wasn't sure what stung most, the rumors or being called a has-been chef. Ryan couldn't believe his eyes. The pictures, the way they doctored them, him and Peyton at the café, beautiful flowers, wine, Peyton kissing him on the side of the head. The headline said, "Are they back together? What will her husband say?"

She started reading some of the tweets. "Old flame and actress back together? "Actress cheats on famous husband with country chef."

"What?! Stop right there," Ryan said. "That's not true."

Lindsey's eyebrow shot up. "Really? It doesn't look that way."

The disappointment on Lindsey's face left no doubt about what she believed. "I've seen enough. Close the phone." He didn't know what to say. He stepped back and looked at Lindsey. "How many people are going to see this?"

"Uh, lots," Lindsey said. "Well, it's definitely trending and there are already over 3000 tweets on the topic."

Ryan felt himself sway, his balance off, a fall inevitable. He grabbed the kitchen counter, knuckles white, and held tight. It was like the old nightmare starting all over again, the publicity, the press. And Jude, what would Jude say?

Lindsey's eyes never left him.

"So, now what?" he asked. "More people will see it?"

"I guess so," she said. "What were you doing with Peyton? I thought you were seeing my mom."

"I love your mother," Ryan said. "Peyton set me up."

"Oh, I see," Lindsey said, not really looking like she saw at all. "Well, whatever. You've got some explaining to do to my mom."

"I know," Ryan said. "I planned to today. I hope she doesn't see this first."

Lindsey hopped down off the barstool. "Don't count on that," she said. "The gossip columns are probably going to jump all over this, and Facebook is already full of pictures. Hopefully it won't hit YouTube. Did they take videos?"

He prayed not. "I never thought…"

"Maybe you should have done some of that before you met with Peyton."

"You don't know what really happened," Ryan said.

"I understand more than you think. Both you and my mom are messed up." She went over to the sink, washed her hands, and then tied on an apron. "Someone better get working today."

Ryan wanted to try to explain, but what could he say? In time, he would make sure both Lindsey and Jude got a full explanation, but for now he had to find Jude and tell her what was happening.

"Do you think you can finish everything here?" he asked.

Lindsey nodded. "It's okay. Sierra will be here soon, so we'll be fine. Go do whatever you have to, and good luck with that."

Ryan looked around in the dining room to see if Jude had come down yet. Luckily, she hadn't. He dreaded talking to her. Maybe it meant she was still upstairs, reading about the mess he'd stepped right into last night. He thought about the headlines. "Actress divorcing famous actor husband Todd Chase." That had to be it. She darn well wouldn't want Ryan back. That certainly wasn't it at all. He was just a casualty of war, indispensable in Peyton's plan to win her husband back. He thought about the look in Lindsey's eyes. She was hurt too, but at least she told him about it.

This was not the time to be waiting around, hoping and worrying. He needed to take responsibility for what happened and tell Jude before she found out on her own. Ryan walked upstairs, heart pounding, and tapped lightly on Jude's door. "Are you awake?" he said. He waited a few minutes until Jude opened the door. She still looked a little sleepy. "Can I come in?" he asked.

Jude wiped her eyes and glanced down at her night-gown. "Is something wrong? Is Lindsey okay?"

"Lindsey's fine," Ryan said, "and I wouldn't bother you if it wasn't important." He knew they'd called a truce and were on better terms, but the strain on their relationship lately had been heavy. He felt terrible, and this was only going to make it worse. It seemed like everything around him was falling apart, and he couldn't quite hold it together. Ever since Peyton hit the island, his life had gone right back downhill again. And everything he'd hoped and dreamed of was going right down with it, as it always had with Peyton Chandler.

Ryan walked over to the picture window. As with so many mornings, another beautiful sunrise was peeking over the Cascade Mountains. The cove glistened in pinks, punctuated with drops of gold. The water was so clear he could see the mussel shells and rocks on the bottom. A lone blue heron stood on one leg, waiting to catch breakfast. Paradise and hell could be so close sometimes. He could feel Jude standing behind him, and he hesitated before he turned to face her.

"So, what is it that's so important?"

Ryan turned to face her. "You might want to sit down, Jude," he said. The look on her face shattered him. He would've done anything to avoid this. He wanted to kick himself for ever choosing to meet with Peyton, even though his intentions had been good. It probably wouldn't have mattered, because Peyton would have found another way to get what she wanted, and it might have been worse. At least he knew what he was fighting against now.

Jude walked over and sat down on a stool at the marble counter separating her kitchen from the living area. Ryan sat down next to her. He wanted to pull her into his arms and hold her forever. He released a sigh. "You know how we talked about my past with Peyton?"

"I know," she said. "You told me already. Why are we going over this again?

Her eyes pierced right through him. "You told me everything, right?"

"Honestly, I did. But Peyton had more of an agenda than I knew, and she maneuvered me into meeting her last night..."

Jude leaned back and raised her hands in front of herself in a protection mode. "Just stop right there," she said. "I've had about enough of your secrets and enough of everything else."

Ryan stood. "I can understand you feel that way, but you need to know, Jude, there are going to be some deceptive report coming out in the media."

Jude tried to stand but he blocked her way. The kindest thing he could do was be the first to tell her. "Last night, Peyton demanded that I meet her at the Captain's Inn."

"Demanded," Jude said.

"It's a long story. That's what I am trying to tell you."

"Just tell me the results." Jude folded her arms across her chest.

"It seems that Peyton had arranged for some paparazzi to be there. They took pictures of us. She'd set the scene with wine and flowers and then leaned over and—"

"Stop," Jude said, "I told you I didn't want to hear anymore."

"I'm sorry. It's all over the news," Ryan said. "Lindsey told me I'm trending on Twitter. You're going to hear about it. There are lies splashed across the media saying actress and chef back together. Is she getting a divorce?"

Jude stood. "I can't keep up with you two any more." She pushed past him and walked over and opened the door to her place. "And now, if you would kindly get downstairs and do your job."

Ryan walked slowly toward the door. He glanced back at her, but the look on her face said it all. He didn't have a chance. He stepped out on the landing and Jude slammed the door behind him. His whole body was shaking. Somehow he made his way down the stairs back to the kitchen. It was going to be a long day. But he was not going to let Peyton Chandler ruin his life or Jude's, no matter what it took.

Chapter Seventeen

Grandpa John leaned back into his well-loved recliner and placed his coffee mug on the end table beside him. It had been quite a morning already, and it was only 8:00. Jude had called his farmhouse about an hour ago and was very upset. He hadn't completely understood their brief conversation before he handed the phone to Lily, but enough to know it was not good. That boy Ryan seemed to be stepping in trouble no matter where he turned. It was the last day of the shooting for the movie, and his grandson, Jason, had a small speaking part today. Lily was supposed to have taken him into town, but she'd reacted to the emergency call to meet with Jude, and he'd stepped in happily to take Jason instead. Ian was busy with the never-ending guests and movie crew coming and going at the B&B, so he'd promised both of Jason's parents not to worry, he'd watch him all day.

"Let's go, Grandpa, we have a 9:00 call."

Jason put out his hand and dragged his grandpa off the recliner.

"Slow down kid, let me get my keys." Jason had shot up in the last few months and enthusiastically stepped up to the job of big brother quite well. He loved watching Jason hold little Gwyn carefully in his arms, as if any wrong motion would cause his sister to break.

They went over Jason's line one more time in the car. They had rehearsed the scene about ten times already, with Jason running down the hill behind his farm yelling, "It's coming! It's coming!" Those were his two lines, but he would get paid well for them. When they arrived in town, he parked in the cast & crew lot on the grassy field behind the library. They walked down and checked Jason in for the day, and then Grandpa John happily took a seat on a bench in the shade.

Watching them shoot take after take made John even more elated that he wasn't in any of the scenes today. It'd been an exhausting few weeks, being an extra in a movie. It wasn't what he thought it would be like at all, but it was good to have a little bit of extra cash. It didn't pay much, but there was time-and-half for overtime, and he'd logged in plenty of that.

The cameras moved into place again as the extras milled along the side for another take. Poor Jason had run down that hill yelling his line several times already. It was a nice clear day with the sky as blue as cornflowers, just the way he liked it, with a slight breeze cooling the pounding summer heat. There was so much commotion going on with this film, not to mention the real-life dramas off set. He was not the only one who would like their peaceful little town back.

"All right, let's do another take," the director said with obvious frustration in his voice. John watched Jason, being a real trouper, come running down the hill waving his hands in the air. "It's coming! It's coming!" Jason yelled as the ambulance followed close behind him. It was the scene where the sick magician had collapsed on the sidewalk after landing on the island during their sail through the San Juan Islands. His wife, played by Peyton Chandler, had frantically called an ambulance. Sirens blared in the distance, while a local boy, played by his grandson, was running ahead to tell everyone it was on its way.

John watched Peyton re-enter the scene and sit down next to her very ill husband on the sidewalk. Tears flowed down her cheeks as she rocked him in her arms. "Oh no! Hurry," she cried. If John didn't know better he would think the scene was real. That woman was a darn good actress. She almost made him believe she cared, but according to the script she'd been poisoning him all along anyway. Typecast, he thought.

"Cut! Cut!" the director yelled. Grandpa John sighed. How many more takes for this tiny little scene? Jason came running over. "Did you see me? Did you see me?"

"You did great! Are they done?"

"Yep, they told me it was a wrap."

"All right," Grandpa John said. "How about I take you down to celebrate with an ice cream? I think the soda fountain's still open, even during the shoot."

"Yes! Let's go."

They wandered down the sidewalk as Jason chattered away. Perhaps adding sugar to his already excited state was not the best call, but Grandpa John had already promised him. He walked on the shady side of the street, saying hi to people and moving out of the way as staff or equipment shuttled around into place. The movie usually shot long into the day because the sun set so late now. It looked like they were taking a break, so that was good. Down time meant the store owners could open to the public briefly and not lose the whole day's business.

After walking into the soda fountain, they sat at the old-fashioned wooden counter. Jean, in her orange apron and crisp white shirt, waved at them. "Now what can I get you two boys today?"

Jason looked at the menu posted on the wall. "I'm not sure if I want a soda or a sundae or a milkshake."

That boy was so cute. Grandpa John couldn't imagine his life without Jason. He was grateful that Ian had decided to move onto the island permanently after he married Lily. Jason was thriving here, and of course Grandpa John was thriving himself having them here.

"Whatever you want," he told his grandson. "You've earned it with a hard day's work."

Jean leaned on the counter. "Well, are you in the mood for something more creamy or more fizzy?" she asked.

"I think cold and fizzy," Jason said. "It's pretty hot out there. And guess what, I just said my line in the movie today!"

"Congratulations," she said. "I always wanted to know a movie star. How does a chocolate soda piled with whipped cream to celebrate your debut sound?"

"Mmm," Jason grinned. "What's a debut?"

Grandpa John laughed. "It means it was your first real acting job for a movie."

Jason sat up straight and cocked his head. "A chocolate soda with lots of whipped cream," he said deepening his voice a little.

"I think I'll have...Let's see." Grandpa John looked at the menu. "I just think I'll have a scoop of chocolate ice cream in one of those house-made sugar cones. They're delicious."

"Coming right up," Jean said.

The ice cream was superb and made right there on the island. It was by far some of the best around, and the creamiest John had ever had. He remembered how he and Maggie used to come down here and enjoy a cone once in a while too. His mind drifted. It had been doing that a lot of that lately, drifting back to the time he'd spent with Maggie, remembering things they'd done together, like having tea on her porch, sharing fresh picked strawberries in the garden, walking along the beach by the house, always laughing together. The distance between them was thinning and he could feel her presence almost daily. For a second, he wondered if that meant anything. He was getting on in years, and he missed her more as time went by. He looked over at Jason. He was so glad Maggie got to meet him before she passed.

"Here you go," Jean said placing the frothy soda in front of Jason. She handed Grandpa John the cone. "Enjoy!"

Jason took the straw and stirred the drink. Froth ran over the top and settled at the bottom of the saucer. Jason scooped some up with his finger and then plunged the straw deep into the tall glass and took a big gulp. "Whoa, that is cold!"

Grandpa John laughed. "It's supposed to be." He licked his cone, letting the sweet chocolate cream melt in his mouth. "So, what shall we do with the rest of the afternoon, now that we don't have to go back to the set again?"

"You know," Jason said, "that was fun, but I don't think I ever want to do it again."

"I understand, buddy. Our destination is yours for the choosing today."

"I'd like to go somewhere we don't go all the time. Can we go off island, Grandpa?"

"As long as we don't go too far," John said. He wasn't comfortable driving long distances, and he wanted to make sure he'd be back before dark.

"We could go to Narrow Waters Bridge and walk on the beach there. I love that trail."

"Okay, that sounds like a plan. Let me call your dad and mom and let them know where we'll be." He pulled out his cell phone and dialed the inn.

Ian answered. "Madrona Island Bed and Breakfast."

"Afternoon, son," he said, "Jason and I were thinking of taking a little ride up to Narrow Waters State Park, to play around the beach, hike in the woods, and hunt for shells. Any problem with that?"

"Let me check," Ian said.

He could hear him calling back to Lily. "Lily wants to know if you guys will be back for dinner." Grandpa John looked at his watch. It was after 2:00, and it was a good hour-and-a-half round trip there and back.

"What if Jason and I just stop for burgers on the way back," John said. "You know that great drive-thru up there, with the homemade fries."

Jason nodded his head eagerly.

Grandpa John listened as Ian gave them a thumbs-up. "All right," he told Ian, "we'll be back way before dark. Don't you guys worry. Tell Lily I hope things went well with Jude."

"Thanks," Ian said. "You two have fun."

Grandpa John turned off the phone. "We're on, buddy. Let's head to the car."

They paid the waitress, got into Grandpa John's truck, and headed North. There was quite a bit of summer traffic clogging the highway, but it didn't take away from the beautiful scenery. Sun moved through the trees as the breeze ruffled their branches. A few bald eagles circled overhead. When they turned the corner at the top of the bay, they could see the Cascade mountain range with Mount Baker standing tall, almost floating in the sky. Locals swore that mountain was on roller skates. No matter where you were, it always looked like it had moved to another place.

Grandpa John headed toward the bridge and decided he'd pay for the parking inside the park. They could park the truck on the sand and walk on the boardwalk that wove along the shore for miles. Memories of walking the boardwalk with Maggie, hand in hand, just the two of them watching the sunset, flooded his mind. "Maggie girl," he thought, "I really wish you were here to see all this." He knew she was here in her own way, and that she'd always be with them in spirit. "As long as my eyes are here, as long as my body is here, my heart will still be with you," he whispered.

The minute they parked, Jason snapped off his seatbelt. "All right, let's go," he said, bounding out of the truck.

They headed down the boardwalk across the white sand strewn with driftwood and into the trees. Jason trotted along saying hi to the different dogs they passed. As they walked, John noticed he was slowing down a little, starting to get tired, which made him think about Betty. He was worried about her. He'd never seen that woman slow down, but the cancer had really taken its toll. He hoped against hope that if anyone could pull through, it would be her. He made a mental note to go visit her real soon.

Jason was waiting for him, sitting in one of the low branches of a cedar, swinging his feet back and forth. "Come here, Grandpa!" he said.

John walked over and patted the boy's back. "Whoa, look at you. Let me get a shot with my phone for your parents when we get back."

Jason posed with a big smile, and Grandpa John clicked the picture. Then he hopped off the tree.

"Where can we go now, Grandpa?"

"I'm a little tired. I'm thinking let's just sit here for a little while and watch the birds go by. Maybe we'll see some whales."

"You think so?" Jason said.

"You never know."

That was one thing about life, Grandpa John thought. You just never knew for sure what was coming next. John was glad he'd chosen to spend this day with his beloved grandson and create a memory they would never forget.

Chapter Eighteen

Jude had chosen Matt's Diner, her favorite not-too-greasy-spoon café, for her get-together with Lily and Kyla. It was a little way out of town, and they would have more privacy and be far away from the movie people.

The familiar chimes over the door rang out as she entered the diner. It had been a while since she'd eaten here, and she'd missed this place with its 1940s décor and waitresses in crisp red aprons. The buttery smell of fresh biscuits and the unmistakable aroma of sizzling bacon filled the air.

The hostess smiled at her. "Morning. You must be Jude," the waitress said. "Your friends are waiting over there."

Jude followed her to the booth where her friends sat. Relief flooded her at the sight of their concerned faces. Lily and Kyla were always there for her.

She slid in across the slightly worn vinyl seat and joined them.

"Coffee for you today?" the waitress asked as she laid a shiny menu before Jude.

Jude flipped the heavy white mug in front of her right side up. "Decaf for me."

For a few minutes, the three of them sipped their coffee in silence. Jude knew they were politely waiting for her to say something first. Kyla was in jeans and had her red hair piled on top of her head and attached with a clip. She looked like she'd stepped right out of a garden and as gorgeous as ever.

A high-pitched bell dinged, and the cook behind the counter yelled, "Order up." The waitress passed their table, her arms laden with piled-high plates of food.

Jude held her menu and tried to focus on the words before her. "What are you having?" she asked Kyla. "Your regular carb overload?"

Kyla laughed. "I just can't pass on their cinnamon roll French toast."

"Why not go for it?" Jude said.

"Agreed," Lily said. "This is the first breakfast I haven't cooked for myself in months. It's nice not to have any worries about a baby crying just as I sit down to eat. Grandpa John is watching Jason for the day, so I'm completely free."

The dark circles under Lily's eyes attested to the little sleep she was getting. Jude wondered how she herself would handle that kind of sleep deprivation, especially at almost forty.

The waitress stood before them, pen and order pad in hand, and scribbled down their orders.

"It's nice to get out of town just the three of us alone having a regular breakfast."

Lily took a sip of coffee. "Like the old days."

This breakfast was going to be anything but regular when she let her friends know her news.

The three plates arrived—one piled with pancakes smothered in real maple syrup, another with scrambled eggs, hash browns, thick crisp bacon, and of course, a steaming hot buttermilk biscuit with their specialty, marionberry jam. The third contained their decadent French toast that was beyond belief.

After a few bites Jude laid down her fork. As hungry as she was, the morning sickness often hit during breakfast. She looked at her friends. "I guess you've seen all the buzz on Ryan trending online?"

Kyla nodded. "It's all smoke and mirrors, and I would know. Peyton is so desperate to get Todd Chase back, she'll do anything. One or the other of them is always making the tabloids with some drama or another."

"Maybe," Jude said. "But after all the things we saw when we Googled him, I don't know what to think."

"That was all in the past," Lily said. "I think Ryan is totally innocent here. When I served breakfast at the inn this morning, there were a lot of heads buried in their phones. The comments were all the same about how well Peyton set the scene and how transparent it was to them. They felt bad for Ryan. I asked one of them to talk to you, but he didn't want to lose his job."

Jude sipped her coffee, willing it to stay down. "That's not all the news" she whispered, looking down at the table. "I'm pregnant."

Kyla's fork dropped, bouncing off her plate and onto the floor. "I've been dreaming about babies all week. I wasn't sure if it was my own, but I was so hoping."

Here Jude had been so worried and concentrating on the problems of pregnancy that she'd forgotten how desperate Kyla was to have a child. "I'm no psychic," Jude said, "but my gut tells me we might all be pushing strollers a year from now."

Lily clapped her hands. "That would be wonderful! The three of us doing birthday parties, picnics, first days of school..."

"Hold on," Jude said. "First I need to make it through a pregnancy at soon-to-be- forty years old."

"You will," Kyla said, squeezing Jude's hand.

"A lot will depend on whether I'm a single mom again."

Lily drew in a breath. "Does Ryan know?"

"No one else knows. Just the two of you now." The room seemed suddenly hotter. Jude pulled her hair off her neck, letting the circulating air from the fan above cool her. The sound of pots banging in the kitchen and orders being called out seemed suddenly louder while neither spoke a word. "I haven't told Lindsey yet either," Jude said.

The waitress swept in and refilled their coffee. "Everything all right for your breakfasts?" she asked.

Lily smiled, "They're delicious."

Lily waited until the waitress was out of earshot and then began again. "I can see why you're concerned with all the Twitter gossip going around, but honestly, I don't trust anything Peyton says or does."

Kyla nodded. "There's a shadow over that woman and it eclipses all light."

Jude took a deep breath. "You know how hard it is for me to trust, and I have no idea how Ryan will feel about a child. He is good with Lindsey, but she's almost an adult."

"Teenagers are almost as trying of your patience," Lily said, grinning. "But you are as healthy as ever and wiser now than when you had Lindsey."

"But I don't want to be a single mother again." Jude willed herself not to cry. These pregnancy hormones had her constantly on edge.

"You won't be," Lily said. "We're your family now, and most of the town folks love you too."

Kyla, with a new fork now, picked at her plate, her eyes focused somewhere Jude always wondered about. She turned her head to face them and spoke softly. "He loves you, as he will the child. But fear is still his companion."

"What does that mean?" Jude asked.

Kyla shook her head. "I just see the image, not the full form yet."

"Try to eat some food," Lily said. "You know the saying about eating for two."

Jude picked at her breakfast, but she could hardly taste anything. She was so tired that it made it hard to work or concentrate. She yawned and put down the fork. "I think I need a long nap."

"Of course you do," Lily said, "and some time off, too."

"That's pretty hard to do with a business that packed with tourists this time of year."

"Then we'll get you off for a few days," Lily said.

Kyla pulled out her phone. "Great idea. We could all use a few days off. Married life is great, but I miss quiet time alone and spending time with the two of you."

"I could really use a few nights uninterrupted sleep," Lily said. "Not that I wouldn't miss sweet Gwen desperately, but sleep, now that would be euphoric."

Kyla typed into her phone. "I'm searching for getaway homes for rent on one of the nearby islands."

"As long as the dates are after the cast wrap-up party in the vineyard," Jude said. "We can't spare a minute until then."

Jude considered the idea of leaving Ryan and Lindsey in charge of the café for a few days after the movie people left. They could definitely handle it, and she would get some precious time away to clear her head and make a plan before talking to Ryan more extensively. And rest. She'd miscarried once before and did not want to exhaust herself. "I love the idea. Let's get something luxurious and pamper ourselves."

"Done," Kyla said. She held the phone up and showed them pictures of a house on Orcas Island. It had tall, wood beam ceilings and large picture windows facing the water. "And look at this kitchen, we can make a feast."

"And this bathtub," Lily said pointing. "Let's get it."

"For two nights?" Kyla asked.

Both women shook their heads and spoke at the same time. "Yes!"

Jude could already feel her stress starting to melt away. At least for two days, Jude would be safe and hopefully find some peace and clarity.

Jude sat down at a small table by the window and put her feet up on the chair across from her. The dinner rush seemed like it would never end, and by the time she finished counting the day's receipts it was after ten o'clock. Ryan had already gone upstairs, and probably to bed, but Jude always did the closing after dinner. Bed was all she could think about, but the thought of standing seemed like too much effort. She dozed a bit and then woke with a start. There was an eerie quality to the café late at night when it was empty of customers.

Finally she woke and switched off the lights and headed upstairs. When Jude entered her apartment, it was completely dark. She flipped the lights on, laid her purse on the counter, and looked around. Usually Lindsey left some lights on for her. Perhaps her daughter had gone out earlier, but if so, why wasn't Lindsey home yet? Jude felt a wave of panic as she hurried to Lindsey's room and flipped on the light, only to see it was completely empty, the bed made. It looked just like it had in the morning when she'd left for work.

Jude walked back to the kitchen and looked on the wall where she kept her keys. The ones to the SUV were missing. Her heart pounded hard against her chest as her mind played out multiple scenarios, none of which ended well. Why hadn't her daughter left a note? Then she thought of Ryan. Maybe Lindsey had told him where she was going.

She hurried over to his place. Hands shaking, she pounded on his door.

Ryan answered in jeans and no shirt looking a little sleepy. "What's wrong," he said.

"Do you know where Lindsey is?" Jude asked.

"She's not back yet?" he asked.

"Back from where?" Jude demanded. Ryan ran his fingers through his long hair hanging loose over his shoulders. "Let me get a shirt and some shoes on and I'll be right over."

Jude paced her living room floor as she waited for him, her mind running over all the possibilities of where Lindsey might be. She felt like an idiot. Why hadn't she tried Lindsey's cell? She dialed, but there was no answer. She hit redial again just as Ryan walked in, cell phone in his hand.

"I texted her," he said, "just in case she didn't have good reception, but no reply."

Jude took a deep breath. "How far away did she go?"

"After you left today, she was banging around in the kitchen. She said you and I were both pathetic with all this Twitter stuff and everything."

"So she was angry. What else did she say?" Jude asked.

"Lindsey said she'd had enough of all of our drama, and this island, and she needed the afternoon off. She told me you said she could take the car anytime to go to the Bluff Park, so I let her go. You know, to blow off some steam."

Jude put her hands on her hips. "You let her go?"

"I'm sorry, Jude, I was trying to help."

Jude calmed her thoughts. This was no time for blame. She needed a clear head. "I don't blame you, Ryan. I know how she gets and would probably have told her to do the same thing."

Ryan sighed with obvious relief. "Let's find her."

"What time did she leave?" Jude asked.

"About four or five. I thought she'd be right back."

Panic welled, making Jude dizzy. "What should we do? It's going on 11:00."

"I'm sorry. I was writing in my room and didn't notice the time. Do you think we should call 911?"

Jude's legs were shaky. She sat down on the couch and Ryan joined her. "I'm here," he said. "Do you want to make the call and then drive out to the Bluff Park and look for her?"

In his worried face she saw love and true concern there, more than she'd ever felt from Lindsey's own father, Mitchell. "Just wait here, Ryan, with me for now, please, and then we can go together."

He took her hand, "Whatever you need." Jude stared at the phone. Before they called 911 she wanted to be sure she wasn't overreacting. Lindsey had not made any friends here. She thought about calling Marco or Becca, but it was so late.

Reluctantly, she dialed 911. "Hello. My 20-year-old daughter is missing. We think she went off to Bluff Park area around 5 o'clock today." Jude went on to give a description of Lindsey, her long blonde hair, 5'7" tall.

"Ryan do you remember what she was wearing?"

He shrugged. "I think dark shorts and a light shirt."

Jude gave the 911 operator the information and the license number to her SUV. They told her they would send someone to the park to check on it. She laid the phone on the coffee table.

Ryan looked at her expectantly. "Should we go?"

"No. They're contacting the onsite ranger and sending an officer. She suggested we wait here by the phone in case Lindsey calls or comes home."

"That's probably a good idea in case she gets our messages."

Jude's stomach twisted. "Do you think she would drive to Seattle?"

"She's a smart girl," Ryan said. "A bit headstrong, but not reckless."

She laid her head on his shoulder and snuggled in close. The warmth of his skin radiating through his shirt comforted her. Having Ryan here for her meant so much. She'd handled everything alone for so long, she'd almost forgotten the relief another caring soul could bring.

They waited in silence, the steady beat of his heart her anchor amidst the chaos.

Finally, after several minutes, Jude's phone rang. She answered it immediately.

"Thank you," she said. "I see. We'll meet you there."

Jude sprang from the couch. "They found her. They're taking her to the emergency room at Island Hospital."

"I'll drive," Ryan said. "Is she okay?"

Jude wiped a tear of relief from her cheek. "She is. They said she was a little scratched up when the found her at the bottom of a steep trail. She'd fallen but should be fine."

"Let's go." Ryan took Jude's hand and they dashed out the door to his car.

The hospital was only five minutes away. Ryan sped into the emergency parking area and they raced toward the front door. An ambulance was out front and two young paramedics were closing the back doors. Jude approached them. "Did you just bring in a young blonde woman from Bluff Park?"

They stared at her a minute, looking uncertain. "She's my daughter," Jude said.

The tall good-looking young man smiled. "Feisty girl. She's fine. Right inside."

"A little embarrassed maybe, but nothing permanent," the other one said, grinning.

"Thank you both," Ryan said before escorting Jude into the reception room where they waited for permission to enter the treatment area. The head nurse greeted them minutes later and took them back where they found Lindsey lying on a bed surrounded by nurses cleaning her scratches and putting small bandages around her hands and face. Lindsey was obviously flirting with the male nurse who had tattoos running down his arm.

"She's enjoying being the center of attention," Jude said to Ryan with a wink.

"Perhaps we shouldn't intrude?"

Jude rolled her eyes and proceeded into the room. A doctor looked up from his computer tablet where he had been typing in notes and greeted them. "I'm Dr. Stuart," he said. "You must be her mother and father."

"I'm her mom," Jude said. "How is she doing?"

"Just fine," he said. "Nothing we can't patch up."

Lindsey met her mother's eyes. She waved weakly and looked guilty. Jude walked over to the bed.

"I'm sorry, Mom," Lindsey said.

Relief and anger balanced precariously in Jude's heart. "How are you feeling?"

Lindsey visibly relaxed and leaned back in the bed. "Not too bad at this point. They gave me something for the pain."

Ryan joined them. "Some hike, huh?"

Lindsey broke a smile. "It was, until I got too close to the edge. There was this sign that showed someone falling off the cliff. It said, 'warning,' so of course I had to go stand right by it to take a selfie."

Ryan laughed. "You are certainly no coward. I have a few battle scars myself. Let's see the picture."

"Don't encourage her," Jude said.

Lindsey introduced her nurses. "This is Lisa, and this is Steve. They're putting me back together."

Jude thanked them. She held her breath as she watched the doctor put a few stitches into Lindsey's badly scraped upper arm.

"Good as new," Steve said, smiling awkwardly at Lindsey. Her daughter's charm had obviously had an effect.

Dr. Stuart gave Jude a prescription. "You can fill this if she needs pain relief for a few days," he said. "But she should be up and around in day or so."

Ryan shook his hand. "Thanks for taking such good care of her."

"Our pleasure," he said.

Jude noticed the smile that passed between Lindsey and the doctor before he left the room. She was making the most of this male attention.

"Out," Lindsey said to Ryan. "I'm going to get dressed."

Jude stayed behind to help Lindsey navigate getting dressed.

"Thanks for coming to get me," Lindsey said.

Jude hugged her gently trying not to touch any bruised areas. "I'll always be there for you. I love you, Lindsey."

Lindsey had tears in her eyes. "I love you too, Mom."

Jude soaked in her daughter's words. "Let's get you home."

They walked down the hall and found Ryan waiting by door.

"So Lindsey," he said as they walked to the car, "how did it feel to be surrounded by all the good looking young men in town?"

"Good, I guess," Lindsey said. "That was one hot doctor."

"And the male nurse wasn't bad either," Jude said.

"That's true," Lindsey said. "Perhaps I'll start hanging out at the hospital coffee shop in the future."

Ryan gingerly helped Lindsey into the back and buckled her seatbelt for her before getting in the drivers seat. "Do we need a late night ice cream run on the way home?"

Lindsey moaned. "Just bed, please."

Jude leaned over and kissed Ryan on the cheek. "Thank you."

"Anytime," he said.

Lindsey leaned forward. "You two sure look a lot happier than you did this morning."

"It'll take more than media lies to tear us apart," Jude said.

Lindsey settled back into the seat with a sigh. "Glad to hear it."

Jude tucked Lindsey into bed while Ryan waited in her living room. She turned off the bedroom light and was ready to fall into bed herself. Instead, she joined Ryan.

"She's resting for now," Jude said, falling into an armchair. "She says she'll still be able to help in the kitchen, she just may have to wear gloves."

Ryan laughed. "You know, she's very talented. Her photos are exceptional."

Jude folded her legs beneath her. She let her gaze rest on Ryan. He had been true to his word and actions."

"Thank you, for everything, tonight and..."

He shook his head. "No need to thank me, I was happy to help."

"I know I haven't been the easiest to get along with lately."

"Totally understandable," he said.

"I've been so focused on my own stuff," she said, "I haven't asked you how you are doing or how the book is coming along."

"With everything else going on, I forgot to tell you. A Seattle agent I met where I previously worked, requested the proposal. I mailed it out yesterday."

"Something to be happy about, at least."

"Hey," he said, "with a little luck we can be signing Island Time Café Cookbooks here next summer, and Lindsey can come back and sign too. She'll definitely be in the credits."

Next summer, Jude thought. Ryan had plans to stay with her, here, together. And Lindsey might return, too. It was time to tell Lindsey the news, that if all went well, Lindsey would have a sibling soon. She wanted her daughter to know first before she told Ryan. It was important that Lindsey felt loved, trusted, and involved in what was coming.

Chapter Nineteen

"Hey, sleepy head," Jude said. "How are you feeling this morning?"

Lindsey moaned a little as she got out of bed. Her still unbrushed hair looked like she'd been in a storm. Some leaf and twig remnants peeked out of the tumbled mess. Gratitude rushed through Jude again. Her daughter was safe and cozy in her pink pajama shorts and tank top.

Lindsey trudged down the hall to the kitchen. She slid carefully onto a stool. "Coffee," she said. "I smell coffee."

Jude went over to the coffee maker and grabbed a couple of mugs from the cupboard. "Cream?" she asked.

"Lots," Lindsey said.

Jude placed her cup of tea down on the counter and the coffee in front of Lindsey, along with a fresh-baked apple spice muffin." She sank into the stool next to her daughter.

Lindsey stared at her. "Since when do you drink tea?"

Jude shrugged. "Sometimes I do." Lindsey had a few bruises from the fall, along with some cuts still covered in white bandages. Otherwise, she looked pretty good. "Any headache?" Jude asked.

"No, just a little shaky."

"I think you'd better rest today. You don't need to go into work. Just lie around and get your bearings back."

"Sweet, a break." Lindsey said. "I don't think I'd be much help in the kitchen, anyway."

When Lindsey held her mug up, Jude noticed her daughter's nails were now neatly trimmed and without polish. Working in the kitchen was giving her a different perspective than her usual fashionista lifestyle.

Jude took her cup to the sink and rinsed it out. "Can I get you anything else?" she asked. "It shouldn't be too busy. We're open for lunch only today. I'll run down and help Ryan, and then come back and check on you, bring you some lunch."

"Thanks, Mom. I'm sorry, again, about running off and acting like that."

"Don't be," Jude said. "I'm sorry that I didn't sit down and talk to you in the first place. I just haven't been feeling well, myself."

Lindsey's forehead furrowed. "Are you okay, Mom?"

"Yes, and no," Jude said. She weighed her options.

Lindsey laid her coffee cup down. "What's wrong?"

"Nothing's really wrong," Jude said, "But..."

"What, Mom?" Lindsey placed her hand over Jude's. "Tell me what it is. I really want to know."

Jude hesitated. "It's not that easy. I, I mean, I just found out a couple days ago that I'm pregnant."

Lindsey's jaw literally dropped. "You're pregnant? At your age?"

Jude laughed and the knots in her shoulders finally released. "I'm only 39 years
old. Lots of people have babies at my age."

Lindsey still looked rather shocked. "You mean, I'll have a brother or sister?"

"That's right," Jude said. "Might be nice."

"Don't expect me to do any babysitting." Her frown made that quite clear.

"No," Jude said. "There won't be anything that you'll have to do, but you can visit and play with the baby."

Jude watched the wheels of Lindsey's mind turning, her mouth twisting one way and then another, until it softened into a grin. "Might be nice, actually. I always wanted a sibling."

Her heart leapt. Jude could imagine Lindsey playing with the baby, especially when he or she was a toddler. There would be quite an age gap, but they would still grow to love each other, and as time went on, the age difference wouldn't mean so much. And Lindsey would not be an only child like Jude had been.

"Oh … wow. Does Ryan know?" Lindsey asked.

"No. No, he doesn't." She took a deep breath as panic crept into her chest.

"When are you going to tell him?"

"I wanted to tell you first. I want you to know, Lindsey, you will always be my first-born and my first love. Nothing will ever change that."

"Oh, Mom, I didn't know. I mean I thought when you let me go live with Dad, you were glad to have your space alone." Tears welled in her eyes.

"My baby," Jude said as she wrapped her arms around Lindsey, careful not to put pressure anywhere. "Not in a million years. Letting you go live with your father was the hardest thing I've ever done. But I wanted you to be happy and have the life you were dreaming of. And to know your father."

Lindsey sniffed. "I guess I knew that deep down, but thanks for telling me. It means a lot."

"I'll always be here for you," Jude said. Her daughter's smile was all the medicine she would ever need.

"What about Ryan?" Lindsey asked. "How do you think he will react?"

"I don't know," Jude said. "What do you think?"

Lindsey smiled. "I think he'll be happy. I really do think he loves you, Mom."

Jude felt her heart swell. Ryan loved her, and she was sure she loved him, too. There was no reason to think things would be different with Ryan when she told him. He was not, and never would be, Mitchell.

"Dad and Ryan are very different," Lindsey said, as if reading her mind. "Ryan spends time with you and me instead of just spending money to impress like Dad does. He sees you as a person, not just arm candy. I think Ryan will make a great dad."

"I do, too," Jude said. "But it's such a big decision. I want to take a few days away with Lily and Kyla and think about it before I tell him. Would you wait, and not say anything until then?"

"Of course, Mom. I won't say a word."

"Lily and Kyla and I are going to go off for a few days. We'll be leaving Friday. You think you'll be okay?"

"Sure. It's just a few bruises and bumps. I'll rest today. I'll be fine tomorrow."

"Ryan will be here, and he'll take care of anything you need."

"Don't worry, I can take care of myself."

"All right," Jude said. She went to pat her daughter on the hand, and then thought better of it. "I'd like to hug you, but I'm not sure where you're hurt."

Lindsey put her arms out. "Just a soft one."

Jude hugged her daughter gently. "I love you, Lindsey."

"I love you, Mom. Don't worry, it's all going to be okay."

Jude couldn't believe Lindsey was reassuring her. "Yes, it will," Jude said. "Now you go on and get back in bed. Do you have a good book?"

"Marco's been giving me lots of books to read. I think he's trying to broaden my reading horizon."

"Marco's a great guy."

"I know," Lindsey said. "Too bad he's in love with Becca."

"I saw a couple cute guys at your bedside the other night," Jude said.

Lindsey smiled again. "Yeah, especially the doctor. How old do you think he is?"

"Quite a bit older than you, if he's been through medical school," Jude said.

"Yeah, I know, but the male nurses looked a little younger." A grin crossed her face. "Maybe while you're gone, I'll go over and have breakfast at the coffee shop in the hospital. I hear they have great pancakes."

"You do that," Jude said. "In fact, you can tell me all about it when I get back from my trip."

Jude watched Lindsey walk back toward her room. Her daughter was here, living with her for the summer, and they were getting along. The first hurdle of telling her daughter about her pregnancy had gone fantastically well. She longed to tell Ryan, but she wanted the few days away with her friends at Orcas Island to get things clear in her mind. Either way, she was having this baby, and she knew she would be a good mother, even if she had to do it alone.

Chapter Twenty

The sun drifted down over the horizon and a cool breeze wafted across Ryan's face as the night sky deepened to indigo over the vineyard. With the movie shoot finally over, the wrap party would be held at Luke's winery tonight. After which, Ryan smiled, the cast and crew would be leaving very soon. It couldn't be soon enough. Each time the door opened at the café, Ryan prayed it wouldn't be Peyton again with some other scheme. But Peyton had gotten exactly what she wanted: the publicity and leverage against her philandering husband. Since Ryan was no longer of use to her, she'd been thankfully ignoring him. But so did Jude, at first. Peyton had done her damage, and now she would be leaving him and Jude behind in her deadly wake. It was hard for Ryan not to want to poison the food that was going to Peyton's elaborately decorated spot at the table.

He let out a deep breath and all his negative thoughts with it. He didn't want his resentments flowing into the food he'd so artfully prepared in Luke and Kyla's beautiful farmhouse kitchen. Lindsey was acting as sous chef, and they'd hired multiple servers for the evening as well.

Luke surveyed the plates and counted them. There were going to be fifty people, cast and crew. On the winery grounds under the pear trees, with a full view of the vineyard, Ian and Luke had set up the long wooden tables with colorful woven runners across them. Bouquets of fresh flowers mixed with fresh rosemary that Kyla had picked and arranged, surrounded thick white candles in glass holders. Silverware were wrapped in white cloth napkins and tied with fresh sprigs of lavender. Everything was extra perfect for this warm August night. Tiny lights glimmered from the trees, and soon everyone would be there and the final scene would be complete.

Luke walked in looking a bit panicked. "Everything ready?" he asked.

Ryan nodded. "Got the wine pairings organized with the courses, whites chilling on the tables in ice, and the reds are open to breathe.

"We are ready then," Luke said. "We just need the people."

"Well, they'll be coming soon enough. Lily's here."

Lily hustled through the front door, carrying platters of baked desserts. It was definitely an island affair. Ian's son, Jason, getting taller by the minute, came running in with his arms full, followed by Ian with more platters.

"Hey, do you need any help? I can carry stuff," Jason said.

"Thank goodness we got Shirley and Don to watch the baby," Lily said as Ryan took the trays. "I'm going to go join Jude and Kyla to help set up the outside bar."

Jason stood tall. "I'm not a baby. I came to help."

"And we can use your help," Ryan said. "I've got something for you to do. The butter. It needs to be put out on the table. It's in those little silver dishes that are shaped like shells. Just put one above every two place settings right near the flowers."

"I can do it," Jason said. He took the butter tray and headed outside, walking slowly to balance everything.

Lindsey rushed over to help him. "I'll be your assistant," she said with a smile that warmed Ryan's heart.

Bailey romped around the floor playing with a bone Ryan had given him. Again, Ryan imagined how nice it would be to own his own home—be married to the love of his life, have a child, and even a dog. He patted Bailey on the head and sighed. It was probably something he would never have.

Car doors slammed and conversation and laughter carried from the parking area to the deck where Ryan stood sipping iced tea. A white Lincoln limousine curved around the road and parked near the tables. The tuxedo-clad driver walked around and opened the door for Peyton. Flanked on both sides by well-dressed men, she emerged in a slinky silver evening gown that clung to her body like skin.

Ryan stepped back into the house. He had no intention of making any contact with her again. One last night and she would be gone. He hoped the publicity would die down so the people in town would stop staring at him and politely and not so politely asking questions. At least Jude believed him now, and that was all that mattered. Even Lily went out of her way to be kind to him. Kyla had come to him and said, "I understand. I know what this publicity thing is like."

They were all standing behind him, and that meant a lot. His heart flipped at the thought that he could still lose

Jude. He would make it up to her after all of this was over. That was the most important thing.

The string quartet began playing, signaling Ryan that most people were seated now. Butter sizzled, water boiled for pasta, and smells of fresh herbs filled the air. Waiters in crisp, white shirts lined up at the kitchen door, and the activity in the room doubled as Ryan and Lindsey prepped the food.

Ian popped his head in the door. "I'm heading out with Luke to handle the wine pairings. Let me know if you need anything."

Lindsey waved. "Will do."

With perfect precision, the dinner service moved forward smoother than Ryan had hoped. Course after course went out with no returns. Each plate was flawlessly executed with local meats and vegetables and paired perfectly with one of Luke's vineyard's offerings. Finally the last set of waiters retrieved the last tray of dessert plates and left the kitchen.

Lindsey clapped her hands, "We did it!"

Ryan gave her a high five. "Couldn't have done it without you."

They stepped out onto the expansive deck and looked down at the scene below.

The sound of laughter and loud, boisterous toasts filled the air. What a relief he didn't have to be down there, where he'd have to paste on a fake smile and mingle with the guests. Instead he could hole up in the kitchen where he felt much more at ease.

Suddenly the piercing sound of a helicopter drowned out everything else.

"Is that a medevac?" Lindsey asked.

When a person on the island needed to be transported to the main hospital in Seattle, the island doctors would have to send for the medevac helicopter. It always worried Ryan when he heard that sound, hoping it wasn't somebody he knew, and he always sent good thoughts to whoever it was.

As it approached just overhead, the sound about deafened them and they covered their ears. It looked like the helicopter was going to land in the open field outside the main vineyard. Sure enough, down it went very slowly until it touched ground. One man jumped out the door and bent down as he exited under the whirling blades. As he ran toward the dinner party, Ryan saw he was well dressed and certainly not for a medical emergency. The man stopped to brush himself off. Then he straightened back his shoulders. His hurried pace slowed as he got closer. The man wore khaki linen pants and a powder blue jacket that set off his deep tan. As he got closer, Ryan thought he might know him. He looked familiar, especially the dark hair with the greying at the temples.

As the man made his grand entrance, the tables quieted and all heads turned as he sauntered up behind Peyton. Ryan knew that face. It was Todd Chase, the actor. Peyton rose, tossing her hair and striking a pose. Ryan could see her mouth open in surprise, her proud stance and how she turned her back to Todd, pretending that her husband was not even there.

There was a stir among the guests as they recognized him. When Todd Chase turned Peyton around to face him, Ryan almost wished he could hear what Todd was saying. The compelling drama continued to build. There wasn't a sound as the scene unfolded and the actor pulled his wife into his arms and into a passionate kiss. There was no mistaking it was mutual, long, and sensual. Todd took Peyton by the hand, and without a backward glance, they ran back toward the helicopter.

"What an exit," Ryan said.

Lindsey sighed. "So romantic."

Ryan had to laugh to himself. And so staged. So this is what it was all about. Make Todd jealous over Ryan so he'd dump his young mistress, come running back and sweep Peyton into his arms and off into the sunset. It all made perfect sense now. Perhaps Jude would believe everything he had told her after seeing this.

Ryan watched Todd escort Peyton up the steps into the helicopter and off they flew. Applause burst out from everyone at the tables, including the serving people as the happy ending unfolded and the helicopter took the air.

All Ryan could think was that it was finally, finally over. He left Lindsey on the deck and went back inside. Ian was sitting at the bar sipping a glass of wine with Luke. The three men looked at each other.

Ian shrugged. "Wow, that was some gesture. I hope our wives aren't expecting helicopters next."

Ryan laughed, opened a craft beer, and sat down to join them. "What a night."

The helicopter had just taken off, the Princess rescued by Prince Charming on a White Horse, or in this case, a private helicopter. All the three women could do was stare.

"Well, that was some exit," Kyla said.

"He swept her off her feet," Lily said with a sigh.

"Just the scene Peyton wanted to star in," Jude said. "All that coming after Ryan. Her sneaky ploys to get her husband back. And she didn't care who she hurt to do it."

"Some people will stop at nothing, especially those with no conscience," Kyla said.

Jude was glad that the dinner was finally over and things would return to their normal summer intensity. The bar at the party was now closed and she was free to wander, but she had kept her distance, greeting people as she needed to, saying her goodbyes, but staying on the sidelines with Lily and Kyla.

"All this time," Jude said, "I let my past cloud my judgment and didn't believe Ryan when he was trying to tell me that Peyton was putting on a show."

"I'll grab a bottle of wine and we can go sit on the deck overlooking the koi pond and unwind," Kyla said. "What can I get you to drink, Jude?"

"Just water," she said.

Jude and Lily stepped onto the deck and happily dropped into comfortable Adirondack chairs to wait for Kyla. It had been an exhausting night.

"Well, that's one soap opera that's finally over," Kyla said when she returned. She handed them each their drinks and sat down.

Jude gazed at the fish in the pond. The sparkly lights in the oak trees glistened on the water's surface, making it appear as though the fish were swimming in liquid gold. "He was telling the truth," she said, "and I was too afraid to believe him."

Lily sighed. "Trust is hard to earn and so easy to lose. Don't beat yourself up, Jude. With all the stress of the filming, your teenage daughter being with you for the summer, and being pregnant, I think you handled things pretty well."

"And," Kyla said, "there were so many intrigues going on besides the movie plot, none of us could keep up. They have to finish shooting the rest of the movie on another island, and surely there will be delays now. I bet the director is pretty upset after this little scene tonight carried off his leading lady."

"Well," Jude said, "as long as she's gone, I'm happy."

"I hear they're painting the town back to specifications starting tomorrow. Did you ask for a different color for the cafe?" Kyla asked.

"No, I just asked them to put it back the way it was, kind of that pretty barn red, fresh white trim. I had thought of leaving it white, but I want everything the way it was before."

"I get it," Kyla said. "I asked them to do a little bit of lavender trim, might as well get the most out of this."

Lily threw her arms back and yawned. "This is a late night for me."

"Is little Gwyn still keeping you awake?" Jude asked

"She's almost sleeping through the night. Thank goodness we have all the help that we do. Shirley has been wonderful, but I'm still a little worried about Betty. She was so sick from the chemo, but at least she's up and about now."

"I'll have to bring over some ginger tea to comfort her," Kyla said, "She is in good spirits, and you know how Betty is, nothing's going to get her down. I think she's going to beat this."

"I hope so, too," Lily said. "I stop by most days to bring her some scones, see if I can tempt her appetite a little. She's never been a big eater to begin with."

"Speaking of eating and sleeping," Kyla said looking at Jude, "how's the nausea?"

"It's good to know why I'm feeling sick every morning," Jude said, "The doctor says I'm due in the spring. Luckily, I'm not showing much yet. But I'm still not out of danger for a miscarriage. I had one after Lindsey was born, and at my age there's more risk."

"Lots of women have children after forty and do just fine," Kyla said.

Lily patted Kyla's hand. "And under thirty too!" she said.

Kyla smiled. "We'll see."

Jude yawned and stretched out her arms. "Ryan hasn't been spending the night in a while. Even though we're reconciled, we're taking it slow. He has no idea. I don't know how he'd feel about being a dad."

"How do you feel about being a mom?" Lily asked.

"I haven't really let myself think about it much yet. It's still a shock," Jude said. "I did tell Lindsey."

Lily perked up. "What did she say?"

"She took it surprisingly well, but I'm not sure I want to raise another child alone again."

"What do you mean alone?" Kyla said, "You have Ryan."

"Do I?" Jude said, "Do I really? Even now that I know he was telling the truth about Peyton, how do I know for sure he'll stay once the baby is born. And as you know, Ryan has a history of being a runner."

Lily shook her head. "He wouldn't run. He seems content, and he's obviously in love with you."

Jude leaned back in her chair and rested her eyes for a second. Perhaps Lily was right. "He told me he was happy here, happier than he's ever been. Between the hormones and the stress, I just don't know what to believe."

"I understand," Kyla said, "but you have a second chance here with a really good man and a new baby."

"I will tell you, new babies are pretty special. Oh," Lily said, putting her hand on Kyla's arm. "I'm sorry Kyla, I know you and Luke have been trying."

"Don't worry." Kyla said. "Things have been looking up for us too. I've been feeling great, so who knows? Maybe we'll all be sharing baby secrets soon."

"That would be wonderful," Lily said.

Jude continued to look out at the pond. A baby? When would she tell Ryan? She knew now that he had been telling her the truth. But did she know everything now? Why hadn't he told her sooner if he loved her? That was the real question... did he love her? But she couldn't wait much longer or he would find out from someone else. A soft breeze raised goosebumps on Jude's arm and caused Lily to draw in her shawl.

"So, I have some news," Kyla said, "My agent called and it looks like my product line is a go. We got a sponsor for the natural beauty aging line."

"Who?" Lily asked.

A smile crept over Kyla's face. "None other than former model, Darcy Devereux."

"You?" Jude said. "Of course that makes sense."

Kyla continued. "We're going to sell it online to start with, maybe even in an infomercial. Who knows! I don't want it to get too big and stressful, but we're going to need a larger place to make the products. Becca has pretty much taken over managing and stocking the store now. Luke says we can convert one of the out-buildings at the vineyard."

"That sounds perfect," Jude said. "I'm excited for you. All three of our businesses are doing well, and that's certainly something to be happy about."

"There's a lot to be happy about." Lily said.

Kyla sipped her wine. "And we are going to have a fabulous time on Orcas. It's all booked. I took care of everything."

Jude reminded herself to count her many blessings. She gazed out over the vineyard. It was almost empty of people now. She saw Ryan in the distance and her heart fluttered. Lindsey was inside helping with the clean up. Servers were clearing the tables and Luke blowing out the candles. It had been a long night, but a good night in the end. And Peyton was finally gone.

Chapter Twenty-One

Ryan walked onto the deck and gave her a lopsided smile. "We're out of here. You ready?"

Jude rose from her chair. "Where's Lindsey?"

"She's still helping out with the kitchen cleanup, and Kyla offered for her to spend the night here. Said they'd run her home in the morning."

"Sounds like she was a great help."

Ryan nodded. "I couldn't have done it without her."

He looked exhausted. Jude was glad it was finally time to go home. She said goodbye to Lily and Kyla and headed to the truck with Ryan.

"Could you believe that grand gesture with the helicopter?" Ryan asked.

Jude laughed. "Yes, not for me. All I need is a good hug now and then."

Ryan stopped walking and took her in his arms, holding her tight. His warm fingers gently lifted her chin so he could look into her eyes. "I hope you know how much I care about you, Jude. I don't have helicopters to whisk you away, and maybe I'm still in a chef coat, but you mean more to me than anything."

He leaned her back against the truck and kissed her. It took Jude's breath away, to have him speak to her like this, and in that moment she knew she had to confess the secret that she'd been hiding or lose him.

"Oh Ryan," she said. "I feel the same." She searched Ryan's deep brown eyes. "Are you done in?" she asked.

"Tired, but also really buzzed. I think I'm going need some down time to unwind."

"What do you say we go back to my apartment? I could make some hot chocolate and we could just talk. I have got some things I want to tell you."

He stared at her, a question in his eyes, "Oh, you do? Anything important?"

She glanced down. It was hard to continue to look him in the eye. "Well, in a way, yes. Yes."

"Now you have me intrigued," he said. "Is it urgent?

"Not life threatening." She forced a smile, hoping she was right. "Let's go back, get you a shower and sit down and talk without any interferences."

Ryan threw his things in the back of truck and opened the door for Jude to climb into the front seat. Once in the driver's seat, he took one last look at Jude and opened his mouth as though to say something, but stopped and started the truck instead. The drive home was silent, the night dark with scattered stars. Traces of twilight lingered in the far horizon as they wound their way home in the deep summer night.

Ryan stopped when they reached Jude's front door. "I'll go to my place and take a shower and join you shortly."

"No rush," Jude said. She watched him walk down the walkway and step inside his place. He'll be right back, she reminded herself. Jude unlocked her door and stepped in. It was warm inside, so she opened all the windows and stepped out on her deck. The almost full moon spilled out a golden glow over the cove. Her stomach was in knots anticipating his reaction. Too many what ifs. She forced herself to think positive. What if he's happy over the news? And he is the right man.

"What if he's not?" a voice softly whispered. "You'll lose him, you'll lose everything, just like you did with your first marriage. She would be forty years old next month. Even if Ryan left, she had her friends, and she knew none of them would judge her. There were always other chefs for the café, but none like Ryan, and definitely none she would love.

Jude turned and walked into the kitchen. Using a whisk, she mixed some dark chocolate powder into the warm milk on the stove and added sugar and a pinch of cinnamon. After pouring the steaming mixture into mugs, she brought them to the couch and waited for Ryan.

Her front door opened and Ryan walked in. His hair was loose from the ponytail, and wet tendrils clung to his shoulders. He'd changed into a grey t-shirt, jeans, and his feet were bare. She wanted to smell the fresh scent of his skin, feel his lips on hers.

She patted the couch next to her. "Come sit down."

He sat near, but not too close. "Thanks for the cocoa," he said, reaching to the table. "No wine for you tonight?" he asked.

"Cocoa felt more soothing." She already that was a partial lie. There was no way she was going to drink when she was pregnant, and she was glad he hadn't noticed until this moment.

Ryan sipped the chocolate and then placed the mug on the table and took her hand. "What is it Jude? You know you can tell me anything."

"I know," she said, forcing herself to make eye contact. "We've had some rocky times lately, but it's so much better now."

He nodded. Worry crept into his eyes, and Jude faltered for a second before continuing. "We both put everything on the table. You told me about your past and I told you mine." Jude paused and took a deep breath. "But there is one thing I haven't told you."

Ryan looked shocked. "What? Why?"

She took a sip of the chocolate and knew it was time. "I had to be sure myself. I had to get to a place where I could deal with it in order to tell you."

"Are you all right? Are you sick? Jude?"

"No. No, Ryan, it's nothing like that."

"Then what is it?"

Jude took another deep breath. "I'm pregnant."

"Oh," he said. His face seemed to pale in the evening light. His pupils dilated and fear crossed his face.

Jude's chest tightened as she held her breath. "I've only known for less than a week. With all the other things going on, the stress with Peyton and my daughter missing, it took me awhile to even figure it out."

"Who else knows?" he asked.

"I told Lindsey first."

Ryan rocked back and forth on the sofa. "And, anyone else?"

"Just Kyla and Lily."

Ryan sat up straight. "So you told them first?"

"They're my family and best friends. You have to understand, Ryan, I needed a little time to register the truth myself. Things were still a little rocky with us when I found out, and the last thing I wanted to do was uproot them even more. You've never mentioned kids, you've never had kids. I had no idea how you'd react."

"You might have noticed I was great with your daughter," he said.

Jude cringed and stayed silent, watching his every move.

Ryan put the mug down on the table, stood, and walked over to the window and stared out at the dark water. Jude's eyes were glued to his back, waiting for him to say something.

When he turned around, his eyes seemed distant. "I don't know what to say. I'm so surprised."

"I'm sure it happened when we were away for the weekend in Canada," she said. "We weren't that careful, remember?"

"Oh, right, right," he said. "I guess I never really thought about it. How did Lindsey react?"

The room and everything in it felt off kilter, and Jude tried to right herself. "I'm not completely sure, but she did show some excitement over having a sibling."

"I see."

Ryan looked even paler. Maybe she should have eased into this conversation more, not told him when he was exhausted.

"Please sit down," Ryan. "Let's talk about this."

He sat beside her, but barely made eye contact. "I need some time to think."

Then Ryan looked her in the eyes and said the words she'd been longing to hear. "I love you, Jude."

"I love you too, Ryan."

"A child," he whispered. "I never thought there would be one in my life. He leaned back into the sofa. "I just don't know what to say."

"It's okay," she said. "I understand. It caught me by surprise too. You'll have a few days alone here to sort things out. I'm going to Orcas day after tomorrow. I hope that will give you the time and space you need."

Ryan nodded almost as if he didn't hear her. "You're tired and it's late. We should sleep on it."

As if he could read her mind, Ryan placed his hand over hers. "I'm here for you. No matter what, I'll be here for you."

She noticed he didn't say "and for the child." Or that he was happy. He didn't say he'd run, but he did stand and move towards the door. He was not spending the night.

"I'll see you in the morning," he said. "Get some rest."

Jude closed the door behind him and listened to his steps fade as he went down the outside walk. When she heard his front door click, she ran into her bedroom and collapsed onto the bed. She'd told him, it was out now. Fear had been written all over his face, and seeing such emotion in him escalated her own fears. She curled up under the covers wanting the total escape only sleep could bring. She thought of calling her friends, but it was already past midnight. She was just going to have to cope alone somehow, go to sleep, and deal with it in the morning.

Tomorrow, she would figure out what to do. Her heart pounded in her ears as she tried to still her panic. Jude ran to the bathroom and started heaving. Morning sickness even at midnight? She wasn't sure what to think anymore.

She at her bedraggled reflection in the mirror. Could her forty-year-old body even handle a baby? It was a quite a shock. But deep down there was this feeling of happiness—a new life was inside her, a sweet baby, and a chance to be a better mom this time. And dare she hope … another chance for happiness.

Jude looked toward the wall that separated her apartment from Ryan's. She doubted he would sleep well tonight, either. In the morning they would talk again. There were decisions to be made. Perhaps a few days away with Lily and Kyla on Orcas Island would help clear her head and give Ryan some space to make a decision himself. Staying with her had to be his choice. She wouldn't want him any other way.

Chapter Twenty-Two

Jude was relieved that they were leaving for a few days. Yesterday she'd felt a little awkward with Ryan. They both stayed busy, and he was kind and helpful, but a good time to talk never revealed itself. The traffic was heavy on the road, but as they made the last turn, the breathtaking San Juan Islands came into view.

"We made it," Jude said as she drove into the ferry line just as the boat began to load.

"A good sign," Kyla said, "considering how long a wait it can be in the summer."

Even though the ferry held hundreds of cars and many walk-on passengers, and luckily they had a reservation, tourist traffic had almost made them late.

The dock worker directed them to park on the outside lane, leaving them a full view of the water if they wanted to stay in the car.

Lily unbuckled her seatbelt. "Shall we go on deck and walk around?"

"Absolutely," Jude said. She grabbed her zip-up sweatshirt and joined them.

They walked to the top passenger deck and stood at the front of the boat. Jude threw her head back and let the wind move through her hair. She was free for a few days, and with her best friends. Puffy, feather-white clouds dotted the bright blue sky, punctuated by shrieking sea gulls overhead.

"It's a gorgeous day," Lily said. "I can't believe we actually made this happen."

They stood on the front deck, sun in their faces. "And we will enjoy it," Kyla said. "Anyone want to join me for a walk?

Lily nodded.

"You two go ahead," Jude said, waving them off. She watched them for a moment as heads turned when they walked by. Kyla, tall and striking with her red hair trailing down her back, contrasted by Lily, blonde and petite, even after having a child.

The ferry glided along the Sound waters and through the San Juan Islands. Houses peeked out from wooded hillsides, their windows reflecting the morning sun. It had been less than two months since she'd been on a similar ferry riding home with Ryan after their weekend escape. Now she was the one escaping. She'd been so sure of his love and hers then. Between the pregnancy hormones, exhaustion from the stress of the movie shoot, and the emotional roller coaster ride concocted by Peyton Chandler, Jude still felt a little numb. Her heart ached at the thought of possibly still losing Ryan, facing pregnancy alone. Her racing mind, clouded by hormones, was not her friend right now. She reminded herself Lindsey was with her. As fragile as their reconciliation was, it was moving in the right direction.

Parents scrambled after their children as they ran by, playing noisily on deck, happy to be on vacation. Would that be her and Ryan some day in the future, watching their child? Her heart longed to be one of the families and couples sprawled over benches, soaking up sun, smiling and laughing together. It was possible. Her life did not have to be a constant repetition of her past. Her friends had found love and happiness, and she needed to believe she could too. She loved Ryan and could imagine happily running the café, together, with their little one beside them.

The winds stirred and Jude decided to go join her friends inside. She found Kyla and Lily sipping coffee at a cozy table by a window. Her friends were steadfast, and these couple of nights away would be a wonderful escape for all of them.

"We got you a bottle of water," Lily said.

Jude opened her drink. "Thanks. I'm so glad we did this," she said, sitting down between Lily and Kyla.

"Me, too," Lily said. "Just think of all the trouble we can get in, and the shopping we can do."

"And don't forget that luscious chocolate shop," Jude said. "You haven't seen that new one yet."

"I'll be the guide for you two on your maiden voyage to Orcas. Once we dock," Jude said, "we'll be driving to Eastsound, then get some lunch."

"You're already thinking of a meal?" Kyla asked. "We just had breakfast an hour ago."

"What can I say?" Jude said. "I'm used to serving breakfast, lunch and dinner."

"Well, forget it," Kyla said, "We're on vacation."

Slowly, the ferry curved around toward Lopez Island. It was a small dock, and the town had just a couple of buildings. A steep drive headed up from the ferry and into the wooded island.

"I've never been to Lopez Island," Jude said. "Maybe next time we'll try that."

"Ian said it's perfect for a bike ride," Lily said, her blue eyes sparkling. "Maybe when the baby's older. You know, Jason loves to ride his bike."

Jude put her arm around Lily's shoulder. "It's nice to be away from it all for a little bit, isn't it? Even though you're thinking about the baby already."

"Caught me," Lily said. "It's the first time I've been away from her for more than a few hours."

"She is in great hands. Think how refreshed you'll be when you return." Kyla laughed. "Three days away. You can sleep. You can do whatever you want, R&R, that's all we're going to do."

Lily smiled. "Well, it's my first time away since we've been married. Speaking of married, how is being a newly-wed suiting you, Kyla?"

"Most of the time, it's blissful. We've both been working pretty hard though, both of us. Sometimes we just pass in the night. I couldn't be happier, really. I think all good married couples deserve a break sometimes." Kyla winked. "Let him miss me a little."

"What a group we are," Jude said. "We can barely leave home for two days without making it a complete production."

"Forget it," Lily said, "We're on vacation and the men will survive."

"I left the restaurant in Ryan and Lindsey's competent hands. Ryan has been nothing but nice, supportive, and helpful, especially since I told him about the pregnancy."

Just as she said that, the ferry horn went off. As the ferry began to back out of Lopez Island slip and turn toward Orcas, Jude could see the great white Orcas Hotel in the distance as they set course toward their destination. She pointed it out to her friends. "That hotel was built turn of the century. It has quite a history and amazing gardens." As they made their approach, Jude saw the tea rose vines draping across the white arbor, and the stalks of hollyhocks and daisies surrounding the wrap-around porch.

"We'd better get back to the car," Lily said.

Jude stood and pulled out her keys. "Right. Forgot all about that. We're not walking off."

They hurried down the metal stairs, and pushed open the heavy door leading to the parking deck.

Jude waved them over. "The car is over here."

Everyone jumped in, none too soon, as the ferry docked in place at Orcas Island. Walk on passengers exited first and climbed the hill to the main street. After the dock was cleared of foot passengers, the cars were directed off.

As soon as Jude drove off the ferry, she turned left. She knew the island. It wasn't complicated.

"We're just going to circle around the top of the U. Then, we'll arrive at the main little town, Eastsound."

"Eastsound," Lily said, "Sounds lovely." They drove along with the windows down, past the rolling fields and the forests that gently sloped up into hills. Music from Jude's iPod drifted through the car.

"I'm glad we made it," Jude said. "I've wanted to show you both this place. There's something magical about it."

"It seems a lot more remote than Madona," Kyla said.

"It is. It's a great place for a summer retreat. I wouldn't want to live here all year round. Winter can be lonely and tough. Plus, there are only a few ferries a day to get off the islands. If you don't have your own boat, or you don't have your own plane, you're pretty much stuck."

"I don't think I'd like that," Kyla said. "I like knowing we can drive off of our island and over a bridge to the mainland."

"I don't have great cell coverage here, either," Lily said. "I was thinking of calling Ian and making sure the baby is all right."

"Shall I pull over and see if we can find coverage? Maybe I should call Ryan, too."

"I know you're anxious to find out how Ryan is feeling, but I do think it was a good idea to give him space," Kyla said. "Come on, ladies, they can live without us for a few days!"

Lily's laugh was weak. "I guess so."

"Being out of touch is part of the island charm," Jude said. "Between the three of us, we should be able to get reception most of the time. And hopefully, none of the guys will be bothering us, and there won't be any emergencies."

"Turn right here," Lily said, holding the map.

"Thanks." Jude made a quick turn. "I don't want to miss this one. At night I've driven right by it before."

On the right was a beautiful U-shaped bay. The tide was coming in strong and high. The sun glistened on the water like sparklers flashing. On the other side was the town dotted with little shops. Jude turned down a small street. "There's usually parking down at the end. And sure enough, there's a spot right in front of a dress shop."

"Anybody hungry?" Jude asked.

"I vote for lunch," Kyla said, looking around, "and then extensive retail therapy."

"Perfect," they both echoed.

"I know a great place," Jude said, "It's just back here down this little path and to the left. It's run by a couple of women. I think it's called Mia's Café."

The café was fairly crowded, but there was a small booth in the back that they were able to slide into.

"Welcome," the waitress said, laying menus before them. "Some of our specials are on the board. We have three different soups, black bean, curry chicken, and tomato bisque."

"Everything looks good," Lily said as she moved through the menu. "Bacon and egg sandwich. Yum, I'm going to have that."

Kyla placed her menu down. "A chopped salad with fresh prawns for me.

Jude didn't feel that hungry all of a sudden. She chalked it up to her pregnancy and ordered soup and bread. "Now, save a little room." Jude turned to her friends when the waitress left. "Because after the shopping, I have a special surprise."

It was a nice change to have someone waiting on her, Jude thought. The food and conversation during lunch took her far away from her worries and she began to feel truly on vacation.

After they finished their lunch, they hurried out and followed Jude to what she said was the best dress shop in town—The Black and White.

"The woman who runs this shop is amazing," Jude said. "She's got to be over 70. She designs these clothes you won't find anywhere else, especially for you, Kyla, with your long legs and model's figure."

They walked around the store exploring the amazing one-of-a-kind little jackets with cuffed sleeves and the silky dresses with unique silhouettes. Everyone was trying on different things, except for Jude. "I don't think I'll be trying on new clothes with this belly," she said. She looked instead at the jade jewelry, little carved boxes, and knickknacks.

Maybe she'd bring something back for Lindsey. One of these bracelets. Jude held them to the light. It looked like something Lindsey might like.

"Sea glass," the white haired, exquisitely dressed woman said. "It's polished and hand crafted by a local artisan."

"Perfect. I'll take it."

While Jude made her purchase, Kyla came out of the dressing room wearing long, sleek pants, with a leather stripe down the side.

"Wow." Lily said. "Those legs really work in those pants."

Kyla smiled. "You don't look so bad yourself, Lily."

Lily had on a pale blue, V-neck sweater and a short skirt. "You think so? I think I'll buy them."

"And I'll take the pants and the top," Kyla said.

Jude could see why. The turquoise shirt accented Kyla's hair, and the pants made her already long legs seem to go on forever.

At the counter, the owner packaged everything and handed out her card. "Come back soon," she said.

After a few more shops, Lily collapsed on a bench. "I'm exhausted. Having fun is hard work."

Jude reached out her hand to Lily. "Hop to it. I think we need to go across the street to the chocolate shop and put our feet up there."

The elegant store was part soda fountain, part coffee shop, and part homemade gourmet chocolatier. Jude pointed to one of the menu items. "This is something you've probably never had before. It's espresso, ice cream, homemade chocolate syrup, carbonated water, and whipped cream. An espresso chocolate soda."

"Oh my gosh," Kyla said, "It must be a million calories."

"I don't care," Jude said. "I'll have a decaf," she ordered, thinking of the baby.

"What the heck," Kyla said and ordered two, one for her and one for Lily.

Drinks in hand, they sat down at the round table and set their packages on the floor.

"This is amazing," Lily said. "You have to try making this at your cafe when we get back, Jude."

"Good idea. Maybe I'll come up with one of my own recipes for one and add it to the menu."

Sugared out and ready for a rest, they went back to the car so Jude could drive them to their rental. The house was advertised as being about a mile out of town and with a view of the water and a trail down to the beach. If it was anything like the pictures, they were going to be very pleased.

They followed the address on the map until they pulled in to a driveway facing the house. It was more beautiful than Jude even imagined. When they walked inside, they found that it was completely open concept with high ceilings, a granite-topped island in the kitchen that ran the full length of the room, and two-story glass windows that gave an impressive view of the water. Two sectional couches faced the French doors that led out to a massive deck.

"I could certainly get used to this," Lily said.

Kyla threw herself on one of the soft couches. "Me, too."

Jude walked into the kitchen, touching the stainless-steel appliances and the island that was twice as big as her kitchen at home. "I think we could all get used to this." She strolled over and opened the doors to the deck. "Come here and look outside."

The women rose with a moan and joined her.

From the deck, Jude pointed out a wood fire pit down on the sand with wood stacked beside it.

"We could have a little fire, roast marshmallows," Lily said.

"Make s'mores?" Jude said.

"You and your chocolate," Kyla said. "Didn't we just have a chocolate soda?"

"All right, well maybe not tonight."

"Let's go see the rest of the house," Kyla suggested.

There were three full bedrooms, each designed in a unique way. One was decorated in a nautical theme, all blues and crisp whites. The downstairs master had a wood carved canopy bed with cream satin linens. The other was a cozy, shabby chic cottage room. Each room had a view of the water.

"This bathroom has a Jacuzzi tub," Lily said when checking the cottage room. "Can I have this one?"

"No problem," Kyla said. "I vote that we give the master to Jude for pregnancy rest."

"Great idea," Lily said. "One question, do we ever have to go home?"

Jude laughed. "We have two nights and two more full days. So enjoy."

"Ladies," Kyla said. "After all that eating, we forgot to stop at the market for food for dinner. I guess we'll just have to go out."

"Forget it," Lily said. "I have a recipe I want to try out on you two. It's only a mile to town. I'll run in to the store. You two relax. When I get back I'll make us something you will absolutely adore."

"You sure?" Jude said.

"Absolutely."

"Luke sent some wine for us, so you won't need to get any."

"How about you, Jude? Should I get you some sparkling cider or something?"

"Sure. Thanks, Lily."

After Lily left, Kyla unpacked the wine and put it on the counter. "This is going to be an incredible evening. Look at the clouds coming in," she said.

"I bet the sunset from here is going to be breathtaking. Why don't we just sit outside for a little while?"

"I think I might take a nap," Jude said.

"Go ahead. When Lily gets back, we can make dinner and then sit out on the deck and watch the stars."

"Sounds good to me"

"Happy napping."

The master bedroom was spacious and pure luxury with a huge king-size bed all to herself. Being pregnant had its advantages. She couldn't wait to sit down on the plush armchair with the footrest that faced out at the water. Jude kicked off her shoes and put her feet up. Even the craftsman ceiling was exquisite wood. Who could ask for more? Maybe she'd make a wish on a shooting star tonight.

She closed her eyes and let the magic of the place fill her. She could hear bird songs out the open window. She almost fell asleep, but then her mind filled with questions. How was Lindsey doing? How was Ryan? She thought of the baby. What a gift it was. Perhaps it was another girl, or a boy? She imagined her and Ryan taking the baby to the park, walking in the sun, wrapping the baby in homemade quilts in the winter. It made her feel warm and happy inside. Getting away from it all gave her a clearer perspective. Ryan was a good man. She knew that. It could be real. She closed her eyes and let herself drift into a peaceful sleep.

Chapter Twenty-Three

Ryan prepped the mussels with thyme and garlic for the photo shoot he and Lindsey had planned for this afternoon. Yesterday, his mind had been elsewhere, thinking about how close he'd come to running after Jude's car and embarrassing himself as she'd driven off with Kyla and Lily. After they'd left, he'd spent all day working on the book, taking advantage of the available time while the café was closed. Today, he hoped his mind would clear more. He loved Jude more than life, but her news had come as such a surprise. More than that, he was afraid. Did he dare hope that his deepest dream was finally coming true?

Lindsey burst into the kitchen filled with energy. "I'm ready to work."

"Hey girl, it's just you and me now," Ryan said.

Lindsey rolled her eyes. "Speak for yourself," she said with a smile. "The café is closed for a few days, my mom is gone, and as soon as we finish this last shot I'm out of here."

"Not to the bluff, I hope," Ryan said with a grin.

She rolled her eyes. "Going to hang out with friends."

Ryan added a sprig of thyme to the white plate on the stainless steal counter. He wiped the edges clean with a towel and stood back to admire the dish. Lindsey focused the camera and took a few shots from different angles.

"Too bad we can't eat this one," Lindsey said. "It looks delicious."

"I'll remake it, minus the shine spray, for dinner for us tonight if you want," he said.

Lindsey shrugged. "I'll probably not be home for dinner, but thanks." She placed her camera in the bag and threw it over her shoulder. "That's a wrap," she said, borrowing the phrase from the movie shooting.

"I get it. You'd rather hang out with the young people," Ryan said.

Lindsey stared at him and he wondered what was going on behind those sparkling blue eyes.

"I'm going upstairs," she said. "See you later."

Ryan cleared off the plate and tossed the food down the garbage disposal. Something didn't sit right with him, the way Lindsey was acting today. He washed and dried his hands and untied the apron. It was his day off, not a day to worry about Lindsey. He was already starting to act like a father, and he had no right. Yet. He planned to take some time to just sit outside on this warm August day and try to get his head around all that was happening.

With the café closed for the day, the best cappuccinos in town were at Marco's place. He hoped he didn't run into Lindsey. She would think he was checking up on her. He walked out the side door and headed over to Books, Nooks and Coffee. A few tourists lingered on the sidewalks, but definitely missing were any signs of movie people. Hallelujah, Ryan thought.

Marco flashed Ryan a smile as he entered. "Afternoon," he said. His little dog, Gatsby, greeted him at the door.

Ryan petted Gatsby, scratching him behind the ears. "This is one cute dog," he said.

He stepped to the counter, the dog at his heels. "I'll have a double cappuccino."

"Wet or dry?" Marco asked.

"Wet is fine." There was no sight of Lindsey in here. He wondered where she'd gotten off to.

Ryan eyed the gluten free cookies, oat bars, and carrot breakfast muffins. "How're the muffins?" he asked.

Marco placed the porcelain cup brimming with creamy, white foam before him on the counter. "Made fresh this morning with golden raisins."

Ryan considered his options and chose the muffin. As he turned with his goodies in hand to find a table, the shop door opened and Ian walked in.

"Great minds think alike," Ryan said.

"Lily left this morning," Ian said, "and as soon as Mary arrived to help, she chased me out of the house to give me some time off from the baby. So here I am."

After Ian ordered coffee, the two men took a seat in the back by the window facing the cove. Ryan sipped his coffee and stared out at the incoming tide as it lapped at the wood pilings holding up the pier. A line to board the local sailboat for their three-hour afternoon cruise was forming on the deck. He ought to take Jude out on that one day, just the two of them. Early next spring there would be three of them.

"So it's just us guys for a few days," Ian said. "Any plans?"

Ryan sipped his drink. "Not really. We closed the café a few days for inventory, and I'm working on the book and other stuff."

"Lily arranged so much help for me while she's gone, I think I'll have time to paint and catch up on sleep."

Ryan broke open the muffin and took a bite. It was surprisingly moist and the flavor bright and satisfying. Surprises were everywhere if you were open to them, he mused.

"How's the baby doing?" Ryan asked.

The smile on Ian's face said it all. "I forgot how much work they can be. Jason is nine years old now. But it's worth every sleepless moment."

The way Ian looked at him, Ryan could tell he'd gotten word. "You know Jude is pregnant."

"I do," Ian said. "How are you doing with that?"

Ryan stared out the window forming his thoughts. "I never imagined I would be so lucky as to have a child and a wonderful woman who loved me. Now that it's happening, I'm afraid I won't make a good dad, or husband."

"I understand," Ian said. "When my first wife told me she was pregnant with Jason, as much as I loved her, my first reaction was to run. I was in my early twenties, teaching art part time, painting some, and longing to travel."

"I'm not sure age matters," Ryan said. "I reacted much the same."

"I'll give you the same words of wisdom my Grandpa John told me," Ian said. "Babies bring luck. He told me to toss aside my fears and be open to life. And so I did. It was the best decision I ever made."

Ryan let out a long breath. "I'm afraid to hope. My past..."

"Is behind you. Where it belongs. You'll make a great husband and father. Look how good you are with Lindsey already."

"Maybe..."

"Maybe nothing," Ian said. "The minute I saw sweet Gwyn look at me, I felt like I'd slay a thousand dragons to protect that little one. As soon you see the baby you'll understand."

Ryan thought about the first time he'd held tiny Gwyn at the shower. The longing that engulfed him had been quite a shock. He thought of the moment Jude told him she was pregnant. Shock was the only way he could explain his reaction.

"What if Jude comes back and asks me to leave?"

"Why would she?"

"When she told me, I should have jumped for joy. Instead, I turned into a bumbling idiot."

Ian picked up his coffee and took a drink, taking his time before answering. "There is always that chance, but I know Jude and she's not a quitter."

A quitter. That was exactly what he had been for the last several years. But Ryan was through running. He'd put down roots here and told Jude everything he thought he'd never tell another soul. This was where he belonged.

"If she'd have me, I'd sweep her off her feet and marry her tomorrow."

Ian laughed. "They won't be back until tomorrow, but hold that thought."

"I could jump on the next ferry and surprise her. What do you think?"

Ian shrugged. "Perhaps it would be best to let those three have their time to figure everything out on their own for now."

Ryan pulled out his phone to check the email with Jude's itinerary for returning tomorrow. He would have everything ready.

Ian pointed out the window. "Wow, look at that yacht docking at the end of the pier. Someone's got some big bucks."

They watched as the crew tied up the lines to the pilings for a secure mooring.

"Pretty fancy," Ryan said. It reminded him of the yacht a director friend of Peyton's had taken them on for a cruise to Catalina one time. He'd rather have a small sailboat, he mused to himself, closer to the water, wind in his face.

A silver-haired man dressed in khaki pants and a blue-striped shirt stepped off the yacht and offered his hand to a young, well-dressed woman. She turned, leaned in and kissed him passionately. Even from this distance their age difference was apparent. Probably newlyweds, Ryan thought.

"Isn't that Lindsey out there?" Ian asked, pointing to the pier.

Ryan stood to get a better look. Sure enough, Lindsey and the newly docked couple were waving at each other as she moved down the pier toward them. Everything fell into place. It had to be Lindsey's father and new wife. What the heck were they doing here? And how convenient for them to arrive while Jude was gone.

"I need to check out what's happening," Ryan said.

Ian rose. "I'll go with you."

"No need, Ian. But thanks."

"I'll just walk you down with, and then we'll head back."

Marco waved as Ryan and Ian rushed out the door. They moved rapidly down the wooden pier. Ryan watched Lindsey throw her arms around the man who he was sure now must be her father. The woman, sun hat and large sunglasses covering her face, shook Lindsey's hand.

"Lindsey," Ryan called out as he made his way down the plank.

She turned and frowned at him. "Are you following me?"

Ryan moved beside her. "Of course not."

"Who is this guy?" her father asked.

Lindsey shrugged. "He's the chef at Mom's café."

Ryan reluctantly put out his hand. "Ryan Folger."

"Mitchell," Jude's ex-husband said, a slick, pearly smile crossing his face. "I'm Lindsey's father. And this is my wife, Kimberly."

"Nice to meet you." Ryan caught his breath and tried to think fast. He introduced Ian and they all shook hands.

"Where did you cruise in from?" Ian asked.

Kimberly flashed a smile at Ian. "We just traveled through the San Juan Islands. They are so beautiful," she said.

Ian nodded. "My wife's on Orcas right now as a matter of fact. Nice place."

"I'm afraid you just missed Jude," Ryan said, watching for a response.

Mitchell put his arm around Lindsey. "No problem. We came to see my daughter."

His possessive attitude turned Ryan's stomach. The timing was suspicious, and his instant dislike of Mitchell did not help. "How long are you staying?"

Mitchell bristled, obviously not used to fielding direct questions. He winked at Lindsey. "We leave in the morning."

And just who was "we," Ryan wondered.

"Honey," Kimberly said. "Why don't you let Lindsey go freshen up while I do some shopping and stretch my legs?" She gazed seductively at her husband. "And then she can join us for dinner on the yacht tonight."

Mitchell kissed her on the cheek. "Run along," he said to his wife. "Buy yourself something nice."

It was obvious to Ryan that Kimberly had very little interest in spending time with Lindsey. So what were they really doing here? Lindsey, alone on that yacht with those two while Jude was gone was just not going to happen if he could help it.

Ryan stepped forward, forcing a smile. "I had a special dinner planned for Lindsey tonight at the café. We're closed to the public, why don't you and your wife join us instead?"

Mitchell looked Ryan over from head to foot. "We have a three star Michelin Chef aboard, why don't you join us?" he said.

Ryan looked at Lindsey and back to Mitchell. "What the heck? It'll be nice to have someone else cook for a change. What time?"

"We dine at 8:00 p.m."

"I'll be there."

Mitchell turned his back as if to dismiss Ryan and addressed his daughter. "Lindsey, I'm going to have a drink on the pier. Go ahead and get ready and I'll see you later."

"They walked back down the pier. When they reached the sidewalk at the end, Ian said his goodbyes. Ryan was glad his friend had been at his side for that confrontation.

Lindsey refused to meet Ryan's eyes during the short walk back to their places above the cafe." At the top of stairs

Ryan blocked the front door of Jude's apartment so Lindsey had to face him before entering.

"Did you know he was coming?"

Lindsey glared at him, reminding Ryan of the bratty girl who had stepped off the shuttle a few months ago.

"Yes and no," she snipped. "Now let me in."

Ryan stepped aside and followed her into Jude's apartment.

Ruffled, Lindsey threw down her purse on the counter. "Why do you care anyway?"

"I'm responsible for you while your mother is gone. And I care about you."

Lindsey took a stance with her hands on her hips. "I don't need a babysitter."

Ryan thought that was debatable. "Pretty convenient Mitchell arriving while your mother is gone."

"I didn't plan it that way, okay? I emailed him a few weeks ago when everything was crazy here. He never answered until this morning. Now if you don't mind, I'm going to take a shower and get ready for dinner."

He looked around the room to see if there were any suitcases packed. Seeing nothing out of order, Ryan walked to the door. "I'll meet up with you here at ten to eight."

"Fine," she said, shutting the door behind him.

Why was she being so defensive if this was nothing but a friendly visit, he wondered. Ryan walked down the path to his front apartment and pulled out his cell phone. Should he call Jude? He dialed her number but it went right to voicemail. He didn't leave a message. He'd hate to upset her when she finally had some time off to rest and enjoy herself on Orcas.

Ryan walked in and laid the phone on the counter. It would break Jude's heart if she got back and Lindsey was gone. He didn't want to overreact. He'd wait to see how the dinner went and if Mitchell was really leaving tomorrow. Perhaps just a little damage control would be enough.

Chapter Twenty-Four

$\mathcal{J}$ude woke from her nap to the sound of Lily and Kyla unloading groceries and banging pots around in the nearby kitchen. It was going to be nice to have someone else cook. Just relax and stop thinking for a while. She stretched luxuriously, and then walked over to the window. The sun was lower in the sky where pale hues of pink and lavender played in the clouds. Such a peaceful place.

Jude slid on her shoes, went upstairs, and glided down the hall to the kitchen. Her beautiful red-headed friend, Kyla, and lovely Lily, looked like models posing in the luxury kitchen. Jude looked forward to chef Lily's gourmet fare.

Kyla was sitting on a bar stool, sipping white wine and watching Lily do her magic. The hand-carved wooden stools lined each side of a granite countertop with a six- burner, stainless steel gas stove directly in the middle. The smell of garlic hung in the air, wafting up to the high-peaked ceilings.

"Smells delicious already," Jude said. "What are you making?"

Lily beamed. "Chicken breast stuffed with sliced mushrooms, garlic, goat cheese, and spinach, then wrapped in bacon and baked to perfection."

216

"Whoa," Kyla said, "That sounds amazing."

Jude heard her stomach growl. "Shall I make a salad?"

Lily pointed to the counter by the sink. "Sure. I got some butter lettuce, tomatoes, fresh, beautiful avocados, and green onion. Just needs to be cut up and tossed."

"I'll make the dressing. Little olive oil, pinch of herbs, and lemon juice," Kyla said.

They worked in the kitchen together in perfect harmony. A sense of happiness melted Jude's knots and worries away. The salty smell of bacon filled the room as the sun sank in the distance. This sense of peace was just what Jude had been longing for.

"Should I bring in some wood so we can light a fire?" Kyla asked.

Lily shook her head. "I don't think it's wise. It's not cold enough yet. Maybe tomorrow morning, if it's foggy."

"Why don't I set out the plates in the dining room?" Jude asked. She eyed the massive table that looked like it was made from one large slab of polished oak. "Or should we sit at the eating bar?"

"I vote for the table by the window." Lily said. "We'll put out a few candles and lower the lights."

They all took a seat when the food was served. Jude was glad her appetite was back so she could enjoy the succulent chicken. "Oh, my," Jude said. "I think I might have to share this recipe with Ryan if you're willing. I guess we could tweak it with a little thyme and call it Lily's bacon thyme special."

"Go right ahead," Lily said. "I created it as I went along, but I think I can write it down for you, and Ryan is pretty good at adapting recipes."

"To us," Lily said holding up her wine glass.

Jude held her goblet of sparkling cider. "To us!"

"I'm having a little déjà vu tonight," Kyla said. "Do you remember the slumber party we had at Jude's house when you first moved to the island, Lily?"

"I do. It was the night after Ian's art opening."

Kyla nodded. "Look how far we've all come since then."

Jude reflected on Lily's plight before she even reopened the bed and breakfast. Now Lily was married to Ian and had a new baby and a thriving inn. And secretive Kyla was married now too, and getting healthier every day. Where did that leave her?

"It's only fair I clear the table," Kyla said. She rose and gathered the now empty plates.

Jude gathered serving dishes and followed Kyla to the kitchen. "I'll help." As she dried dishes, she glanced out at the low clouds lining the mountain peaks like a veil. Deep blue skies were advancing as a soft wind blew away the remaining clouds. Jude laid down the dishtowel and turned to Lily. "There will be stars tonight. Let's go take a look."

"We can bundle up, sit out on that deck, and watch to our heart's content," Lily said. "I'll go find some blankets and sweaters."

After they finished cleaning, they went outside with blankets in hand. They walked from the deck down the stairs to the cedar Adirondack chairs gathered around the fire pit at the water's edge. In the cove before them, Jude watched a lone boat weave back and forth against the breeze as darkness descended into the night.

"It's a little nippy," Lily said, wrapping herself tight in a quilt.

"If you need more blankets, let me know," Kyla said. "I can go back and grab a few more."

Lily shook her head. "No problem. I'm good." Lily reached out and took Jude's hand and then Kyla's hand in hers. "I am so glad we took this time to be together. I've missed you both so much. Being a new mom, I hardly have any time to myself. Not that I'm complaining."

"I remember," Jude said. "I barely had a life between the baby and trying to have a marriage. I don't know how you're doing it all with the B&B, and Ian's art shows, and raising young Jason, too."

"Oh, Jason's a big help. He loves the baby," Lily said. "But I have to admit, sometimes I wonder where the instruction booklet is for motherhood."

"There is none," Jude said laughing. "That's the secret."

"I've called my mother more times lately than I think I ever have, and I appreciate her more than ever." Lily sighed. "I can really understand now why she took me away from my dad and worked so hard for so many hours to give me a good life. When I hold that baby and look into her eyes, I know I would do anything for my little Gwyn."

"Of course you would," Kyla said. "Don't worry. Motherhood is something I think we all respond to differently. It's something I would like to try, but it scares me, too," After coming from kind of a crazy mother and a broken home, I wonder what kind of mother I'd be."

"A great mother," Jude said. "Your mom and grandma love you. And with a husband like Luke..."

"Yes," Kyla said, "Luke would make a wonderful dad, but his family is very difficult as we all know!"

"At least they're far away." Jude said. "This time around, I want to be a better mother than I was when Lindsey was young. I'm certainly older and wiser."

"And it won't be the destructive marriage you had before with Mitchell," Lily said.

Kyla nodded in agreement. "You have to remember, Ryan might be scared right now and wondering what it all means to be a dad, but I'll tell you, I know in my bones that he'll be a wonderful father and this will be the marriage you always dreamed of."

"I hope so," Jude said. "Sometimes I wonder if I'm truly lovable."

"What?" Lily said. "You? The whole town loves you. We love you. Everybody loves you."

"Yes, but they don't know me in the same way."

"What do you mean?" Kyla said. "We both know you exceptionally well."

"It's different with a man," Jude said. "It's been so long. After Mitchell put me through everything, I haven't had the confidence I used to. I doubt that someone will ever be right for me or even stay with me."

"Of course he will," Lily said. "You've got to let go of the past, Jude, so the new can come in."

"No man is perfect," Kyla said.

Jude imagined being married to Ryan. Her heart skipped a beat. The past was behind her and her future? Dare she hope?

"Enough about me," Jude said. "How is married life, Kyla?"

"Truthfully, I couldn't be happier, and that's what scares me. I've had a life where being happy was elusive at best and now, every day I wake up and thank God for Luke and count my many blessings. I have a wonderful man, a beautiful home in a vineyard, Tea & Comfort is thriving, and my health is stronger than ever. But..."

"But what?" Lily asked.

"It is cold out here." Kyla wrapped herself in the fleece blanket and paused before answering. "I think of my mother and the life we had growing up. Do I deserve this happiness after everything I've done? How I hurt Luke..."

"Wait a minute," Jude said. "You deserve massive amounts happiness. You've earned it every step of the way."

"Luke is such an incredible man. Even his family is starting to come around some. His brother Stephan mostly leaves us alone, but his wife stays in touch. His dad calls occasionally, and his mother sends wonderful cards and gifts. I guess she's hoping for another grandchild."

"All right," Lily said, "you'd better get working on that."

Kyla grinned. "As soon as I get home I plan to. We let so much stand in our way sometimes. It's time we let our light shine."

"So true," Lily said.

"You're right." Jude patted Lily's head, "You're both right." Jude stared up to the night sky. It was so clear out here far away from city lights. Millions of stars twinkled, their winking lights reaching out to the threesome, specks on a sheltered beach. "Fear is such a heavy burden. It's hard to let it go, but it's definitely time."

"Let's all close our eyes," Kyla said, "and imagine throwing all our fears out into the ocean and watch them float away with ease and grace."

Jude closed her eyes and let the stillness of the night fill her. She visualized her fears filling an iridescent bubble before her, floating and ready to be released.

"Let's all do it together," Lily said. "One, two, three throw!"

As the words left Lily's mouth, a loud splash sounded in the water just off shore.

"What was that?" Lily asked.

Jude wasn't quite sure, but the timing was amazing. They stood and walked down to the water's edge. "It was probably a fish or seal or something, but I can't see anything."

"You never know," Kyla said. "I think that worked pretty well."

"Agreed," Lily said.

Jude felt lighter, like a weight had been lifted off her chest. She took the first deep breath she had taken in a long time. A wave glided in toward her, its foam shimmering in the moonlight. Moment after moment, the sea advanced and receded, just like life. All of it was beautiful if you looked closely.

"I'm going back to the chairs," Lily said. "It's freezing out here."

"We're coming too," Jude said.

"I have a confession," Lily said as she took the steps two at a time. "When I went into town to the market today, I tried calling Ian. But I could not get a signal anywhere."

"We forgive you," Kyla said. She pushed open the sliding glass door and they stepped inside.

"He's probably so engrossed in his painting he wouldn't have heard the phone ring anyway," Lily said. "It's probably the first time he's had uninterrupted hours to paint in months, so I don't blame him."

Lily slipped off her jacket and draped over the back of a chair. "I'm happy he is getting some time for himself, too. Being a parent is a full time job."

"I wonder what it'll be like to be a mom at forty years old," Jude said. "By the time the baby is in college, I'll be almost sixty."

"So many women are having children late now," Kyla said. "You're as strong as ever and you'll have lots of help. You two take a seat at the counter, I'll make us some hot tea."

"That's true. And things are going better with Lindsey. She seems excited at the prospect of having a little brother or sister."

"Everything will work out," Lily said.

"I hope so."

"It will," Kyla said. She placed the hot teas for each on them on the counter and took a seat.

"You seem so sure," Jude said.

Kyla continued. "Only one thing is in the way. Ryan is waiting for you."

"What does that mean, Kyla?"

"He's waiting for you..." Kyla's blue eyes pierced into Jude's. "He's waiting for you to trust him."

Kyla's deep red hair glowed as she said the words that touched deep inside Jude. "Trust, has always been a big issue for me," Jude said.

"It is for all of us," Lily said. "It took me a long time with Ian, but look where it led me."

Jude asked herself if she was truly willing to share her heart with Ryan. Certainly she had more than enough love to give. She thought about the hummingbirds when they'd first arrived today and how they fought at the glass feeder. They would rather fight the other bird off rather than share the nectar. Jude didn't want to be like that. Her feeder was full, and sharing was what made it worth it. "I want to trust him," Jude said. "I hope his first reaction to the pregnancy will change."

Lily giggled. "All men freak out a little when they first get the news, even Ian. Just let him have a little time to adjust to the idea. I bet he's going to sweep you off your feet the minute you get home."

"What if he packs up and leaves?" Jude said.

Kyla's voice was firm. "Ryan is not Mitchell, and you are not a young, twenty- year-old dependent on a husband to provide."

Jude considered Kyla's words. She certainly was a stronger person now and would handle things better as well. "All right. I get it. Onward and upward toward happiness."

Lily clapped. "That's it. Risks can pay off. Look at me."

"And look at me," Kyla echoed. "After moving all the way across the country away from him, what if I'd run when Luke arrived on Madrona Island? Imagine everything I would have lost."

"I was petrified when I left Brad and then reopened Grandma Maggie's bed and breakfast. Ian scared me the most. But then I found that letter in one of the old Guestbooks at the inn. It was from Grandpa John to Maggie. It said, "When the Heavens see fit to send love your way, only a darn fool would turn down a gift like that."

"I couldn't have better mentors leading the way," Jude said.

Lily squeezed Jude's hand. "You helped both of us to remember to be strong when times were tough by sharing your love and your friendship."

"I never thought of myself as a mentor," Kyla said. "But I kind of like it."

"Friends forever," Lily said. She pointed to the sky. "Look!"

Jude searched the sky. Sure enough, a shooting star came right at her, almost like a piece of a meteor was going to land at her feet.

"Did you see that?" Lily said.

"It was amazing," Kyla said. "Did you both make a wish?"

"Of course," Jude said, hoping it would come true.

"I think I'm going to head to bed," Lily said. "Tomorrow, on our only full day here before we leave, let's get up early while the mist is on the lake and rent those paddle boats we saw. Can you handle it Jude?"

Jude patted her belly. "I sure can. I used to be pretty good at racing those things when I was a kid at camp."

"Whoever wins pays for breakfast," Kyla said.

Chapter Twenty-Five

At 7:45 p.m. sharp, Ryan knocked on the door of Jude's apartment to meet with Lindsey for dinner with her father. She opened the door wearing a fancy white sundress that showed off her tan. Her makeup was heavy, and she looked more like the city girl who had first arrived here on the shuttle.

"Dad just texted me," Lindsey said. "He wants us to meet them in the bar on the pier for a drink before dinner." She fidgeted around. "Are you okay with that?"

Ryan's hackles went up. Had Mitchell been in the bar all this time? It was almost 8:00 p.m. What about dinner? "I guess I have to be," he answered.

Lindsey took the stairs two at a time. Ryan hurried his pace to keep up with her. He was not letting her out of his sight tonight.

Lindsey slowed as her heels caught in the planks lining the pier. She tossed her hair and walked slowly, stepping over the cracks.

She glared at him. "I was thinking that since we're all done with the food shots for the book, I could leave with

Dad and Kimberly and spend the last weeks of summer cruising with them."

Ryan felt a punch in his gut. There was no way that was going to happen. "I thought you were happy here. You and your mom are getting along so well."

Lindsey shrugged. "Dad says we'll sail through the islands, eat at all the best places, and he'll take me shopping for back to school."

Buying her off, Ryan thought. Anger seeped up his spine. "What about your agreement with your mother to spend the summer here, with her?"

"You two have a lot to work out. I'll probably only be in the way."

"We do," Ryan said. "But you are part of it too and you are never in the way." He stepped in front of her and met her face to face. "You know that isn't true. You'll break Jude's heart if she comes home and you're gone."

Lindsey narrowed her eyes. "What makes you so sure?"

"You have no idea how much your mother has done for you and would do for you."

"And why is that?" Lindsey said. "Because she never tells me. Now please step aside or join me, because I'm going to meet my dad."

Ryan shifted to his right, opened the door into the bar, and followed Lindsey in. The decibel level of the music was high, but topping the noise and chatter was the booming laugh of Mitchell sitting at the bar, half hanging off the stool next to his wife. Their level of intoxication was obvious.

"Well look who's here," Mitchell said, putting out his arms to Lindsey. "My beautiful daughter. And...the chef."

Ryan reached out to shake Mitchell's hand. "The name is Ryan," he said. "Are we eating here now?"

Mitchell laughed and slurred his words. "Whatever makes my daughter happy." He slid off the stool and attempted to hug Lindsey, but almost fell on her.

Lindsey pushed him upright and Kimberly moved in to support him from the other side. "Dad, don't you think we should get some food? I'm hungry."

Mitchell snapped his fingers toward a waitress. "Can we get some food here, honey."

The waitress nodded, but moved in the other direction. Ryan couldn't blame her. "This island has the worst service," Kimberly wined. "Even in the dress shops I could barely get anyone to wait on me."

The uncomfortable familiarity of the scene, and the awareness that this was not where he wanted Lindsey to be, propelled Ryan forward. "It's getting late. Why don't I just take Lindsey back to Jude's café and I'll cook something there for us."

Mitchell pulled loose from his wife's grip. "Back off Mr. No Star Chef or whatever your name is. Lindsey's coming with us." He grabbed his daughter's arm and pulled her toward him. "We'll set sail tonight," Mitchell said, "and you can't stop us."

Seething, Ryan stood right up in Mitchell's face. "Get your hands off her. You're drunk and not thinking about what's best for your own daughter."

The crowd noise dimmed as the scene between the two men unfolded. Ryan didn't care. He was not backing down and allowing this man to endanger Lindsey, no matter who he was.

Lindsey's eyes were filled with panic. Ryan reached out to her. "Let's go home. Your mother loves you more than anything, and her love doesn't come at a price. She would never jeopardize your safety the way your father is."

"My daughter can do a lot better than working in some hot kitchen with a mother who couldn't care less about her. Where the hell is Jude, anyway?"

Lindsey writhed free of Mitchell's grip. "Dad, calm down. Mom is on a retreat. She's, she's not feeling well."

A sneer crossed his face. "When did she ever? Moping around, whining and complaining all the time."

Lindsey looked at Ryan and then back at Mitchell. "I don't want to just sneak off."

"You're the one who emailed me the SOS, baby girl. This podunk island wasn't on my itinerary."

Lindsey stepped closer to Ryan. He put his hand on her shoulder and stood firm. "Lindsey doesn't need rescue. You might have thought more seriously about that when she was a baby and you walked out."

Ryan felt a jolt move through Lindsey's body.

"Is that true Dad?" she asked.

Mitchell's face reddened, and then he lunged to grab Ryan but missed and almost fell himself. "Shut up or I'll..."

The restaurant cleared around them. All eyes focused their way. Ryan pushed Lindsey behind him and stood tall. "Or you'll what? I think we better take this outside."

Mitchell and his wife followed them outside to the pier. Ryan did not want the whole town knowing about this and seeing what kind of father Lindsey had.

"You have it all wrong," Mitchell said, frowning at Lindsey. He leaned against the railing of the pier for support.

"My crazy ex-wife took my only child and moved to Madrona Island. Wouldn't even let me see her."

"You may have fooled Lindsey with your lies, but you're not fooling me. And I will make sure Lindsey knows the truth, all of it, tonight!"

Mitchell's bloodshot eyes narrowed. His curled lips trembled with hatred. 'Lindsey," Mitchell said. "Go get your things and leave with us right now, or I'll stop paying for your college. You can let your deadbeat mother support you."

"No, Dad. I won't go with you."

Ryan smiled inside and wanted to pat Lindsey on the back, but he let her own the moment.

"What garbage has you mother been telling you? Or this guy?"

Lindsey shook her head. "She never said a bad word against you, Dad."

"And there was plenty to say." Ryan stepped forward, his eyes never leaving Mitchell. "Jude saved your butt once years ago when Lindsey was a baby. And she's been a damn good mother. She may not have told Lindsey about your little accident, but I can. I'm not under the same threatening contract you have with her mother."

Mitchell raised a fist, glaring Ryan down.

Ryan lifted a fist too, but dropped it immediately. "You're not worth it," he said. "Get out of here, Mitchell, while you can still walk and have some dignity left in front of your daughter."

Kimberly lent her shoulder to Mitchell for support. "C'mon, honey, let's go."

"Lindsey," he said, his words like steel. "This is your last chance. You can come with us right now, or not at all."

Lindsey had tears running down her cheeks. She stepped back toward Ryan. He put his arm around her waist and pulled her slightly behind him in case Mitchell got violent again. A cool wind hurled across the pier where they stood.

"She's staying here with us, Mitchell. You can take your threats and sail away." Lindsey leaned against him, tears spilling onto his back. Ryan's heart broke for her.

Mitchell slammed his fist on the railing and staggered. Ryan wondered if the man, even with his wife's help, could even make it down the plank walkway and back to his yacht. And what if her father fell in the Sound? Damn, Ryan didn't want to have to jump in after him and yank him out before he froze to death.

"Kimberly," Ryan said, "you might want to text your staff to help get Mitchell back to the ship safely."

"I'm fine," Mitchell said, trying to regain his balance. "More than you'll both be when I'm through with you." He straightened his back and, leaning on his wife's shoulder, stamped toward the boat dock.

Ryan saw some of the yacht crew running out to help Mitchell and was grateful he could finally leave with Lindsey. Clouds had rolled in as the drama unfolded, and the cold winds off the cove chilled to the bone. Lindsey was shaky, but he supported her down the pier as fast as they could walk. Until they were almost safely back to Jude's apartment, Ryan did not take the time to look out at the cove and make sure the yacht had left the dock until they were almost safely back to Jude's apartment. Thank goodness the yachts lights were on and it was moving across the cove. His adrenaline had lowered now, leaving his legs a little shaky, as he led them upstairs.

Inside, Lindsey curled up on the couch and Ryan handed her a throw from the bedroom to wrap herself in. A soft rain coated the windows. He hoped Mitchell had the sense to go right to bed and not try to sail too far in this.

"I'll make you some tea," he said. "The good stuff from Kyla's shop."

"Thank you," she said. "I mean, you know, not just for the tea." Lindsey wrapped the wool blanket tightly around her and stared into space.

Ryan poured the boiling water from the kettle through a strainer filled with loose tea into a mug. He added some local honey to the mug and brought it over to Lindsey.

"What contract were you talking about that my mom made with my dad?"

"I'm sorry I disclosed that back with your dad, but your welfare was at stake. The fact is, I promised your mom I wouldn't say anything. That is something for Jude to tell you about herself.

"She won't and you know it," Lindsey said, raising her voice. "Please tell me. I'm not a kid anymore. I don't know what to believe. All I've ever been told is that my mom took me away from him ..."

Ryan was conflicted. If he broke Jude's confidence and told Lindsey more about her dad, Jude might never forgive him. But if he didn't, he risked Lindsey shutting down toward her mother and leaving on her own. It would break Jude's heart, and nothing was worth that. It burned him to think about how long Mitchell had been lying to his own daughter.

Ryan turned to face her. "Did you ever consider Mitchell was the one not telling the truth? Your mother always put your needs first. As you said yourself, she never badmouthed your dad. And believe me, he deserved it."

Lindsey warmed her hands on the mug and pouted. "I know he drinks too much sometimes and does dumb things."

"Like driving drunk and jeopardizing their marriage?"

"Why didn't my mom stand beside my dad? Make sure he got help? He was her husband after all. She left him at a time when he needed her most."

Ryan knew that what he was about to say might ruin his relationship with Jude forever. He also knew Jude would never say it, and Lindsey would go on believing her father was the victim in all of this. The lie had gone on long enough.

"What never came out was that your dad was with another woman while your mom was home one night, frantic with worry and taking care of you."

"Oh," was all Lindsey said. Her face began to crumble.

"And when Mitchell finally got home, Jude confronted him." Ryan paused. "I'm sorry to say it, but your dad told your mom to take you and get out if she didn't like it."

Lindsey's eyes widened. "I don't believe you, he'd never —" She stopped herself mid-sentence and took a deep breath. Her composure was crumpling, and along with it the vision of her father. "I once saw him chase a guy off the freeway who cut him off, pull the man out of the car, knock him out, and leave him unconscious on the pavement."

"Real nice," Ryan said with distain.

"Why didn't my mom tell me all this? Why did she let me go live with him?"

"She wanted you to feel safe and loved. That's why she moved to Madrona Island to start a new life for you both.

When your father finally resurfaced, she saw how much you wanted to live with him. Jude didn't want to stand in the way of you having a relationship with your dad, and she certainly didn't want you to grow up having bad feelings about him. She hoped Mitchell was telling the truth when he told her he'd changed and was happily married now. But it about broke her heart to let you go."

Lindsey put her tea down with a trembling hand. Ryan watched her fight back tears and wished he hadn't been so harsh.

"All those things I accused her of," Lindsey said. "I left her for my dad. Will she ever forgive me?"

"She loves you. And all she wants is for you to be happy."

Lindsey broke down sobbing. Ryan scooted in next to her on the couch and patted her shoulder. "I'm here," he said. He reached over the table to retrieve a tissue for her.

She blew her nose, then looked up. "Thanks, Ryan. And thanks for telling me. Are you going to get in trouble with my mom?"

"Probably," Ryan said. "But at least we'll both be here when they return. I really should call her and let her know what happened tonight."

"Do you have to? She'll be home tomorrow anyway and she needs some rest."

Ryan knew how much Jude and the others were looking forward to their time on Orcas. The crisis had been averted, Mitchell was long gone, and it was almost midnight. "How about I call her in the morning? I'll tell her everything is fine, but give her a little head's up."

"Okay." Lindsey sniffed. "But don't worry. I'll be on your side when she gets home. I'll tell her I made you tell me."

"Hey," Ryan said, "I'm still the adult here and have to take responsibility."

"My mom is lucky to have you," she said.

"I'm the lucky one." Ryan stood to leave. "I'll be right next door if you need anything, any time."

Lindsey stood and gave Ryan a hug. "I'm lucky to have you, too."

Ryan walked back to his apartment and fell into the recliner. His head was spinning and Lindsey's words almost had him crying too. He'd grown to love that girl and her mom. Relief flooded over him when he considered the disaster that had been averted earlier that night. It would have been over his dead body that Lindsey went out to sea with that drunk who called himself her father and went out to sea with him. He'd call Jude in the morning. Let her get one night of rest and make a decision in the light of day. After she returned he'd confess everything to her. He prayed she wouldn't hold it against him.

Now more than ever he wanted this relationship to work. After tonight, he was sure he would be a good father to the baby and Lindsey. If Jude would have him, he would get down on one knee and propose to her as soon as she returned. Tomorrow he would go shopping for a ring at the custom jeweler on the South end of the island and think of some special way to propose.

Chapter Twenty-Six

Ryan jumped into his morning shower in hopes it would wake him up. He'd slept hard last night after all the commotion with Mitchell. Now, a feeling of dread shot through him. His muscles tightened even as the hot water pounded on his shoulders. He had betrayed Jude's trust. He had told Lindsey what Jude had specifically asked him not to. Mitchell wasn't the great guy that Lindsey had thought he was. He hoped Jude would understand that the circumstances had warranted his actions.

When he turned the water off, he heard his cell phone buzz. He grabbed a towel and leaned over to see his phone on the counter. It was a text from Lindsey.

"Come to breakfast. Wait to call my mom till we talk. Okay?"

He texted back that he'd be right there, then dried off and threw on some jeans and a t-shirt before heading over to Jude's apartment. He knocked on the door.

"Come in," Lindsey said.

The fragrant smells made his stomach growl. He walked toward the kitchen, "You need any help?"

"No. You go sit down," Lindsey said. "You're always the chef. I'm serving breakfast this morning."

Ryan took a chair at the dining table. It was set with fresh flowers, silverware, cloth napkins, and wide square plates. "Hmm, something smells good," he said.

"You bet it does. Smoked salmon and cream cheese omelet, French roast coffee, local and organic of course, crispy apple smoked bacon, and fresh-baked chocolate chip scones."

"Scones? You have been busy this morning," Ryan said.

"I just woke up early, filled with energy. Thought I'd cook breakfast."

"I'm happy to hear it," Ryan said.

He watched her pour two mugs of steaming coffee and bring them over to the table. She placed them beside the crystal goblets of ice water. "Do you want any fruit or juice?" she asked.

"No, I think we've got quite enough here."

Lindsey dished out the food and brought the plates to the table. "Dig in."

Ryan ate a few forkfuls of the fluffy eggs and sipped the deep, rich coffee. "Delicious," he said between bites.

Lindsey popped a slice of bacon in her mouth. "Taste the crisp I got on the bacon. It's so good," Lindsey said.

"You had a good teacher," Ryan said.

Lindsey pretended to scowl. "I know."

"But you picked everything up so fast," Ryan said. "You really are quite skilled in the kitchen."

"I was thinking," Lindsey said, "you think I'd have a shot at the Food Network? You know I kind of like the movie stuff, and I like cooking. Maybe TV?"

"Sure thing," Ryan said. For a moment he hesitated, remembering his good friend and all his success as a celebrity chef, and then the drugs and scandal. But Lindsey was tough and had his and her mother's love behind her. "It can be a hard life, Lindsey," he said." It can be hard to keep your feet on the ground. But you're a pretty level-headed kid most of the time."

"I'm not a kid," Lindsey said. "I'm twenty years old. Twenty-one soon enough."

Ryan dipped his scone into the last of the egg mixture on his plate and savored the flavors in his mouth. The windows were open and he could hear the seagulls outside screaming and diving for mussels they could drop on the pier to break open for a fresh breakfast.

"Lindsey," he said, "I really think we should let Jude know what happened last night before she gets home."

"I did," Lindsey said, I thought I should call her, that she should hear it from me. But it went right to voice mail. They probably took the early ferry."

Lindsey looked at the clock at the same time as Ryan. It was just a little before nine. "Then they'll be here in a few hours."

"That was a good thing you did reaching out to her. Why don't you try again?"

"What do you think she'll say?"

"I don't know," Ryan said, "but I know she loves you."

Ryan brought the dishes into the kitchen and placed them under running water. He tried not to make too much noise so he could hear the conversation. Lindsey was out on the deck, but the glass doors were open. Of course he could only hear one side of the conversation. He heard her skipping a little bit of the story, but she got out that her dad had been here and he'd wanted her to go with him. "And I didn't," Lindsey said quite loudly. "He got a little crazy."

Crazy, Ryan thought. That was certainly the right word. Drunk, crazy, and vicious.

He scrubbed the pot a little more fiercely thinking of Mitchel. "I'm okay mom," he heard her say. Then he heard his name. "Ryan was there for me. Yes, he's a good guy. We're fine. Don't rush."

Upon hearing those words, Ryan couldn't help but smile. He knew Jude would certainly rush home now. He loaded the dishwasher and then stopped when he heard Lindsey say, "I love you," to her mom. It was the first time he'd heard her say that to Jude, and it made everything worth it.

Lindsey walked back in and joined him in the kitchen, putting away the dishes that he'd dried.

Unable to wait any longer, Ryan turned the water off and faced her. "So?"

"I told her what happened. I told her that I didn't want to go with him and you took good care of me and everything's fine, right?"

"Right," Ryan said. "You didn't tell her anything else?"

"I did tell her I knew more of the truth now, but when she gets home I'm going to ask her to tell me the whole story. I...I hope she won't be too upset."

Ryan dreaded hearing what was going to happen when Jude found out he'd broken her confidence. "You mean because I told you about your dad?"

"I'm really glad you did, and I think it's time my mom told me herself. If she says anything about you, I'll take full responsibility."

"That's good to know," Ryan said, "but I'm the one that made the decision."

"It was a good decision, you'll see. But maybe it would be best if you weren't here when my mom gets home, so I can talk to her first."

"I think I should be here too. At least when she first arrives," Ryan said. "I want her to know that I take responsibility for what I did."

"All right. I'm going to clean myself up a little. You might want to do the same. She laughed in a kidding way.

"Do I look that bad?"

"Hmm, no you never look bad, Ryan, but you know that ponytail could use a little work."

Ryan tugged on his hair. "Well I just threw it together when you invited me over for breakfast."

Lindsey laughed. "Go on. She'll be home in an hour so. When you hear her pull in, just come on over."

"Okay will do."

Ryan walked back to his apartment and sat on the sofa to wait for Jude's return. Worry crept into his thoughts. What if this was the final breaking of trust between him and Jude? After the way he'd acted when she told him she was pregnant, he wouldn't blame her if she ended things between them. And now this? But he would explain to her that when she first told him about the baby, he'd been shocked. And afraid. Not of the commitment or his love for Jude, but afraid he wouldn't be a good enough dad. Or husband.

"Face it," he told himself, "when things got tough in the past, you never stuck around that long before." But he was absolutely sure now that Jude was the woman he loved and wanted to spend the rest of his life with. He would face the challenges ahead of them, and hope and pray she would understand that everything he'd said and done to protect Lindsey, he done out of his love for Jude.

Jude pulled into her driveway, grabbed her suitcase, and headed upstairs. She was anxious to find out exactly what had happened with Mitchell and Lindsey. Her daughter assured her on the phone that everything was fine, but Jude was not convinced. As she reached the top of the landing, she saw Ryan walking out of his apartment toward her. "What happened?"

Ryan put his arm around her. "Everything's fine now. Come on in. Lindsey's waiting."

"Wait," she said. "Can't you brief me a little?"

"Lindsey wants to be the one to tell you everything. I'll be right there with answers to any questions you may have." Ryan took the suitcase from her. "Go on in. You must be tired from the trip."

"Not really. I'm just nervous," Jude said.

When they walked in, Lindsey jumped up from the couch and gave Jude a hug. "Did you have fun?"

Jude thought for a moment. "Actually, we did. We had a great time. It's absolutely beautiful. I'd love for the three of us to go there some day, but honestly, I really need to know what happened with Mitchell."

"Why don't you sit down, Mom," Lindsey said pointing to the couch.

Jude took a seat and folded her arms across her chest. "Ryan," she said, "after Lindsey's call this morning, it made me wonder why you didn't call me last night."

Ryan sat down across from her. "By the time everything was settled, it was close to midnight."

Jude's heart softened a little when she saw the concern in his eyes.

"I didn't want to upset you," Ryan said. "I knew you wouldn't sleep and there was no way off that island that late except by helicopter. Besides, you were coming home in the morning already. I hope I made the right decision."

"You're right," Jude said. "I would have had to be scraped off the ceiling from anxiety if you'd told me about it last night."

"You needed a vacation, Mom. We both decided to wait. And you need to take care of yourself," Lindsey said, "with the baby coming and everything."

Jude patted her belly and smiled. "I am a bit more tired than normal, so thanks." She looked at both of their concerned faces. They looked nervous and hopeful for her approval. "You made a good choice by waiting," she said, "but I want you to tell me everything that happened."

"You want something to drink first?" Lindsey asked.

"I just want the whole story."

Ryan looked over at Lindsey and nodded.

Lindsey pushed back her hair and shuffled around in her seat. "Remember when that whole thing with Ryan trending on Twitter happened? I was pretty upset, so I emailed Dad." She grimaced. "Kind of a distress call to his yacht. I wanted to get off the island, escape. I thought I could just hang out and cruise in the sun before the last few weeks before school starts."

"Oh," Jude said. "I'm sorry you were that upset."

"It didn't last. I was just pissed and thought maybe you two didn't want me around. I didn't think Dad would even answer."

"But he did." Jude felt her heart beating hard in her chest. She'd come so close to losing the closeness she'd built with her daughter."

"No. He never did answer. Then I completely forgot about him until I saw them dock last night."

"Them?" Jude said.

"Dad and Kimberly. His newest wife."

"They showed up in the late afternoon," Ryan said. "Lindsey went down there to talk to them and I followed. I met Mitchell, but I don't think he was too happy to see me there."

"Oh I'm sure that was a great joy," Jude said.

"Well, we can talk more about that later," Ryan said. "He obviously had his eye on Lindsey and a plan in place."

"He sure timed it well," Jude said. "How did he know I'd be gone?"

"I don't know," Lindsey said. "I didn't tell him."

Jude threw up her hands. "Your dad always did seem to know how to get what he wanted. And then what happened?"

Lindsey told her the story of how the day had unfolded.

Jude shuddered just thinking of her daughter on the yacht with her drunk father. "Thank you for being there, Ryan. It means a lot to me."

A smile spread across Ryan's face. "And to me," he said.

"And me," Lindsey said. "Especially later when we went back for dinner and Dad took a swing at him and almost fell over."

"What? Are you all right Ryan?"

"Fine," he said. "Mitchell was out of his depth and very intoxicated."

Lindsey nodded. "Ryan told him we weren't going anywhere with him. Dad said some not very nice things about you, and this place, and that I needed to pack my bags and go with him immediately." She turned to Ryan. "He was great Mom. Ryan stepped in and told Dad there was no way that I was going anywhere with him. And I told him too! Then when we tried to leave, he threatened me."

Jude was shaking with anger. "He threatened you?" she asked.

Ryan spoke up. "He didn't want to take no for an answer. "But there was no way I was going to let him take Lindsey, especially in the condition he was in. And certainly not without your permission."

Ryan is such a good man, Jude thought. How could I have ever have doubted him? What if he'd been gone when Mitchell arrived? But she didn't need to worry about that because Ryan had been there, and Lindsey had made a good choice herself.

"How did you finally get Mitchell to leave?"

"Well," Lindsey said, drawing out the word. "Ryan said some things."

"I'm sorry, Jude. Everything was intensifying and Mitchell was standing his ground. I told him that if he didn't get out of here now, that I would tell his daughter about his shady agreement with you."

Jude faltered. He'd broken her confidence, but he'd saved her daughter.

"I said what I needed to say to get him to leave. I think we've heard the last from Mitchell for a while."

"Phew." Jude let out a big breath. "You did what you needed to do. I hate to think what would have happened if you hadn't been here, Ryan."

"But I was here," Ryan said. "I always will be if you'll let me. I'm really sorry about what I had to say and what came out after."

"After?" Jude asked.

"Mom, don't be mad at Ryan. I was a mess, crying. He kept telling me to wait for you, but I needed to know the truth about my dad. I begged Ryan. I'm sorry now that I wasn't there for you, Mom. That I believed Dad at all. But Ryan loves you, and his words to me made all the difference."

Jude stared at Ryan, but he wouldn't meet her eyes. "How much did you tell her?" Jude asked.

When he looked up, Jude saw only love in his eyes. "Just enough to know that her father was not the man that she ..."

Lindsey looked at her, tears welling in her eyes. "Please tell me the truth," Mom.

Jude felt her stomach churn. Had she made the right decision back then? "Lindsey, I wanted to tell you but I ... I didn't want you having resentment towards your dad or ill feelings. It was hard enough not having him here most of the time, and you seemed so happy to finally have a relationship with him."

"I think I understand," Lindsey said, "but I'm not a child now and I need you to tell me everything."

"You're right. You deserve to know everything, and you will."

Jude glanced at Ryan. His face had gone white. "Ryan, you look like you're going to pass out on us. I understand why you told her. And I thank you. It should have come from me sooner."

"I'm so relieved to hear that," he said. "If I'd lost you on top of everything..."

"You're not going to lose me Ryan, especially now."

He sat down beside her and took her into his arms. "I love you so much, Jude. I'm sorry for the way I acted about the baby. I was afraid, but I think I will make a good dad." He turned to Lindsey. "And with your daughter's blessing, I'd like to be a good husband if you'll let me."

Jude's breath caught when his eyes met hers, looking through to her very core. Lindsey gasped beside them.

"Are... Are you asking me to marry you?" Jude asked.

Ryan's smile was radiant. "Absolutely. I know this isn't very romantic, but I'll make it up to you. I don't want to rush you but.... He put his hand on her belly."

"I will," Jude said, throwing her arms around him. "Don't worry about rushing. Doing it soon is a good idea. But I don't want to jump into a wedding, and I don't want anything big. The café is all booked for the last week of August. A nice, quiet, little ceremony in September sounds wonderful."

"But then I won't be here, Mom, I'll be back at school," Lindsey said.

"Oh, right," Jude said. "This is all happening so fast. We'll figure it out."

Ryan stood. "I'll whip something up downstairs and give you two a little time to talk alone before you come down."

Lindsey jumped off the couch and pulled her mother with her. "Group hug to celebrate," she said.

Jude threw her arms around Lindsey and then motioned for Ryan to join them. For a moment she remembered the young eagles they saw on Orcas, learning to fly with their mother, gliding back and forth across the sky. All the struggles had led to here and now, and the three of them were learning to fly together.

It had been a long day. Jude felt like she'd been on an emotional roller coaster that never returned to the station. And it wasn't over yet. She turned on the bedside lights, propped up her pillows, climbed in under her silk duvet cover, and waited for Lindsey.

"Hi, Mom," Lindsey said from the doorway. "Can I join you?"

Jude patted the side of her bed. "Come in under the covers, like you used to when you were little."

Lindsey smiled. "When you told me bedtime stories."

Jude wished that was all she was telling Lindsey tonight. After her daughter was cozy and snug in the bed next to her, Jude began. "Are you sure you want the whole story?"

Lindsey nodded. Jude stroked Lindsey's fine hair. She could still see the little girl inside her, and she wished she could spare Lindsey the truth, but that was exactly what had gotten them here. She looked at the pictures of Lindsey on the wall, her first birthday, the Christmas parade, and so many more until Lindsey had left with her father.

"From the beginning then," Jude said. "When I found out I was pregnant with you, we'd only been married a short while, but we were both very excited. Your dad bought us a nice house in Bellevue, with a fenced yard and a bright nursery for you. I thought he'd settle down after you were born, and we'd be a happy family of three. But he wasn't even there for your birth. His mother, your grandmother, came and made some excuse."

"You must have felt so alone," Lindsey said.

"I did, but I talked myself out of it after Mitchell came home with flowers and excuses. Instead, I focused on how beautiful you were, and motherhood was everything I'd ever dreamed of." Jude remembered holding Lindsey in her arms and watching her blessedly sleep. Her old rocker was still in the corner of her bedroom draped with a hand-knit shawl made by her own mother.

Jude took Lindsey's hand. "You started having colic, and couldn't eat without throwing up. Nothing calmed you. You couldn't sleep, and neither could I. I was sure it was my fault somehow, but the doctor said there wasn't much that could be done about it."

Lindsey squeezed Jude's hand. "I bet you were exhausted. Where was Dad during all of this?"

"To be honest," Jude said, "Mitchell started staying out later and later, spending nights at his parents' so he could sleep. Your grandmother said they'd pay for a nanny to come and help a couple days a week. But I didn't want a stranger, I wanted my husband."

Jude reached for a tissue and wiped her eyes. "I'm sorry," she said.

"It's okay, Mom, cry all you need to. I would have. What did you ever see in Dad?"

"I was young when I met him. He swept me off my feet. He introduced me to sailing, fine food, and good wine. He'd grown up with only the best. But when we settled into the suburbs, he rebelled. He was used to being free and doing whatever he wanted. It took the worst night of my life to realize exactly what I'd gotten myself into."

Lindsey put her head on Jude's shoulder. "It must have been so hard."

Jude touched her head to Lindsey's and closed her eyes to enjoy the moment of having her daughter beside her again. "Just know," she said, "you were all that really mattered to me. Still are."

Lindsey nudged in closer. "Is that when you made the agreement?"

"Yes," Jude said. "One night, after a particularly exhausting week, Mitchell didn't come home at all. When he finally did, he was bruised and bleeding and said he'd been in a car accident. Everything changed after that. I found the police report that showed Mitchell had been driving drunk and hit a young boy on a bike."

"What...what happened to the kid?"

"Both of his legs were broken. Your dad's family made a private settlement with the boy's family to cover it up and keep it from getting out to the public. As you know from what Ryan told you, he was with another woman too. After I found the police report, I confronted him with my knowledge. He threatened to take everything from me if I told a soul. And perhaps, he said, it was time for me to leave."

Jude paused, remembering the horrible confrontation. All Mitchell's parents had cared about was protecting their precious son's reputation. They were fine with buying Jude off with the building they owned on Madrona Island, even if it meant losing touch with their only grandchild. Jude decided to leave that part out; it would only hurt Lindsey more.

"So we moved here," Jude said, forcing a light tone. "Your grandparents signed over this property in Grandview as a divorce settlement so you and I could live in the apartment and remodel the café below. I always loved to cook, and I thought it would be a peaceful, friendly, safe town to raise you in."

"So that's why I hardly ever saw Dad or my grandparents. They didn't bother to come over and were happy we were far away."

Jude cringed. It was the truth, but it cut deep. "You can see why I kept some of this from you."

Lindsey squeezed her eyes shut. Jude watched her daughter's chest rise and fall as she took deep breaths and processed her feelings. She opened her eyes and tears streaked across her cheek. "Did Dad ever tell the truth?"

"I don't know, Lindsey. I do think he loves you in his own way though."

"Maybe. Right now I just want some time away from him." Lindsey turned to Jude. "It must have hurt so much when I left the island to go live with him. I'm so sorry, Mom."

"Don't be," Jude said. "You were just being a normal teenager. Your best friend had moved away and you were restless on the island. Your Dad lavished you with expensive presents, took you out on his yacht, and then to Europe. I wasn't surprised you were enchanted by the prospect of an exciting new life. You would have hated me if I stood in your way, and in the end, despite my pain over losing you, I wondered if it might be the best thing for you after all. He could offer you so much, private schools, top notch colleges, and the excitement you craved. It took everything in me to let go."

"I don't know how you did it. And how I could do what I did."

"We're together now," Jude said. "Things worked out. Island Thyme Café thrived and the town rallied around me. It may not be the most exciting town, but people here care about each other, support each other, and tell me my mochas always cheer them up."

Lindsey laughed. "You do make the best mochas ever."

"Thanks. Maggie, who owned Madrona Island Bed and Breakfast, was my first true friend. I miss her."

"I remember her brownies the most," Lindsey said.

"After you left, I closed down the café and stayed with Maggie for a few days." Jude remembered that first morning after Lindsey went off with her father. It was so quiet. Jude's passion for living, for the café, her passion for everything came crashing down while sadness and the emptiness engulfed her. Jude, the upbeat one with the smile that everyone in town came to see at the cafe. Jude, the one who always saw the good in everything, now saw nothing but darkness.

"I wish you could have known Maggie better," Jude said. "She gave me the best room in the inn, the honeymoon suite with a frilly canopy bed, a soaking tub, and a gorgeous view of the water."

"I'm so glad you had friends like that," Lindsey said.

"I don't know what I'd have done without Maggie, or what I'd do without Kyla and Lily now." Jude leaned back into the down pillows and remembered the trays waiting outside the B&B suite each morning with fresh brewed coffee, home-baked scones, scrumptious egg dishes, and a little hand-written upbeat message from Maggie. In the afternoons, they'd walked the beach and talked about their children, life, and love. And Jude had healed slowly from the inside. Before she left to go back home, Jude had written in the B&B guestbook:

Thank you, Maggie, for all that you do for everyone lucky enough to know you, and for me. I'll never forget it.

Jude never had. She'd gone back to work and thrown her heart and soul into expanding Island Time Café. Once in a while she'd think about finding love again one day and hoped that Lindsey would want to come back. And here she finally was.

Lindsey put an arm around Jude's shoulder. "We're in this together now. All four of us."

And Jude knew her daughter had finally come home.

Chapter Twenty-Seven

Ryan laid out the homemade potato buns on the counter in preparation for the day's chicken thyme sandwich special.

"The grill is hot and ready," Lindsey said as she handed Ryan the garlic butter to brush across them before grilling them.

"I have a favor to ask," he said.

"Sure. What?"

Ryan finished buttering the insides of the buns and placed his knife on the cutting counter. "Do you think you can get your mom out of the restaurant Tuesday afternoon before our date night?"

Lindsey smiled and narrowed her eyes. "Just what do you have planned?"

"Obviously a surprise," he said.

She gave him a pleading look. "And you won't tell me? I won't breathe a word."

"I'll just say I will be preparing something special for your mother, and I don't want her to find out until dinner."

"I thought you were taking her out to that French place off island?"

"We are. Dessert is another matter." Ryan had sketched out the design and bought baking paper and a clean paintbrush and wooden ruler. Now he just had to prepare it and chill it and hide it from Jude.

"Two specials, salad instead of fries," a waitress yelled into the kitchen, leaving the check on the assembly area Ryan had set up for smoother service.

Ryan raised the burners under the cast iron skillet and put two marinated chicken breasts into the sizzling oil. "Let's go Lindsey, we have some hungry customers and more coming."

The café was busier than it had ever been. The town had gained some notoriety after the movie shoot, and tourists poured in. Labor Day Weekend was the culmination of summer, and after that he hoped business would slow a little. Jude needed more rest, and the profits from summer would allow them to be open fewer days each week for the winter season. He looked over at Lindsey, who had become invaluable in the kitchen. He would miss her.

"How's your packing coming along?" Ryan asked. She was leaving for school in a week, and Jude had taken her shopping for clothes and supplies. Mitchell had sent a cursory apology in an email and told Lindsey her tuition would be covered until she graduated.

Lindsey looked up from her station and brushed the hair off her forehead. "I had to buy another suitcase to put everything in."

"I bet you didn't mind that," Ryan said, grinning. "Are you planning on taking any photography classes? You have the eye of a pro."

He loved seeing that grin spread across her face. "I'm going to try to add some at least for winter quarter. Speaking of pictures, any word from your agent?"

Ryan flipped over the chicken and inhaled the scent of garlic and thyme. His stomach groaned for lunch, but that would have to wait until the rush slowed down. "Actually, I have a call scheduled with her Tuesday morning, after she gets back from the holiday weekend. She said she had news about the cookbook."

Jude pushed open the kitchen door looking a bit frantic. "Party of ten just sat down. Thought I'd warn you."

Ryan saluted. "Got it boss." He felt invigorated just seeing her sweet face and knowing this was his life now.

"The chicken's ready." Lindsey pointed to the pan. "And don't worry, I'll book a little Mom and daughter bonding day over mani & pedis to make sure I keep her out of the restaurant all of Tuesday afternoon."

Jude put on one of the new, loose dresses she'd bought when she was out shopping with Lindsey today. Lindsey had fixed her hair into a fancy updo, and she liked the new look. Her nails matched the rosy trim on the sleeves, and her toenails sparkled from her sandals. Butterflies swarmed in her stomach. Tonight was her first date night with Ryan since he'd mentioned marriage.

The knock at the front door had her heart pounding like her first high school crush. Ryan, dressed sharply in all black, stepped in holding a sizeable bouquet of yellow and orange sunflowers. "For you," he said.

Jude held the flowers close. "I love these colors. They're so happy."

"As am I," Ryan said. "And I hope you are too."

Jude leaned over the flowers and kissed him. "I am, very happy."

"I better get them in water," Jude said.

"Then we can head out," Ryan said. "We have a bit of a drive ahead of us and a seven o'clock reservation."

As they made their way off island, Jude looked out the passenger window admiring the Madrona trees lining the slope down to the cove. She glanced over at Ryan's profile. He looked especially handsome in a dark, button-down shirt. His sun-streaked hair was pulled back into a ponytail that rested over his collar. The musky scent of his aftershave lingered between them. It was hard to believe this was really happening to her. This man loved her, and she him.

Ryan pulled into a parking lot Jude had never been to before. The restaurant looked like a Chalet straight out of the French countryside. Red flowers draped over window boxes at the entrance. Fragrant smells and soft music greeted them as they walked in. The dining room was filled with dark wood booths and tables. Blue and white tablecloths were complemented with flickering candles and glass vases filled with fresh daisies.

"I hope it's as good as it smells." Jude said.

Ryan winked. "Better."

She glanced down at the pink bakery box Ryan had carried in. She wanted to ask, but said nothing...yet.

The hostess smiled when Ryan gave their name and took them to a private table in the corner by a window.

Ryan handed her the mystery box, and she nodded and took it back toward the kitchen.

Ryan winked at Jude. "Later."

A bottle of what looked like champagne was chilling at the table, and noticeably missing were menus. "I see you have this well planned," Jude said. His grin and sparkling eyes let her know she was right.

The waiter, French accent and all, uncorked the bubbly gently. It released a soft hiss. He poured some for Ryan's approval. After he nodded, the waiter poured the fizzing golden liquid into their tulip-shaped glasses. Ryan held his up for a toast.

"It is Chateau De Fleur Non-alcoholic Sparkling Wine Champagne," he said clicking his glass to hers.

The champagne tasted slightly floral with hints of spice. It melted down her throat. "Magical," Jude said between sips.

"The chef is serving us his special seven-course menu tonight," Ryan said.

"It's a good thing I had a light lunch."

The hors d'oeuvres started with Oysters Mignon on the Half Shell, followed by, as the waiter said, "Coquilles St-Jacques, gratineed scallops. The courses just kept coming, one more magnificent than the next: Salade Lyonnaise with hard boiled eggs, cheesy French Onion Soup, and the restaurant's signature entrée, Coq Au Vin.

Jude rubbed her stomach. "This is one of the best meals I've ever had." She placed her fork down on the table after two hours of fine dining. "Thank you for arranging this. It was very special."

"I hope you left room for dessert," Ryan said grinning. He motioned to the waiter and asked for espressos for two, and to make one decaf.

"Oh Ryan. I'm going to gain too much weight eating like this while I'm pregnant. At least can we wait a bit?"

"No problem," he said. "And don't worry, after this I'll make sure I only make you the healthiest meals."

They sipped their coffee, and Jude thought about all the things they had overcome together in so short a time. Now they had so much to look forward to.

"I have some news to tell you," Ryan said.

Jude's breath caught.

"So," he said, "remember I told you about the literary agent pitching the Island Thyme Cookbook? We got a book deal!"

Jude exhaled unaware she'd been holding her breath. "We?" she asked. "Congratulations to you!"

Ryan reached across the table and took her hands. "It's your café and our cookbook. I'll write it and we can share the profits."

"That is so sweet, Ryan. Thank you."

"One other thing." He sipped the cappuccino and put the cup down before looking her in the eye. "One of the top five-star restaurants in New York offered me a position as executive chef."

She held her breath, willing the room to stop spinning.

"Jude," Ryan said. He tipped up her chin so that she would look into his eyes. "The reason I'm telling you this is because I replied with a resounding no! As I will to anything that could ever takes me away from you."

She took his hand to her lips and kissed it. "You had me worried for a second."

Ryan nodded to the waiter. "Jude, from now on, I will do everything in my power to wash all your worries away."

With that the waiter walked out with the pink box and laid it in front of Ryan with a small plate. Ceremoniously, Ryan opened and brought out a handmade dark chocolate box and placed it gingerly on the plate between them. "I made this for you," he said.

It must have taken him hours to make. He had decorated the box with carved red hearts and white diamond shapes. The chocolate was smooth, perfectly formed.

Ryan lifted off the lid, took something out, and placed it in his hand. Then, as Jude watched, heart pounding, Ryan got down on his knees before her.

"Jude, will you make me the happiest man in the world and be my wife?" He opened his hand revealing a braided golden ring with diamonds sparking throughout.

Between happy tears, Jude said. "I will, I absolutely will."

Ryan stood and placed the ring on her finger and the whole restaurant broke out in applause. He threw his arms around her and sealed the engagement with a kiss.

The owner of the restaurant ran out holding a magnum of Champagne "Félicitations à vous, let us all drink to the lovers, les amoureux."

A waitress handed Jude and Ryan glasses bubbling with the non-alcoholic champagne and led the toast, "Congratulations! To your happiness!"

Jude toasted and placed her glass on the table. She held her hand up and admired the ring.

Ryan pointed to the band. "I had the jeweler carve some of the strands to look like sprigs of thyme and place the marquise diamond right in the middle."

"How clever," she said, brushing her fingers over the strands.

"I've been thinking," Ryan said. "We could knock out the dividing wall between our apartments and make my bedroom the nursery."

"What a great idea." Jude could see them decorating the new baby's room and then going back to the bedroom they shared together as husband and wife. "Shall we go soon," she said. Jude wanted to be alone with Ryan, to hold him in her arms, and finally let go and open her heart completely."

"One other thing," he said.

"More?" Jude put her hand to her heart. "Not sure I can take it."

Ryan grinned. "You said you wanted a quiet, small wedding. So how does a honeymoon cruise to Alaska and being married by the sea captain sound? It is Lindsey pre-approved as well."

"Perfect. I've always dreamt of seeing Glacier Bay and the coastal towns." She stopped and came down to earth for a second. "When would we go? What about Lindsey and school?"

"I already thought of that and booked all three of us a flight to Anchorage. Lindsey will join us for a few days on the cruise for the ceremony, and then when we port in Juneau, she can fly back to school. We will continue on for another week and celebrate our honeymoon."

Jude looked at him in wonder. She'd never believed she would find a man like this. Or that she would ever heal from the pain of her past and open her heart again. Now here she was about to marry Ryan, welcome another child, have Lindsey at her side, and be a happy family again.

Epilogue

Grandpa John surveyed the gathering from his favorite spot on the porch swing of the bed and breakfast's wrap-around porch. Golds, reds, and yellows tinged the leaves like a watercolor painting welcoming the late fall. Although the chilled air called for a jacket, the day cooperated with not a rain cloud in sight. Gretel's tail thumped on the porch by his feet, and he reached down and scratched the dog's head.

Mary rushed out the front door carrying a tray of food. "John," she said, "what are you doing sitting on the porch? Come join the party."

"I'll be along soon. Just resting my feet."

He watched her move through the crowd. It seemed everyone in town was here for Jude's fortieth birthday. A few days ago, they'd celebrated Lily and Ian's first wedding anniversary. His grandson, Ian, was easy to spot, carrying sweet Gwyn in his arms. His great-granddaughter, no less. Lily was at Ian's side, her head on his shoulder as they watched the musicians on the lawn. Grandpa John scanned the area for Jason.

"Surprise!" Jason said, popping up on the porch. The boy ran over and wrapped his arms around John with a tight squeeze.

"I love you, Grandpa."

"Love you too. Are you having a good time?"

Jason fidgeted on the porch. "There aren't many kids here. When do you think we can eat the cake?"

John laughed. "I'm sure it will be soon." He pointed to a boy who'd just arrived with his mom. "Isn't that your friend from school?"

Jason perked up. "I'll see you later Grandpa."

He dashed off with his youthful energy sparking around him. John wondered if he himself even had the energy to get out bed some days. He was getting old. No doubt about it. For a moment he felt Maggie's warm presence beside him on the old swing. He closed his eyes and imagined the sweet scent of gardenias that lingered wherever she went.

"Oh Maggie," he whispered. "I wish you were here to see all of this."

A soft laugh trickled inside his head. Maggie's laugh. She was here, in his heart, in his soul. "Look Maggie," he told her silently. "You granddaughter, Lily, is so happy now, and a mother. And you don't have to worry about Jude. She found a darn good man. Married and a baby coming too. Even Lindsey will be home for Christmas."

Laughter and song lyrics filled the air, bringing him back from his drifting. In the distance he saw Becca and Marco dancing. New love, and Shirley and her new husband dancing beside them. Old love. He'd had it with Maggie.

John sighed. The pain of loss never left him, but he'd made a promise to Maggie to watch over those she left behind. And he'd kept it.

"How you doing?" Betty asked. Zinger pounced up the steps in front of her and barked at Gretel to play. John was glad to see some color back in her cheeks.

"How are you doing is the question," John said. "I saw you mowing the lawn yesterday. Did the doctor okay that?"

Betty snickered. "The doctor told me I could come do his next! Full remission, she said."

"I don't know how you do it, Betty. You're a tough one."

"Don't know what else I'd do," she said. "Can't just lay down and die, I wouldn't know how." She started down the steps and turned. "And I've got so much to do, including wishing that girl a Happy Birthday."

"More power to you," John said.

Gretel finally rose, tempted by Zinger to play. "Go ahead," he told the dog, waving her on.

"See you later," Betty called behind her.

Betty and Shirley had been his neighbors for years. Time had flown by, so many memories. For a moment he was back with Maggie, and the party was for the grand opening of the Madrona Island Bed & Breakfast so many years ago. He could see Maggie cutting the ribbon with a radiant smile on her face. John looked out expecting to see Maggie in the crowd.

"Time to sing Happy Birthday," Ryan called out. "Come over all and join us."

Everyone gathered around the cake. John rose slowly and walked over toward all his friends and neighbors. Kyla motioned for him to join her and Luke, and of course their dog Bailey who was happily wagging his tail. Another happy couple. Oh Maggie, I wish you were here to celebrate with us, he thought.

Voices rose in the chorus, "Happy Birthday to Jude!"

The sheriff patted John on the shoulder. "Good to see you here."

John nodded. "And you." Everywhere he looked he saw someone he knew. Someone who had touched their lives. There was, Kelly, the reporter, taking pictures of the party for the paper, Audrey the librarian, and Cherise from the art gallery where Ian sold his work. Under the old apple tree, the dogs played in the fall leaves. And for a moment all was well with the world.

He had kept his promise to Maggie, to watch over them all. He'd seen them open to love and all the pain that can go with it. But what else was there that really mattered? Just love.

If you enjoyed this book, please sign up for my mailing list to receive updates and special offers at http://eepurl.com/biKrpH

Reviews are always appreciated on Amazon https://www.amazon.com/Andrea-Hurst/e/B001JS0Y76/

Goodreads   https://www.goodreads.com/author/show/6553580.Andrea_Hurst

Join me on Facebook at – https://www.facebook.com/andreahurstauthor
www.andreahurst-author.com

If you've missed any of the series here is a summary below.

Book One – The Guestbook

EVERYONE REMEMBERS THEIR FIRST LOVE ...
BUT SOMETIMES IT'S THE SECOND LOVE THAT LASTS
Evocative and heartfelt, The Guestbook is the profound story of one woman's journey toward hope, renewal and a second chance at love on a lush Pacific Northwest island. Curl up with your favorite cup of cocoa and enjoy.
~Anjali Banerjee - author of Imaginary Men and Haunting Jasmine said about this women's fiction romance

Fleeing her picture-perfect marriage among the privileged set of Brentwood and the wreckage of a failed marriage, Lily Parkins decides to move to the only place that still holds happy memories, her grandmother's old farmhouse. The lush and majestic setting of the Pacific Northwest calls to her and offers a place of refuge and perhaps renewal. Her grandmother has passed away, leaving the Madrona Island Bed & Breakfast Inn to Lily. Left with only an old guestbook as her guide—a curious book full of letters, recipes, and glimpses into her family history—Lily is determined to embrace her newfound independence and recreate herself, one page at a time. With the help of the quirky island residents she has befriended, she slowly finds the strength to seek out happiness on her own terms. But as soon as she has sworn off men and is standing on her own two feet, Lily meets Ian, the alluring artist who lives next door, and her new life is suddenly thrown off course. The last thing she wants to do right now is to open her heart to another man. Ultimately, Lily must decide if it's worth giving up her soul for security or risking everything to follow her heart in this romantic love story.

Book Two – Tea & Comfort

This second volume features the puzzling yet sensuous, Kyla Nolan. The story unravels the mystery behind her hasty departure from her glamorous New York life as a top model and her transformation to shop proprietor, herbalist, and local tea leaf reader on Madrona Island. Follow her battle with a reoccurring illness and the return of Lucas, the wealthy winery owner and former fiancé whom she left behind. Can a love that was so based on outside trappings survive illness and loss? With a touch of the paranormal, and her island friends, Kyla comes to terms with her fears and her heart's longings.

Book Three – Island Thyme Café

Recipes from the book
Island Thyme Cafe

Lily's Bacon-Wrapped Stuffed Chicken

Ingredients:

1 package of sliced bacon

2 cups thick-sliced mushrooms

2 cups fresh spinach leaves

1 package of sliced Provolone cheese (smoked or plain)

Fresh Thyme sprigs

Salt, pepper, and garlic flakes

Medium/large boneless, skinless chicken breasts

Preparation:

Preheat the oven to 375 degrees. While the oven is preheating, cook bacon (two to three pieces per chicken breast) on the stove for about 3–4 minutes until slightly cooked, but bacon is still soft. Pat dry with paper towels and put aside.

Wash off the chicken with cold water. With a small, sharp, knife, cut into chicken from the side to create a deep pocket in the center. Spread the chicken open. Put in a layer of raw mushrooms. Next, cover in a thick layer of spinach.

Finally, cover both of these with strips of Provolone slices, approximately one slice per chicken breast. Salt, pepper, and garlic the inside. Fold the chicken closed tight as you can. Wrap each breast in at least two slices of bacon.

Put chicken in a deep-dish pan. Fill the bottom of pan surrounding chicken with thick sliced mushrooms, salt, pepper, garlic. Place fresh thyme sprigs on mushrooms and chicken. Bake until center of chicken is cooked, approximately 45 minutes or until done.

Chef Ryan's Island Thyme & Sea Salt Butter

This butter can be served at the table for buttering bread or rolls, or used to cook with over chicken or pasta.

Ingredients:

2 sticks of unsalted sweet butter softened

¼ cup fresh minced thyme

Salt to taste, approximately 1 tsp.

1/2 garlic glove chopped fine

Preparation:

Combine all ingredients and mold into preferred shape. Chill in refrigerator, or leave out at room temperature to serve. This is also great to use for cooking poultry, pasta, etc.

Jude's Magic Hot Cocoa

Ingredients:

3 ½ cups of whole milk

1 cup of whipping cream

½ cup of sugar

1/3 cup Hershey's Unsweetened Cocoa Powder. We recommend Pernigotti Ilcacao Amaro, the best Italian cocoa powder. Can be ordered on Amazon.com

¼ teaspoon Cinnamon

1/8 to ¼ teaspoon culinary lavender to taste

½ tablespoon pure vanilla

Preparation:

Put the milk and cream in a pot on medium heat and warm. Slowly add sugar and mix well, add cocoa and mix with a whisk to keep from burning and to get all the chocolate off the sides and blended. Add all other ingredients and continue stirring until warmed.

Serve immediately. Approximately 4 servings

Strawberry or Blackberry Thyme Lemonade
Ingredients:

1 cup sugar or to taste, honey can be used instead

4–6 sprigs fresh thyme, plus more for garnishing

1 ½ to 2 - cups strawberries or blackberries, cleaned and sliced

10–12 fresh-squeezed lemons

1 cup water

Preparation:

In a small pot, add a cup of water, the sugar and thyme. Bring to a low boil and cook, stirring lightly until the sugar is dissolved. Let cool and remove the thyme.

Combine the above mixture with the berries, lemon juice, and 5–6 cups cold water in a large pitcher. Chill for 30 minutes or more. Serve over ice, garnished with fresh thyme sprigs.

Aknowledgements

This was a bittersweet book for me to write. I enjoyed returning to Madrona Island to complete the third book in the trilogy, but it was hard to type "the end." I'd like to thank the numerous people who supported me on this writing journey, and all the readers who kept encouraging me to finish *Island Thyme Café*.

Special thanks to: Rebecca Berus for her expertise with plotting and for sharing brainstorming walks on the cliffs of Fort Casey while I worked out the storyline. To Sean Fletcher for his encouragement during the dark moments of writer's block. To my developmental editor, Cate Perry, for her unwavering support and friendship.

To Justin Hurst for believing in me.

And to my Beta readers for their fast and thorough reading of the initial manuscript, a heartfelt thanks to Cameron Chandler and Sheila Myers. To Jean Galiana, who has read and made excellent suggestions for all three books in the series, a big thank you!

A very special nod to my plot party gang: Audrey Mackaman, Sean Fletcher, and Rebecca Berus.

And to my expert virtual assistant who keeps me organized, Geneva Agnos https://www.facebook.com/VirtualAssistantGeneva/?fref=ts

Last but not least, gratitude to my beloved dachshund, Ferdie, for making sure all the dogs on Madrona Island were included.

Author Bio

When not writing, visiting local farmer's markets, or indulging her love for dark chocolate, Andrea enjoys working with other authors as a developmental editor and workshop leader. Her passion for books drives her to write stories that take readers on a journey to another place and leave them with an unforgettable impression. She lives with her rescue dachshund, Ferdie, in the Pacific Northwest, on an island much like the fictional Madrona, with all of its natural beauty and small town charm.

Her published books include the Amazon bestseller, *The Guestbook, Tea & Comfort,* and *Island Thyme Café.* Her other publications are *Always with You, The Lazy Dog's Guide to*

Enlightenment and *Everybody's Natural Foods Cookbook,* and she co-authored A *Book of Miracles: Inspiring True Stories of Healing, Gratitude, and Love* with Dr. Bernie Siegel.

To be alerted of upcoming new releases and receive contest and giveaway notifications, please follow her on Facebook where she shares beautiful pictures of the island, new recipes and, of course, photos of Ferdie. Newsletter subscribers enjoy special bonus content as well.

Author Website - www.andreahurst-author.com

Facebook - https://www.facebook.com/andreahurstauthor

Made in the USA
Columbia, SC
13 January 2020

86762076R00169